WIZ'S FIRST TASK: SAVE THE DRAGON FROM HIS WIFE

With her husband held captive in some secret dragon's lair, Moira wasn't about to let the conversation wander off into a comparison of computerized vending machines: "Well, can you trace him or not?"

Jerry rubbed his chin. "That's hard. See, the path shown on a message like the one Wiz sent isn't completely reliable. You can fake some of it. It's going to be hard enough just to figure out where he's connecting to the Internet, to say nothing of where he is in our world."

"Maybe not so hard," Danny said. "If we can rig up a little perl script and plant it on all these sites we may be able to trace him back to where he's really connecting."

Moira's face lit up. "Can you do that?"

"Well, we're going to have to get into a pile of computers, including that Coke machine at MIT, but . . ." His eyes focused on something far away. "Let me think about this and see what I come up with. But we should be able to do it."

"And then?" Jerry asked.

"Then," said Moira grimly, "we go to his rescue whether he wants it or not."

BAEN BOOKS by RICK COOK

The Wizardry Consulted

Rick Cook

BAEN

THE WIZARDRY CONSULTED

This is a work of fiction. All the characters and events portrayed in this book are fictional, and any resemblance to real people or incidents is purely coincidental.

A Baen Books Original

Baen Publishing Enterprises
P.O. Box 1403
Riverdale, NY 10471

ISBN: 0-671-87700-3

Cover art by Courtney Skinner & Newell Convers

First printing, December 1995

Distributed by Simon & Schuster
1230 Avenue of the Americas
New York, NY 10020

Typeset by Windhaven Press, Auburn, NH
Printed in the United States of America

Once again, for all the people who helped. Paul for some code and a lot of brain-picking. Greg for details. Pete for inspiration and some truly wicked war stories. Bill and Mary for introducing me to "Malkin." Bob Jernigan for a line of APL. The Bixen for their usual support and help. And various people on the Internet.

ONE

FLUFF THE MAGIC DRAGON

True, it is nonsense. But it is important *nonsense.*
—Philosopher Ludwig Wittgenstein On His Life's Work
(Quoted on the title page of *The Consultants' Handbook*)

"You know one of the nice things about peace?" Wiz Zumwalt remarked to his cubicle mate. "It's boring."

Jerry Andrews turned away from the glowing letters of golden fire hanging in the air above his desk.

"Are you being sarcastic?"

William Irving Zumwalt, "Wiz" or "Sparrow" to one and all, twisted his wiry frame in his chair and brushed a lock of dark hair off his forehead. Like Jerry he was dressed in the flowing linen shirt, breeches and high, soft boots that were this world's equivalent of jeans and a T-shirt. In spite of the clothes he still managed to look like a programmer.

"Heck no! I was just thinking how nice it is. No one's trying to kill me, no one's trying to destroy the world. No dwarf assassins, no elvish magic. Just peace and quiet. It's boring, but you know something? I *like* being bored."

Wiz sighed and looked out the traceried window into the rose garden below. Now that there were only three

1

programmers left in the World, the Stablemaster had reclaimed their old quarters for his cows. In place of the Bull Pen, Danny, Jerry and Wiz had a spacious workroom in the main tower, with windows surrounded by climbing roses, and a view of the rose garden and the western wall of the Wizard's Keep. Beyond the towers of the west wall, the green hills ran off into the purple distance.

In Wiz's time in this world peace had been a scarce commodity. His first weeks after being shanghaied here were spent running for his life from the Dark League of the South. What with one thing and another, especially a red-haired hedge witch, he had discovered that the magic in this world could be made to work like a computer program. That led to a hacked-together magic language and a battle of magic that destroyed the Dark League. Then he'd been kidnapped by a remnant of the Dark League and spent weeks dodging wizards in the freezing, deserted City of Night. That was when Jerry, Danny and some other programmers were brought here from San Jose to help him. That in turn led to a couple of computer criminals finding their way to this world and that had ended in another enormous battle. In between there had been the job of teaching this world's wizards how to program and months of delicate, wearing negotiations with the non-humans of the world who were upset by humans' new magical powers. It had only been in the last few months that teaching and negotiating had tapered off and Wiz could get back to serious programming.

"Yep," he repeated, taking his eyes away from the landscape. "It's wonderful."

"You sound as if you're trying to convince yourself." Jerry sounded amused.

"I'm already convinced," Wiz said firmly. "I'm bored and I like it."

Jerry leaned back in his chair, which squeaked in

protest, and put his ham-like hands behind his head. He was several inches taller than Wiz and a lot heavier, although he had dropped perhaps forty pounds since coming to this world a couple of years ago. Even powerful wizards here got more physical exercise than their software counterparts in Cupertino. Like Wiz he was tanned, but unlike his friend, who drew his dark hair back in a shoulder-length ponytail, Jerry's lighter brown hair was neatly trimmed above his collar. "I'd rather think of it as having enough time to work on interesting projects. Now that we've got wizards and apprentices trained in the basics of the magic compiler we've got the time for refinements."

"Speaking of which, what is that you've been hacking on so furiously?"

"Kind of an experiment," Jerry said, turning back to the code. "I'm trying to see how well the magic compiler works in a more conventional computer language."

"You're translating the thing into C?"

"Well, no," Jerry said. "I thought I'd try something that was a little less tied to computer architecture. Something more general."

Wiz looked over his shoulder at the lines of luminescent characters suspended in midair. Then he squinted and leaned closer.

The magic compiler was written in a combination of this world's runes, the English alphabet and various made-up symbols. To the uninitiated a spell listing looked like someone's graphics card had barfed on the screen. But even compared to that, this listing was strange. In addition to the "normal" symbols, there were tiny squares, triangles, right angles and things that were even less comprehensible. Wiz scanned the display several times, frowning.

"If I didn't know better, I'd swear that was . . ."

"Yep," Jerry said proudly. "APL."

Wiz groaned.

"Hey, you're a fine one to complain. Who wrote the first spell interpreter in a hacked-up version of Forth?"

"That was different," Wiz said with some dignity. "Forth was exceptionally well suited to what I needed to do."

"So is this," Jerry informed him. "APL is an extremely elegant language. You can express a whole series of complex mathematical operations in a single line of code simply, unambiguously and logically."

Wiz tore his eyes away from the mess above Jerry's desk and poured himself another mug of blackmoss tea." *If* you've got a computer that can produce hieroglyphics and *if* you never need to remember what you did."

"Nonsense. It's no harder to write understandable code in APL than anything else. You can even write incomprehensible code in C."

"I rest my case."

Before Jerry could reply the door banged open and Danny limped in.

"How's the back?" Wiz asked, grateful for a respite from what promised to be a full-scale language debate.

"Getting better," the young programmer said, plopping himself down in his chair. He leaned forward almost forty-five degrees. "See? No pain."

Considering the extent of his injuries, Danny was lucky to be alive, much less walking around. A blast from a guard's weapon had nearly burned him in half during the great battle for Caer Mort almost three years before. Magic had saved him and magic had healed him, but not even the world's most skillful healers could restore him fully in safety. So for months he had been going to the healers in the Wizard's Keep for a combination of physical therapy, massage and healing magic. Gradually but steadily he was improving.

The third member of the software development team

was several years younger with fresh good looks that made him look younger still. Even before his ordeal he had been slender, but the rigors of his recovery had taken flesh off his bones until he was positively skinny, despite the best efforts of his wife June and the castle cooks to feed him up.

He looked over at the characters above Jerry's desk. "What's that?" he asked, levering himself out of the chair and limping over to join them.

"APL," Wiz told him. "He could have been doing something useful and he's been writing an APL interpreter."

"Well, whatever makes you happy," Danny said with a shrug.

"Like figuring out how to tap into our world's telephone system, I suppose," Jerry retorted.

"Hey, we *needed* an Internet connection. We have to keep up with what's going on back in the real world. Besides," he added, "you're the one who's on that thing four hours a night."

"I have a lot of newsgroups I have to keep up with," Jerry said virtuously. "There's a lot going on there."

"Well, better keep it away from the wizards," Wiz said. "I'm not sure what they'd make of some of those newsgroups."

"You mean like the **alt.sex** groups?" Danny asked.

"I was thinking more of **comp.language.flames**, but yeah, the **alt.sex** groups too. Especially **alt.sex.gerbils. duct-tape**."

"That's bogus," Jerry said. "The real name is **alt.sex. bestiality.hamster.duct-tape**."

It was Danny's turn to look smug. "You mean that's another group. Just because it's not in the official **alt** hierarchy you can't find it."

Wiz wasn't sure whether he was joking or not. The Internet, an international computer network originally built around universities and research institutions, was famous for the depth and breadth of the knowledge contained in its newsgroups. However, even Internet's staunchest advocates had to admit that not all the newsgroups were research-related—or even serious. Hidden away in various places in the sprawling multidimensional message space were some decidedly odd things, including some highly unofficial newsgroups. But you needed to know how to use the net to get to them. Danny's knowledge of the ins and outs of the net was extensive.

Danny was no sooner settled back in his chair than there was a discreet knock at the door. In all the Wizard's Keep there was only one person who knocked so delicately, so discreetly and so exquisitely.

"Come in Wulfram," Wiz called.

"Excuse me, My Lord." The castle seneschal was calm, dignified and more than a little bit stuffy. "But . . ."

Before he could finish the door banged open again and two children and a dragon charged into the room.

"UncaWiz, UncaWiz," shouted Caitlin, the daughter of one of the guardsmen. She was a couple of years older than Danny's son Ian, with dark curly hair, flashing dark eyes and a single black eyebrow stark against her pale, fair skin. She was utterly charming, she knew it and she used it shamelessly.

Right on her heels came Ian. He was barely three and well into the head-down-and-charge stage of childhood locomotion. Without pausing he ran full-tilt across the room and bounced into Danny's lap.

But the real attraction was the third member of the group, who charged into the room just as heedlessly, got his feet tangled up with the rug and his own tail, caromed off a pile of manuscripts and executed a neat bank shot to end up beside Ian and Danny.

Little Red Dragon, or LRD to the programmers, was

little only in comparison to the eighty-foot cavalry mounts in the aeries below the castle. He—Wiz thought he was a he—was nearly ten feet long from snout to tail tip. His scales were darkening from scarlet to maroon and the blue edges were going from turquoise toward navy and his combination of exuberance, dragonish temper and size was making him increasingly hard to handle. Dragons do not become intelligent until they are nearly full-grown. LRD was a long way from full grown and somewhat further than that from intelligent. But LRD and Ian were inseparable, so the dragon was allowed in the programmers' workroom and their quarters in the Wizard's Keep.

The seneschal knew when he was outclassed. With an exquisite sigh of resignation he stepped away from the door to await the wizards' pleasure.

"The dragon's got a new name!" Caitlin announced. "We had to come tell you because you can't call him LRD any more."

"Not LRD?" asked Danny, looking down at his son squirming in his lap.

"No! Fuf-fee," Ian pronounced distinctly, reaching up and hugging the scaly monster's neck. LRD looked pleased.

"I beg your pardon?" Wiz said.

"He means Fluffy," Caitlin said with five-year-old superiority.

"Fluffy!" Ian repeated with three-year-old emphasis.

"Okaaay," Wiz said, "his name's Fluffy."

"He's taking us on a adventure," Caitlin announced. "We're going across the river to hunt for mushrooms."

"All by yourselves?" Danny asked. "What does Shauna say?"

"Oh, Shauna can come too," Caitlin said. "Fluffy says it's all right."

"Where is Shauna anyway?" Wiz put in.

"Here, My Lord," the nursemaid said, puffing with

exertion as she came into the room. She dropped a perfunctory curtsy to Wiz. "Sorry, My Lord, we were down in the orchard and they just took off running. The whole pack of them." She turned toward her charges and planted her hands on her ample hips. "No manners in the lot of them. Just up and whooping off like a tribe of savages. They ought to be ashamed of themselves, bursting in here like that and disturbing wizards at their work. Why it would have served them right if they'd interrupted a powerful spell and been turned into a parcel of frogs!"

The boy, the girl and the dragon recognized their cue and they all managed to look properly abashed.

"Maybe it would be a good idea to take them over to the woods," Danny said. "Let them run off some of this energy."

"Well . . ."

"Please Shauna," Caitlin wheedled.

"Peese," Ian chimed in.

"Whuf," added the dragon.

Shauna considered and then relented. "Well, all right, My Lord. But just to get them out of your hair." She turned and glared fiercely at the children. "And this time that beast—" She jerked her head at the dragon. "That beast has to swim the river. Near to upset the boat last time, he did, and the boatmen won't take him any more."

"Come on," Caitlin whooped and dashed for the door. Ian jumped out of Danny's lap and pounded after her and the dragon followed, nearly knocking Shauna down as he charged past.

"Here now!" she yelled. "Just slow down, the lot of you." With an apologetic glance over her shoulder, she followed her charges out the door, calling to them to come back.

The racket died down as dragon, children and nursemaid vanished down the corridor.

At that point Wiz's wife Moira came into the room,

a wide-brimmed straw hat thrown back over her shoulders, setting off her freckled, slightly flushed skin and cascade of red hair. She was wearing a peasant blouse, a brightly colored skirt and she had a basket of fresh flowers in her hand. To Wiz she looked like a vision out of a Monet painting.

"Was that LRD?" Moira asked as she came over to kiss her husband hello.

"No, that was Fluffy."

Moira arched her coppery eyebrows over great green eyes. "Love, even for you that is incomprehensible."

"Wasn't my idea." Wiz shrugged. "Caitlin and Ian insist LRD's name is Fluffy."

"Where did they get that, I wonder?"

Wiz shrugged again. "Maybe the dragon told them."

Moira just sighed and shook her head.

"Normalcy," Wiz sighed. "It's wonderful."

Jerry snorted with laughter.

"What's so funny?"

"Two kids go tearing out of here chased by a dragon, and you say it's normal."

"The dragon doesn't bother me, I just think of it as an overgrown St. Bernard."

A discreet cough reminded him of the waiting seneschal.

"I'm sorry Wulfram. Now, you were saying?"

"There is a dragon to see you, My Lord."

"A dragon?"

"A *large* dragon," the seneschal amended with gloomy glee. "He is sitting on the East curtain wall and—ah—urgently desires an audience."

For a minute no one said anything.

"Oh boy," Wiz said at last.

"So much for normalcy," Moira said.

"Just think of it as an executive vice-president from the home office," Jerry suggested.

TWO
ENTER THE DRAGON

First, know who you're working for.
                              —The Consultants' Handbook

Their guest was perched precariously on the east curtain wall of the castle. The walkway on top of the wall was wide enough for eight men to pass abreast, but the dragon gripped it with his talons the way a parakeet grips its perch. Its enormous scaled head stretched well above the watchtowers. Wiz couldn't see its tail, but judging by what he could see the dragon was a monster, two hundred feet long if it was an inch.

Although the courtyard and walls were deserted, the dragon had an audience. Wizards and others crowded the windows and doorways looking out into the East Court. There was another group at the double gate that led into the courtyard.

Even in silhouette Wiz recognized the bulk of Bal-Simba, the leader of the Council of the North, in the front. The large black wizard nodded to him over the heads of the others as he came up.

Next to him was the one-armed Master of Dragons who commanded the council's dragon cavalry and

Arianne, the tall blond woman who was Bal-Simba's assistant.

The crowd parted as Wiz approached and he saw that the courtyard was not completely deserted. Out in its center sat Fluffy, née LRD. He was gazing up at the visitor and his tail switched back and forth like a fascinated cat's. Caitlin and Ian were back in the shadows at a side door, huddled up against Shauna's skirts like frightened chicks with a mother hen.

Wiz ducked back from the doorway.

"Quick," he said to Bal-Simba, "tell me everything you know about dragons."

The giant black wizard shrugged. "Easily done, since I know little enough. Adult dragons are morose, fierce and solitary creatures. They are greedy for treasure, skilled in magic and grow in size and intelligence seemingly without end."

"How smart do you think that one is?"

Bal-Simba looked appraisingly at the shadow darkening the doorway. "I would say very smart indeed. Like lizards, dragons never stop growing, but their growth tapers off as they age. That one must be very old to be so large."

"Great."

He looked at the Master of Dragons, but the one-armed man just shrugged. "Lord, I can tell you of the care and training of young dragons, but I know nothing of them after they mature. As their brains begin to grow the psychic bond with their riders loosens and they become unmanageable. We release them long before they attain full intelligence."

Wiz looked again. This dragon was not only bigger than the ones he knew, it was different. The scales had darkened to a dull gray-green, there were spines along its back and its teeth were much longer. The body was leaner and the whole effect was more predatory. The cavalry mounts were fearsome, but this thing was positively terrifying.

"Do not worry Wizard," a voice at once warm and soft as honey and hard and cold as iron rang in his head. "I will not eat you. Not yet, anyway."

"Uh, thanks," Wiz said. Bal-Simba frowned and started to speak, but Wiz motioned him to silence. Obviously Wiz was the only one who could "hear" the dragon.

Again the honey-and-iron voice rang in Wiz's skull. "You may call me Wurm."

"Hello Wurm," Wiz said. He took a deep breath and stepped out into the courtyard. The afternoon sun had warmed the flagstones and the air was balmy and sweet with the scent of roses. None of which made Wiz feel any less like a turtle on a freeway.

"Since my presence here seems somewhat disconcerting, may I suggest that we come to the point?"

"Sounds good to me. Ah, what is the point?"

"I have a proposition for you."

"'Proposition' as in 'job'?"

The dragon "shrugged" in Wiz's mind. "If you want to put it so crudely."

Wiz shook his head. "Sorry, I don't hire out. There's enough to do here."

The dragon "sounded" amused. "I think once you have heard the terms you will reconsider."

In spite of the mildness of the afternoon Wiz realized there was a trickle of sweat starting down his back. "Okay, what are the terms?"

"If you do this thing I will reward you richly. Gold, jewels, a heap of treasure higher than your head." A dismissive mental "shrug." "The usual."

"What if I don't take the job?"

The dragon craned his neck high into the sky and peered down at Wiz as if he were something small and soft that had just crawled from beneath a rock. "Then," Wurm said with chilling calm, "I shall burn the town to ashes and ravage the countryside for miles around. And I shall continue until you do agree. Or until I am slain."

Looking up at the monster, Wiz had no doubt Wurm could do it, or that he would.

"Uh, let me think this over, will you?" Wiz ducked back into the doorway where the others were waiting.

"How hard is it to kill a dragon?"

"Difficult," Bal-Simba said in a low voice. "Dragons are inherently magical and their magic is extremely strong. Besides which they are large and powerful beasts." He looked intently at Wiz. "Has it come to that?"

"No, but it might. He wants me to take on a job for him and he's got a real strong negative incentive plan."

"If we must fight him we had best buy time," the giant black wizard said. "I would advise you to ask him his proposition in detail."

Wiz stepped back out into the courtyard. "Okay, look. I can't decide on the spur of the moment, but I am willing to listen. Why don't you tell me the details?"

The dragon paused, as if thinking. "Very well then. Come with me and I will show you what I wish."

"Now I don't know about . . ."

"Do you fear for your safety, Wizard?" Again Wurm sounded amused. "I told you I will not harm you and I will not. Besides," and he lowered his huge head almost to Wiz's level and cocked it like a chicken watching a worm, "what could I do to you elsewhere that I could not do to you here?"

"It's not that," Wiz assured him hastily. "It's just that it's not easy for me to just pack up and go. I mean I've got responsibilities here and . . ." Wurm raised his head above the castle wall. Then he daintily lifted a foreleg and inspected his three black front talons, each longer than Wiz was tall.

"I'm in the middle of these spells, you see . . ." Wiz continued weakly.

Without pausing to inhale, Wurm breathed a roaring jet of lambent blue flame perhaps fifty feet long. Wiz flinched back from the heat and noise. Behind him he heard screams as people stampeded for safety. But the dragon's head was turned away from the Wizard's Keep. Wurm extended his index talon until it was immersed in the fire. He held it there until the tip glowed bright red. Then he reached down and whetted the heat-softened claw on the rough stone of the castle wall. He left three smoking, foot-deep grooves in the stone before he was satisfied. Then he turned his attention back to Wiz.

"Now Wizard," the dragon said mildly, "you were saying?"

"Can you give me ten minutes to pack?"

THREE

HE WHO RIDES A DRAGON ...

Initial client contact is often the most delicate part of the project.

—The Consultants' Handbook

"I do not like this," Moira said as she and Wiz walked back out to the courtyard a few minutes later. Bal-Simba and the others were trailing by a few yards to give them some privacy.

Wiz grimaced. "It's not my idea of a summer afternoon's stroll either, but we don't have a lot of choice."

"We could refuse the dragon now," she said fiercely, "and fight him if he wills it!"

"And get a lot of people killed unnecessarily." Wiz shook his head. "You heard Bal-Simba. We can't protect the town right now, much less the countryside. In a few hours we'll have the spells ready to hunt him down, but now we've got to buy time."

"And you are to be the sacrifice," Moira said bitterly. Then she sighed. "Oh, I know you are right, love. And so is Bal-Simba. But for once I wish it could be someone else."

15

Wiz stopped under the final gate and pulled her close, almost losing his staff in the process. "Come on, it's not that bad. I've only got to stall him for a few hours and, hey, maybe the dragon wants something easy." He kissed her and felt her relax in his arms. "Don't worry, I'll be fine. Honest."

Moira broke away from him and tried to smile. "I know, love," she said softly.

"Besides, I've got this." Wiz held up his hand to show off his ring of protection. "Anything dangerous happens and this spell kicks in immediately. So quit worrying." He leaned close and kissed her again. Then he let go, turned and stepped out into the courtyard.

Wurm was where Wiz had left him. "Are you ready, Wizard?"

Wiz slipped the leather thong of his staff over his head and shoulder. Then he exhaled and tried to sound chipper. "Ready as I'll ever be."

The dragon bent its enormous neck down and Wiz swung his leg over. Then the beast raised its head and the spines moved together, cradling Wiz gently but firmly between them. Wiz made himself as comfortable as he could and tried not to think what would happen if the dragon arched his neck further.

Instead Wurm raised his head and Wiz was carried aloft with the swooping suddenness of an amusement park ride. Before he could adjust to his new perspective the dragon pushed off the wall and unfurled his gigantic wings with a beat that sent wind swirling through the courtyard, kicking up stray leaves and blowing grit back in Wiz's face. Wiz squinched his eyes shut involuntarily and nearly lost his lunch as his inner ear, deprived of a visual cross check, protested strongly. By the time he got his eyes open, the Wizard's Keep was dwindling toy-like below and the land was spreading out like a patterned quilt beneath them.

✧　　✧　　✧

Bareback on a dragon was not the most comfortable way to travel, Wiz discovered. At least not when you were riding a monster like Wurm. Unlike the cavalry mounts, Wurm was so large that a human could not straddle his neck comfortably. Trying to sit astride was like doing the splits. By extending his legs forward along the dragon's neck Wiz could bring them comfortably close together, but that left him supporting most of their weight with his stomach muscles. Eventually he settled for a jockey-style seat with his legs drawn up as if his feet were in very short stirrups. If he shifted position frequently his muscles didn't protest too badly.

To keep his mind off his muscles—and his predicament—he studied the scenery passing beneath them. As nearly as he could estimate from the size of the fields below they were about as high as an airliner flies. But airliners are heated and pressurized and there was no sign of either on Wurm's neck. Still, legs and back aside, Wiz was as comfortable—well, as physically comfortable—as he had been back in the courtyard of the Wizard's Keep. Wiz spent a few minutes considering the implications of that for this world's physics and then finally dismissed it as magic.

After an hour or more Wiz began to fidget, and not just from the cramps. They were passing beyond the lands of man and well into the Wild Wood. "How much further is it?" he asked.

"Far enough," his host/mount replied.

"I mean when will we get there?"

"When we arrive." The dragon sounded amused. "You mortals, always so fastened on time and distance."

"I thought dragons were mortal too. I mean you die don't you?"

"Even the ever-living can die, Wizard, as you know. Mortal implies a finite life-span."

"Well, don't dragons grow old and die?"

"Grow old, yes. But I have never heard of a dragon dying naturally."

That had several implications and Wiz wasn't sure he liked any of them. "How old are you?"

"I do not know. Even if I had remembered to count the seasons, we do not become self-aware until we are nearly full grown. Ask the little one in the courtyard how old he is and see what you get for an answer."

"The little one . . . oh, you mean the young dragon."

Again the amusement in Wurm's "voice." "There was no one else in the courtyard as I recall."

"That's the pet, uh, playmate of a friend's kid. He calls him Fluffy for some reason."

"That is because he is," Wurm said in Wiz's head.

"Fluffy?"

"Of course. Can you not sense it?"

Wiz wasn't sure whether the dragon was joking or not and considering the circumstances he didn't want to find out.

"In any event," Wurm went on, "the experience will probably help him. Your kind is spreading everywhere and knowing humans well will serve him even better than it has served me."

"You were a cavalry mount, weren't you?" Wiz asked with a sudden burst of insight.

"I was."

"I thought you said you didn't remember before you became intelligent."

"I said we could not count. Just because we are not intelligent does not mean we do not remember."

Wiz wondered if dragons bore grudges.

"In probability it helped me," Wurm said, so quickly Wiz's next wonder was if dragons could read minds. "Most of my kind die before they attain reason. A few score years fed and cared for undoubtedly bettered my odds."

"But don't your parents take care of you?"

"We are able to care for ourselves from the moment we hatch," the dragon said. "Our mother is long gone before our birth."

"I'm sorry."

"Why? It is the way of dragonkind since time began. We avoid the entanglements of those who are born in groups of their kind and it ensures we will be strong and clever—those who survive."

Wurm didn't say it but the subtext was clear: This was one strong, clever dragon.

They flew a while more in silence.

"Wurm? When you were in the cavalry whose side were you on? I mean who . . ."

"Does it matter, Wizard?" There was a trace of irritation in the dragon's thought. "It was long ago, it happened and it is done. That is enough."

Wiz didn't try to make any more small talk.

Northward they flew, and eastward, for what seemed like hours. The sun rose to noon and sank toward the western horizon as they traveled. Below them the neatly tended fields and villages of the World of humans gave way to the rolling green of the Wild Wood and that in turn to a land of jumbled mountain ranges and steep, narrow valleys. Then gradually the mountains flattened and the valleys widened into gently sloping grasslands. The forest did not come back, save in scattered patches, but the land was green and pleasant. Squinting ahead Wiz could see more mountains rising off in the distance.

"Yonder lie the Dragon Lands," Wurm informed him. "Do you wish to turn back now, Wizard?"

Wiz hesitated. Part of him wanted more than anything to turn around and go home. But there was another part of him that drove him grimly onward. There was a problem here and he had to solve it. *Had* to.

Besides, if they turned around now it meant more agonizing hours riding dragonback.

"No," Wiz told Wurm. "Let's go on."

Wurm's expression didn't change but Wiz felt the dragon "nod" mentally. There was a small distant part of him that told him he ought to be worried about that.

Wiz glanced at the sinking sun and estimated the distance to the mountains. "Is that where we're heading?"

"Our destination is somewhat closer," the dragon said and, without word or warning, winged over and dropped steeply. Wiz whooped in terrified surprise and wrapped both arms around the spine in front of him. He had a confused, whirling view of a broad grassy valley cut by a meandering river with a substantial village or small city nestled along its banks. Then everything was hidden by Wurm's enormous wings as they locked to brake for a landing.

"Dismount. We are here."

"Fine," said Wiz, trying to throw his leg over the dragon's neck. He found it was numb from hours of sitting and he had to use both hands to hoist the leg over so he could slide off.

He tried to step away from Wurm's side and his knees nearly buckled.

"Where is here?" he asked to cover his embarrassment.

"The Dragon Marches," Wurm told him. "Here the lands of mortals run to the borders of the Dragon Lands."

They were on a grassy knoll beside a dirt road that wound through the valley toward the village in the distance. Dotted here and there he could see clusters of buildings that looked like farmsteads. The fields were laid out in strips, most emerald green with growing grain.

The air was cool but not unpleasant and the breeze whispered gently through the grass.

Wiz took a couple of tottering steps. His legs were more or less working again, but his lower back ached terribly and his butt was on fire as the circulation returned.

"I didn't think people could live beyond the Wild Wood because of the magic."

"Humans have spread further than your Council of the North ever knew," Wurm told him. "Here there is magic, but less than in the Wild Wood."

"So I see." Wiz shaded his eyes against the setting sun. Off toward the village he saw movement on the road, as if people were coming this way.

"Okay," Wiz grunted, stretching backwards to try to get the kinks out of his back, "now what's this job of yours?"

The dragon regarded Wiz with an unwinking golden eye.

"It is not my job, precisely," Wurm told him. "Rather it is for them. The ones who live in this valley."

"I thought you . . ."

The dragon breathed a thunderous snort of amusement. "What need would I have of mortal magic? It is the inhabitants of the valley who need you."

Wiz looked down the road. There was definitely a crowd of people headed toward them.

"Okay, why do *they* need me?"

"Why to defend them against dragons," Wurm told him. Then with a sudden motion and a thunderclap of air beneath his enormous wings the dragon launched himself into the sky, leaving Wiz to face the people of the valley.

"Remember, Wizard," Wurm's voice came into Wiz's mind. "Your duty is to them. Fulfill it well."

There were perhaps a hundred people coming up

the road in a compact mass. *Welcoming committee?* Wiz thought. *But why didn't we just land closer to the village?* Most of them were carrying things, as if they had left their work to come welcome him. As they drew closer he could hear them, a low rumble that somehow didn't sound like cheering. In fact it sounded downright ugly.

By then the crowd was close enough that he could make out details. They were all men, mostly roughly dressed and all carrying something. Some of them had pitchforks, some of them were carrying flails and pruning hooks and some of them just had big sticks. None of them looked in the least bit friendly.

"Uh, hi," Wiz said, smiling weakly.

Moira fidgeted in the window seat looking north. Outside the bottoms of the clouds were turning pink in the setting sun. To the embroidery in her lap she had managed to add perhaps a dozen stitches.

"Negotiation or not, he should have been back by now," she announced.

Bal-Simba looked over from the oversized arm chair across the room. "Long before now," the black giant amended. "At the very least he should have contacted us."

By unspoken consent they had gathered in the programmers' workroom. Danny and Jerry worked at their desks, Bal-Simba had settled himself into his special chair and relayed instructions through his assistant, Arianne. June, Danny's wife, was sitting in the corner with Ian asleep in her lap and Moira was in the window seat looking out the way Wiz had gone.

The first several hours after Wiz's departure had been a rush of frantic effort as programmers and wizards alike prepared for battle with the dragon. In several places in the castle wizards of the Mighty were still casting spells and apprentice programmers were still laboring, but in the main preparations had been complete for a couple of hours. Now as the long summer day drew to a close there was nothing left to do but wait and watch for some sign of Wiz or the dragon.

Danny turned from his workbench. "Time for the locator spell?"

Moira stood up. "Past time."

Once before Wiz had been kidnapped. As a result all the programmers carried a spell which would locate them anywhere in the World.

Jerry took down a beaten copper bowl from the top of a corner cabinet. The bowl was nearly hidden by scrolls and papers and he almost caused a small avalanche as he worked it free.

"We need some water," Jerry said looking around.

Moira snatched up the vase she had filled with flowers only hours before, tossed the flowers on the floor and extended it to Jerry.

As Jerry poured water into the bowl, Arianne entered, perhaps summoned by Bal-Simba. She stood beside him while they completed preparations.

Finally Jerry took a splinter from a vial and floated it carefully on the water's surface.

arg wiz locate exe! Jerry commanded.

As the five leaned over the bowl, the needle spun twice around widdershins, quivered and then slowly drifted off until it was pointing firmly south.

"South?" Danny protested. "But they went north."

"The needle points south," Moira said. "They must have circled around when they were out of sight of the castle."

Jerry frowned. "Hold it." He reached into the bowl and nudged the sliver of wood gently with his finger. The needle swung aimlessly and finally stopped, pointing in another direction entirely.

"Northwest?" Moira said, "but . . ."

Jerry tapped the needle again. The sliver bobbed aimlessly.

"Shit! We've lost him."

Almost unnoticed by the others, Bal-Simba whispered something to Arianne. The tall blond woman nodded and hurried from the room.

"But the locator . . ." Moira began.

"Has been masked," Bal-Simba said, rising from his chair to join them.

The hedge witch rounded on Jerry. "You *swore* to me that the spell could follow him anywhere. No matter what."

Jerry spread his hands helplessly "It should. I don't understand it."

"I do, I fear," Bal-Simba rumbled. "The dragon is shielding Wiz's location from us."

Moira clenched her fists and hissed something very unladylike under her breath.

"I suspect he had no intention of attacking us at all," the giant wizard went on slowly. "That was simply a ruse to distract us while he made off with Wiz. And while we prepared for the attack which would never come the dragon wove his spell masking their whereabouts." He scowled fiercely. "As Wiz would say, we have been slurped."

"That's suckered," Danny corrected.

"What it is does not matter," Moira snapped. "We have to find him."

Bal-Simba shrugged. "Easier said than done, I fear."

Danny twisted the ring on his finger. "I thought these things could punch through any counter-magic."

"Any human magic," Bal-Simba said. "Dragon magic is different and of a very high order. This Wurm is extremely powerful even for a dragon, I think."

"What do you think he wants with Wiz?" Danny asked.

Bal-Simba only shrugged. "Who knows the mind of a dragon?" Then he caught Moira's expression. "But I do not think he intends to kill him," he added quickly, "or even harm him, necessarily. Beyond that? I would not venture to guess."

"Wait a minute," Jerry said. "Can't Wiz contact us?"

"He can if he is unconstrained," Bal-Simba said.

They all fell silent. Everyone in the room knew what it took to constrain a wizard from communicating.

"Well, how do we find him?"

"The Watchers are being alerted now," the giant black wizard said. He turned to Jerry. "My Lord, can you release the recon demons?"

"I'll get on it immediately. It will take a while to extend their coverage though."

"As quickly as you can, then. Now if you will excuse me . . ." He turned and hurried from the room.

FOUR

MISDIRECTION FOR THE DIRECTIONLESS

Sometimes the problem you're hired to solve is not the real problem.

—*The Consultants' Handbook*

Okay, Wiz admitted and he leaned against the bars of his cell, *maybe it wasn't my best opening line.*

At least they hadn't killed him. On the other hand, there was no guarantee that they *wouldn't* kill him. And considering the way they'd acted that was a definite possibility. In fact that option had strong minority support in the mob. What had passed for cooler heads had held out for "The Rock," whatever that was. Wiz had a suspicion he'd find out soon enough and an even stronger suspicion he wouldn't like it.

After a brief argument over his fate, they had hustled him back to town with a pitchfork in his back. Now he was on the second floor of a fairly substantial building. More precisely, he was in jail.

Wiz had never seen one of this world's jails before but he had no doubt that he was in one now. There were bars running from floor to ceiling on three sides and a windowless stone wall on the fourth. There was a narrow bunk bolted to the wall and a chamberpot underneath. The layout reminded Wiz vaguely of a Western movie set, but the substantial bars were no stage props. The cells to either side of him were empty. The place was clean enough, but smelled faintly of must and dust, as if it wasn't swept regularly.

From the glimpses he had gotten as the mob frog-marched him through town, the place was larger than it had appeared. In fact it was a good-sized town or even a small city, enclosed in stone walls. Most of the buildings were built of a combination of timber and stone, but a few of the more imposing ones were all stone. That included this very imposing jail off the main square of the town.

There were offices of some sort down on the ground floor and every so often someone would mount the narrow staircase to peek in. Somewhat less frequently the jailer, a thin, sour-looking man with jug ears and a big nose, would come all the way into the room to check on him. He was careful not to get too close, Wiz noticed, and if he had the keys he wasn't carrying them.

Wiz toyed with the idea of creating a spell to unlock the door but he decided the best thing to do was to wait and see. If he was going to solve these people's problem he needed more information and he wasn't likely to get that as a fugitive from justice.

Still, it wasn't a very comfortable situation. Wiz sat on the edge of the bunk and wondered how he had gotten into this mess.

Let's see, he thought. *A dragon wants me to protect these people from dragons. The people who live here want to string me up because I'm working for a dragon— only I'm not working for a dragon, I just agreed to find out what the dragon wanted. Except the people still want to string me up for associating with dragons and I'm*

still not sure what the dragon really wants and . . ."
And he was getting a headache.

For some reason he remembered visiting a psych major buddy in her lab long ago and far away. Sybil had been running rats through mazes as part of some kind of project and while they talked she kept a stopwatch on the rat and its frantic efforts to escape. It had been a long time ago and Wiz found he couldn't remember what Sybil looked like very well, but he had a crystal-sharp memory of the expression on the rat's face.

There was a stirring in a corner of the room off behind the stairs. Wiz looked again and someone stepped out of the shadows. Someone tall, slender and wearing a jerkin and tight trousers. Then she took another step out into the full light and Wiz saw it was a woman. A young woman, actually, he amended, with dark hair down to her shoulders, dark eyes and fair skin. She strode lightly across the room with the easy grace he associated with gymnasts or dancers. Somehow Wiz didn't think she was either of those things.

She stopped several paces from the bars and put her hands on her hips. "So you're the wizard, eh?"

Wiz nodded. "Who are you?"

"Name's Malkin. I'm here for stealing. What'd you do?"

"Not much of anything, actually. My name's Wiz."

"You came here riding a dragon, didn't you? That's enough."

"Well, if you knew why did you ask?"

Malkin shrugged.

"And," he added, "if you're a prisoner too, how come you're on the outside?"

Malkin grinned and held up a key ring. "Like I said, I steal things."

"And you're still hanging around here?"

His new acquaintance grinned. "Jail's as good a place as any to doss," she said lightly. "Besides, listening is more fun than escaping. They're arguing about you in the sheriff's office."

"What are they saying about me?"

"They want to take you to The Rock."

"What's The Rock?"

"That's where they chain out the condemned for the dragons to eat," Malkin told him. "Supposed to keep the dragons satisfied so they don't eat anyone important."

"Does it work?"

"Nah. But the dummies keep doing it anyway." She shrugged. "You're an outsider, so you're natural."

"Not much tourist business here, is there?" Wiz asked sourly.

Malkin shrugged again. "Anyhow, the folks who brought you want to take you to The Rock right away and the sheriff doesn't want to until the mayor and council have a chance to see you. So far the sheriff's winning. That means you've got a few hours because it will take them that long to get most of the council together."

"Does the sheriff think the mayor won't want to see me killed?" Wiz asked hopefully.

"Nah. But ol' Droopy's a stickler for protocol. If he isn't consulted he'll make the sheriff's life miserable for weeks. So it's better for the sheriff to wait."

Wiz opened his mouth to reply but Malkin faded soundlessly back into the shadows. An instant later the jailer poked his head up the stairwell.

"Who are you talking to?" he demanded.

"Myself," Wiz said brightly. "I often have long conversations with myself. I find I'm excellent company. I play bridge with myself, too. You don't happen to have a deck of cards, do you?"

The jailer looked at him oddly and ducked back down the stairs.

Wiz lay down on his bunk and thought hard. Unless these people had some very powerful magicians, something he had seen no sign of, he could get out of here any time he wanted to. But that wouldn't help solve his problem. Given a little time to prepare spells, his magic would probably let him beat a dragon—provided it wasn't too big or too powerful. But he didn't think that he could take on all the dragons in the Dragon Lands alone and win. That obviously wasn't the answer.

He might be here to help these people but they felt he had a higher and better purpose as dragon bait. They didn't want help, they wanted a sacrificial goat they could hang all their trouble on. Yet he *had* to help them! It was imperative that he solve their problem.

Wiz chased the problem round and round in his mind without finding even the beginnings of a solution. He did, however, find an increasing sympathy for that long-ago rat in the nearly forgotten psych lab. He wondered if the rat had ever found the solution to its problem. Then he wondered what constituted a "solution" to a psych maze from the rat's point of view. The patch of sunlight from the window in the side wall finished its journey up the wall and gradually dimmed out at dusk. Outside the street noises quieted and died as the city settled into sleep. Eventually Wiz did the same.

Gently, soundlessly, the searcher floated north into the graying dawn. Physically it looked like a smear of smoke or a wisp of gray silk about the size of a hand-kerchief. Magically it was nearly as uncomplicated. All it did was gather sense impressions and pass them on to a slightly larger, somewhat more substantial entity floating along well behind it. It had only limited mobility and moved mostly by floating on the wind.

By itself it wasn't much, but the searching spell cranked them out by the tens of thousands. The searchers fed back into hundreds of the larger concentrators and they fed into dozens of high-level analysis demons. Given time they could find anything in the World that was in the open and unmasked. Slowly, inexorably, the net of magical watchers was spreading over the face of the World.

The rising sun tinted the underside of the clouds orange but the mountains below were still in deep shadow. Soon the sun would break above the horizon and bathe the mountain peaks in fire. It would be a glorious sunrise but the searcher was incapable of knowing or caring. It floated where the wind took it, working generally north on the air currents.

The searcher saw the speck detach itself from a peak and waft into the air, but it attached no more significance to it than to the pinkened clouds or the dark valleys. Analysis was for the higher echelons. So it faithfully recorded the speck's growth and resolution into a dragon, climbing to just below the bottom of the clouds. It watched without apprehension as the dragon approached, its great wings cleaving the air in mighty beats. It felt no fear as the dragon swooped down with its wings slightly folded to increase the speed of the dive, and no terror as a gout of dragon fire blotted out its existence. All of this it simply recorded and transmitted back to the collector, neither knowing nor caring that another dragon had flamed the collector minutes before.

Its killer, a young female only recently sentient, felt a pang of fierce joy at having destroyed the intruder. She gloried in her strength and prowess as she climbed toward the clouds to begin her day's hunting—and to kill any more of the strange creatures who invaded her territory.

Back at the Wizard's Keep, Jerry Andrews studied the results on his display and frowned.

"A problem?" Arianne asked mildly. Bal-Simba had been up late and his assistant had taken the early watch. Jerry had been up all night and probably wouldn't crash for a few more hours.

"Something's happening to the searchers." He took a long pull on the mug of blackmoss tea on his workbench and swiveled to face the tall blond woman. "We've got good coverage on the lands of man and the Wild Wood, but when we move outside that territory we start losing them."

"Losing them?"

"The search demons. Mostly they're being destroyed. Some we're just losing contact with. I think those are local magical effects. But a lot of them are being attacked by dragons."

It was Arianne's turn to frown. "That could be natural. Dragons are common beyond the borders of the lands of man and they do not like other flying objects in their air." She paused.

"Do you think it's natural?"

"I do not know," the wizardess said slowly. "I would not count on it."

"Wurm's doing?"

"It may be. However, dragons are solitary creatures. It takes a great cause to get them to cooperate, even slightly."

"Which means that kidnapping Wiz is a very big deal for the dragons."

"What it means, I think, is a problem for Bal-Simba when he awakens, and possibly the Council of the North. It is far beyond my abilities to decipher. What does this do to your search?"

"Complicates the hell out of it." Jerry swiveled back to the columns of glowing letters above his bench. "We're not getting any searchers more than a couple of hundred leagues beyond the borders of the known world. Unless we can change that we're going to be limited in where we can look." He took another pull on his tea mug. "Somehow I don't think we're going to find Wiz in the known world."

FIVE

A SUDDEN CAREER CHANGE

Never tell them the truth until you check to find out what the truth is today.

—The Consultants' Handbook

"You still here?"

Wiz jerked awake and there was Malkin standing just outside his cell.

"Of course I'm still here. I'm in jail!"

Malkin shrugged. "So? You're a wizard, aren't you? Why don't you just magic yourself out of here?"

"I can't do that," Wiz said miserably.

"Well, don't you know other wizards? They could get you out of here."

"I can't do that either," Wiz said.

"Why not?"

"I just can't. I've got to solve these people's problems."

"Look," said Malkin, obviously exasperated, "the folk hereabouts don't want you to solve their problems. They want to stake you out like a pig at a barbecue."

"I can't run away," Wiz said simply. "I've got to stay, don't you see?"

33

"I see they're right," Malkin said. "Them as says wizards is all cracked."

She was right, he knew. The smart thing would be to magic himself out of the place, walk the Wizard's Way back to the castle and return with enough help to clean up the whole situation. But he couldn't do that. He just *couldn't*. There had to be a better way and he had to find it on his own. Malkin sniffed and Wiz looked miserable as he pondered the trap he was in.

And then, in a blinding flash, he had it!

The misery and indecision were gone and his brain shifted into overdrive as he saw the possibilities. He started to smile. Then he started to grin. Then his expression became positively maniacal with glee.

Like most programmers, Wiz preferred straight talk and plain dealing. But he wasn't a fanatic about it. It was obvious the only thing straight talk and plain dealing would get him in this situation was a quick trip to The Rock.

Malkin edged away from the bars. "Are you all right?"

"Never better," he assured her. "Never better. It's just the solution is so obvious."

"What is it then?"

"Well," he told Malkin slowly. "There's reality, and then there's Creative Reality."

"Creative reality?"

"It's kind of like Creative Accounting—except they don't send you to prison if they catch you at it."

"Meaning what?" the girl said with a frown.

"Meaning that a true master of Creative Reality borrows their watch and tells them what time it is, and then gets paid for it," Wiz told her. "That's the first rule of Creative Reality. You make people pay you to solve their problems—and then you make them like it."

"But these people don't want you to solve their

problems," Malkin said in the same exasperated voice. "They want you for a sacrifice."

Wiz's smile got even broader. "That's normally the way it is for the masters of Creative Reality. Kind of the job's ground state."

"The only thing that's going to get ground is you if you don't get out of here."

"Oh, not at all. Look, the first secret of consulting— that's what we call applied Creative Reality—is that people don't need an outsider to tell them what to do about their problems. They know they've got problems and they usually know what their choices are. What they don't know is how to get from where they are to a place where they have made a choice. So they bring in a consultant and most of the time half the people in the organization don't want advice, they want a scapegoat—a sacrifice. Now they've got an outsider in the game they can blame their troubles on. But the game's rigged against him from the first."

Now Malkin was intrigued rather than exasperated. "Yeah. So?"

"So what the successful consultant does, once he's dealt into the game, is cheat like mad."

"I still don't see . . ." Malkin began, but there was some commotion on the stairs as the warder made his way up. The thief slipped into an adjacent cell the instant before the warder's head poked through the floor, quickly followed by the rest of him. He stood by the stairway, drew himself to unaccustomed attention and announced: "His Honor, Mayor Hendrick Hastlebone, Lord Mayor and head of the wool merchants guild and the honorable members of the city council. Mayfortunesmileonthe-honorablemayorandcouncilors." Then he relaxed and slumped again.

The mayor was a portly individual with basset eyes, a substantial paunch and a considerable appreciation of his own importance. He was dressed in a short robe of green velvet trimmed with gold. Around his neck hung a heavy, gaudy gold chain of office topped off with a jeweled and tasteless medallion.

One of his councilors was tall and lean, one was short and bald and the others were pretty much nondescript. They wore either the short robe and hose like the mayor or long robes with deep hanging sleeves and they all had heavy gold chains around their necks, only slightly less gaudy than the mayor's. They advanced in a tight knot with the mayor in the lead until they stood before Wiz's cell.

Wiz stood waiting for them, not quite leaning against the wall, but giving the impression that he was completely at ease. He watched the mayor carefully and just as the man drew breath to speak he cut him off.

"Good of you gentlemen to come."

The mayor was caught with his mouth open. He closed it, scowled and tried again.

"Who are you?"

"My name's Wiz Zumwalt."

"A wizard?" one of the councilors interjected. Mayor Hastlebone glared over his shoulder, but Wiz and the others ignored it.

"I'm a wizard by training, but by profession I'm a consultant. I solve other people's problems for a living."

The mayor raised an eyebrow. "Most folks have enough to do solving their own problems."

"That's why we consultants are so rare. And so much in demand."

The mayor snorted.

"Now, I understand that *you* have a problem with dragons," Wiz said. "I can show you how to rid yourselves of your dragon trouble—for a very reasonable fee, of course."

"Of course," said one of the councilors, the lean one,

an individual with an oily manner and a puce wool robe that clashed horribly with his complexion.

"What makes you think you know how to handle dragons?" the mayor demanded.

"I come from the Valley of Quartz—Silicon Valley— and we have no problems at all with dragons there."

"We have our own ways of handling dragons," one of the councilors said.

"I'm sure you do," Wiz said, assuming a manner he had seen so many times when consultants made a pitch. "And what you've accomplished here is really remarkable—all things considered. But perhaps you could benefit from a more professional, scientific approach to your problem."

"How did you get here?" a hatchet-faced man in a malachite green robe demanded in a tone that indicated he knew the answer perfectly well.

"By dragon. It's a very expeditious manner of travel." Wiz smiled. "You ought to try it sometime."

That set them buzzing. The mayor turned his back and the whole group huddled together, muttering to one another. Once or twice someone poked his head up out of the pack and craned his neck to get a better view of their visitor. Wiz stayed where he was and tried desperately to look as if he didn't have a care in the world.

"Very well," Mayor Hendrick said finally. "If—*if* you can completely rid the valley of dragons, what would be your fee?"

"One tenth of the town's produce for a year," Wiz said as blandly as he could manage.

"Preposterous!"

"Hardly. The dragons cost you more than that in a bad year and probably almost that much in most years."

"Absurd," said the mayor, with a little less conviction.

"Quite reasonable, actually."

"It would be worth it if he succeeded," said one of the councilors, a portly man in a forest green short robe and rose pink hose.

"Utter nonsense," said another councilor.

"Are you afraid he might succeed?" asked a silver-haired man in sea blue.

The mayor's face turned red and a vein in his temple started to throb.

"Gentlemen, gentlemen," interposed a pudgy man with a rim of white hair around a sweat-shiny scalp. "Suppose it got about that this wizard had made his offer and we had refused out of hand? Can we afford *not* to let him try?"

The councilors nodded and muttered among themselves and even the mayor seemed momentarily lost in thought.

"Very well," Hendrick said at last. "You shall have your opportunity. But," and he stepped close to the bars and wagged his finger under Wiz's nose, "we expect results. We only pay for results."

The fact that he didn't haggle over the price told Wiz the mayor didn't expect him to complete the assignment successfully.

"Plus room and board, while I work," Wiz said.

The mayor opened his mouth to object, caught the mood of the council and merely nodded.

"Oh yes, I'll need a local assistant."

Hendrick didn't look pleased. "Don't know that I can spare anyone."

"What about the young lady over there?" Wiz pointed to Malkin, sitting demurely in her cell. "I believe she is available."

The mayor turned to look at Malkin and a smile spread slowly over his face. Wiz didn't need to read minds to know he saw a way to get rid of two thorns in his side when Wiz failed.

"Very well. Warder! Release the prisoner into this wizard's keeping."

As soon as the cell door was unlocked Malkin threw herself about the mayor's neck, weeping and thanking him for his generosity. Since she was nearly half a head taller than the mayor, the result was incongruous to say the least.

Mayor Hendrick was still trying to brush her off when someone burst into the office below shouting for the watch.

There was a mutter of conversation downstairs and then two sets of feet came pounding up the staircase.

"Dragon!" panted the lean straw-haired man in the lead. "Dragon's hit the Baggot Place. Got Farmer Baggot and his whole family."

"Ate them all?" demanded the mayor.

"Not yet," the man gasped. "Least not when I left. He's got them penned in the farmyard."

The mayor turned back to the cell and smiled at Wiz in a way that wasn't at all pleasant. "Well, Wizard," he said, "it seems you face your first test."

SIX

MORE THAN ONE WAY TO
SKIN A DRAGON

First get them talking.

> *—The Consultants' Handbook*

The Baggot Place was about a mile out of town. Since the mayor and council didn't offer to provide transportation, Wiz and his new apprentice had to walk.

It was a fine morning for walking. The sky was clear, the air was cool, the sun golden, and the morning light made the dew on the brilliant green grass sparkle and glitter as far as the eye could see.

They weren't the only ones on the road. Ahead and behind them, people were trooping out of town along the road. Occasionally an apprentice or schoolboy would overtake them and run on ahead.

"Are you sure we're going in the right direction?" Wiz asked Malkin.

"This is the way to the Baggot Place and that's a fact," Malkin replied, tossing and catching something shiny as she strode along, her long legs letting her match Wiz stride for stride.

"Then why are all these people coming this way? Don't they know they're headed toward the dragon, not away from it?"

"Course they know," Malkin said. "They want to see the show."

"The show?"

"The dragon burning down the farm. Or maybe even you destroying the dragon." The way she said it made it obvious which way Malkin thought it would go.

"Hmmpf!" Wiz snorted. Then he got a closer look at the shiny thing his companion was juggling. It was a heavy gold chain with a big medallion attached.

"Where did you get that?"

"Pinched it when old baggy eyes wasn't looking," Malkin said gaily. "He never even noticed it."

"Well give it back!" Wiz commanded. "Preferably so he doesn't know you took it."

Malkin turned sullen for a moment and then brightened. "You mean un-steal it? Put it back around his neck so he doesn't notice? Now that could be fun."

Wiz groaned. Obviously his new associate's profession was an avocation as much as a necessity. Kleptomania he hadn't counted on.

"Why'd you spring me anyway?" Malkin asked, tucking the chain away in her jerkin.

"Because I needed someone who knows this place to tell me what's going on. And so far you're the only honest person I've met." Then he eyed the bulge in Malkin's clothing.

"So to speak," he added.

Little knots of citizens had already gathered on the hill overlooking the farm. They stood about in groups of two or three and gossiped and pointed down at the farmstead below. Wiz noticed none of them ventured even a little ways down the grassy slope toward the stricken dwelling.

As Wiz and Malkin toiled up the road the crowd's excitement grew.

"The wizard's coming!" an adolescent male voice shouted. "Here comes the wizard." Heads turned and people shifted to catch a glimpse of Wiz and Malkin as they climbed toward the brow of the hill.

The farmstead at the base of the hill was built of warm yellow sandstone with a dark slate roof. There was a three-story farmhouse, a large stone barn and several stone outbuildings, all clustered tightly around the farm-yard. Where the buildings did not touch they were connected by a high stone wall.

Protection against dragons, Wiz realized. Only this time it hadn't worked. Wiz could hear the terrified lowing of cattle in the barn and in the courtyard he saw the flash of sunlight off scales as the dragon moved.

The gawkers edged closer to Wiz and Malkin, some of them shifting their position so they could see both the wizard and the farmhouse at the same time.

Obviously they expected him to produce a white horse and suit of armor out of nowhere and ride down to do battle with the monster. Or at the very least start throwing lightning bolts.

But Wiz didn't have a spell for horse and armor handy and he suspected lightning bolts would only annoy the creature. Besides, he doubted he could kill it before it burned the farmstead to the ground and killed every-one inside.

In fact, Wiz realized, he didn't have the faintest idea just *what* he was going to do next. So far everything had been reaction and reflex. Now he needed some-thing more and he simply didn't have it. He felt the townspeople's eyes boring into him from all sides and he flushed under the weight.

Well, he wasn't going to accomplish anything from up here. He'd have to confront the dragon.

"You wait here," he told Malkin. "I'm going to go down there and try to talk him out of this."

Malkin looked at him. "You're going to go in there?" she asked. "Just like that?"

"Well, yes."

"And you're going to talk to the dragon. Get him to release his prisoners?"

"I hope so."

Malkin eyed her erstwhile employer. "Around here we've got a name for people what talks to dragons."

"Traitor?" Wiz asked apprehensively.

"No. Lunch."

It was a long, long way from the top of the hill to the farmyard gate. Well, Wiz acknowledged, it may have only been a few hundred yards, but it *felt* like a long, long way. By the time he got to the door of age-grayed oak planks in the yellow stone wall he was sweating, even though the dew was still on the grass.

Wiz stood before the gate for a moment, gathering his courage and mentally reviewing his plan. But his courage wasn't cooperating and reviewing his plan only reminded him he didn't have one, so he took a deep breath and knocked on the gate.

The door opened a crack and a three-foot talon hooked through the slit and pulled it wide. Suddenly Wiz was face to face with a very large dragon.

It wasn't a monster on the scale of Wurm. Objectively he knew the creature couldn't be much more than a hundred feet long. But objectivity doesn't count for much when you are one easy snap away from a set of jaws that are longer than you are high, all studded with fangs as long as your forearm. It doesn't help any when those jaws start salivating as soon as you come into view.

"Helllooo," the dragon's honey-and-iron voice rang in Wiz's skull. "Do come in." The last part was said pleasantly, but there was no doubt it was a command.

Wiz stepped through the gate as if it was the most normal thing in the world. He found himself standing between two enormous clawed forepaws and staring at an expanse of armored chest.

The dragon stretched his neck out until his head was nearly twenty feet above the ground. Then he cocked his head to one side and regarded Wiz unblinkingly. Wiz resisted an impulse to wave inanely to the beast and a much stronger impulse to turn and run. So he just stood there, hands at his side and with what he knew must be a monumentally silly smile plastered on his face.

"My, you are a bit odd, aren't you?" the dragon said at last.

"I beg your pardon?"

"Normally the only humans who approach us are warriors who come blustering and bashing, or magicians who come hurling all sorts of dreadfully tacky spells. But you're not doing either. I wonder what you could be?"

"I'm a negotiator. I'm here to arrange for the release of the hostages."

"Hostages? Oh, you mean those." The dragon jerked its head toward a corner of the farmyard and Wiz saw several people huddled together. One young man scrambled to his feet as if to dash for safety through the open gate, but without turning his head the dragon lifted his tail and brandished it threateningly. The youth turned white and sank to his knees.

"Actually they're not hostages. More in the nature of provisions."

"That's what I wanted to talk to you about," Wiz said.

"You're not frightened, are you?"

"No," Wiz lied.

"Oh, I do hope you're not," the dragon said. "These—" he twitched his tail at the cowering knot of people "—are frightened positively speechless and I was so hoping for some amusing conversation before dinner."

"Uh, I don't suppose I could convince you to make a meal of beef?"

The dragon licked his chops and his fangs glinted evilly in the morning sun. "Oh, certainly. As a second course."

Then he was all mock civility again. "But I am being churlish. Allow me to introduce myself. I am called Griswold."

"Pleased to meet you," Wiz lied once more. "I'm Wiz Zumwalt."

"Ah, yes," Griswold said, regarding him closely. "And a wizard too, I see. My, my. How opportune of you to come to call."

Wiz was feeling that it was less opportune by the moment, but he didn't say that.

"Yes, ah, now about releasing these people . . ."

"Oh, quite out of the question, I can assure you. But surely you knew that before you arrived?" The dragon heaved a great gusty sigh. "You humans, always thinking that wishing for something can make it happen. You are amusing, but you are so dreadfully illogical."

"And dragons are logical?"

"Of course."

For a mad instant Wiz tried to imagine what the NAND diagram for a logical dragon would look like.

And then he saw his opening.

He hesitated. The last time he had tried this with one of this World's creatures he had nearly lost his soul. But he didn't have much choice. He sure couldn't fight the monster, he didn't think he could out-magic it on the spur of the moment and he didn't have any other ideas.

The people of this world didn't think in the abstract.

Abstractions and mathematical thought tended to puzzle and confuse them. Wiz devoutly hoped the same was true of dragons.

He cleared his throat. "Then surely you are skilled in all forms of applied logic. Riddles, say?"

"Dragons are excellent at riddles," Griswold said loftily. "Surely you're not proposing playing the riddle game with me?"

"Yep. And if I win you turn these people loose and agree never to bother them again."

"And if *I* win?" Griswold asked, leaning forward so Wiz had to crane his neck to meet the dragon's eye.

"You get them."

"My dear boy, surely it hasn't escaped your notice that I have them already. No, you'll have to offer something more." The dragon licked his chops in anticipation. "Yourself, for instance."

It occurred to Wiz that the dragon had him too, but he tried to ignore that.

"All right, but if I win I want a larger prize, too."

Griswold looked amused. "Gold? Jewels?"

Wiz almost agreed; then he caught sight of a farm implement leaning against the wall. It was a pruning hook, its two-foot curved blade wickedly sharp along its inner edge.

"Uh, no," Wiz said. "I was thinking of something a little more personal."

"What then?"

Wiz smiled as unpleasantly as he could manage. "Well, dragon skin *does* have a number of magically useful properties."

The dragon hesitated for an instant. "Done and done," he exclaimed.

"Fine. I'll go first,"

Griswold nodded. "Tell me the riddle, then."

"It isn't one I tell you. I have to show it to you."

The dragon brightened. "Charades? I haven't had a good game of charades in ever so long."

"Here are the rules," Wiz told him. "**emac**." Instantly a two-foot-tall demon wearing granny glasses and a green eyeshade popped into existence next to him.

Griswold watched him closely, alert for any sign of treachery.

"**APL dot man list exe**," he commanded.

The demon drew a quill pen from behind one bat ear and began to scribble furiously. Line after line of fiery letters grew before them. Each line defined one of the commands of Jerry's version of APL. There were a lot of them and the emac took several minutes to write them all in the air.

"Hmm. Ah, yes," Griswold said.

"Now, have you memorized them?"

"Of course." The dragon didn't sound quite so confident now.

"Fine," Wiz said. "**emac**."

"**?**" replied the editing demon.

"**clear end exe**." The emac rubbed the air furiously and the characters vanished. The demon bowed and it vanished as well.

"Now." Wiz picked up a stick and scratched furiously in the dirt.

$$\rightarrow \square I O \leftarrow 1 + L \mid - \ominus \partial \triangleq \phi \overline{\Phi} \boxplus \rho \Psi \triangle 2 \ulcorner \ast 0$$
$$\times ! ? \sim \circledast 1$$

"I'll bet you can't tell me what this does."

Griswold craned his neck forward to stare at the symbols in the dirt.

"Um, ah . . ."

"Come on," Wiz said. "It's perfectly logical and quite unambiguous. What is the result?"

"Well . . ."

The dragon drew his brows together in a mighty frown. He stuck his forked tongue between his ivory fangs and let it loll out one side of his mouth. He cocked his head nearly upside down to get a better view of the characters.

Whistling tunelessly, Wiz strolled over to the wall and picked up the pruning hook. He ran his thumb along the edge nonchalantly and hefted it experimentally.

"You're forfeit, you know," Wiz said, turning back to the dragon.

"Time," Griswold said desperately. "Give me more time!"

Wiz had never seen a dragon sweat before. He decided it was an interesting effect.

"Can't you solve it?"

"Of course I can solve it," Griswold said pettishly. "I just need a little more time." His voice rose to a whine inside Wiz's head. "The rules didn't say anything about a time limit."

"Very well." Wiz laid the pruning hook aside and gestured magnanimously. "I will give you until the Moon is full again to solve the riddle. Now go."

Griswold sagged with relief. "Thank you," he practically blubbered. Then he hesitated and looked back at the humans huddled behind him. "Uh, I don't suppose . . . just one . . . for a snack, you know?"

"GO!" Wiz roared, reaching for the pruning hook. Muttering to himself, the dragon leapt into the sky.

"Whhhoooooo," Wiz breathed and collapsed against the wall, using the pruning hook for a cane. He was immediately engulfed by the hysterically grateful Baggots, all of whom were laughing, crying and hugging him simultaneously. Since the entire family apparently enjoyed garlic as much as they disdained bathing, and since their idea of a thankful hug could snap the spine of an ox, Wiz was less appreciative than he might have been. In fact, by the time he got out the farmyard gate he was limping and holding his ribs.

SEVEN

SETTLING IN

Always live better than your clients.
—The Consultants' Handbook

News travels fast. The mayor and council hadn't been at the Baggot Place, but they knew all about it by the time Wiz and Malkin made their way back to town. They were gathered inside the gate in a tight cluster when the pair strode back through.

While the town guard held back the common folk, the mayor and councilors pressed forward, eager to be associated with their new hero.

There seemed to be twice as many councilors as there had been in the jail. A couple seemed to be in open-mouthed awe of him. Most of the others looked gravely pleased. A minority eyed him speculatively, like a group of cats trying to decide what they could do with a new and rather strange baby bird which had just dropped into their midst. With a sinking feeling Wiz realized he wasn't out of the woods yet.

"Well, Wizard, it seems we owe you a debt of gratitude," the mayor said, loudly enough to be sure the crowd heard him.

"All part of a consultant's job," Wiz said airily and equally loudly. "We exist to solve our clients' problems."

"Well, you've made a very good start," said one of the councilors, a handsome silver-haired man with an air of smooth sincerity.

"Almost too good," came a voice from the crowd. "Like it was planned."

"Of course it was planned," Wiz lied glibly. "You don't think even a consultant would face a dragon without a plan, do you?"

"Some folks," Malkin put in, "don't even plan where their next pot of ale is coming from." She turned to face the heckler. "Do they, Commer?"

The crowd laughed and that was the end of it.

"Now as I was saying," Mayor Hendrick went on, "let me be the first to welcome you to our city."

"On behalf of the council," a small, overdressed councilor with a fringe of dark curly hair added sharply.

The mayor looked annoyed. "On behalf of myself as mayor and the council," he amended.

"Thank you," Wiz said. "I'm sure this will be the beginning of a very productive relationship." *Push it when you're hot.* "Oh, and I'll need living quarters for my assistant and myself."

"We have just the place." Mayor Hendrick beamed. "A fine old house in the very center of town. In fact we will give it to you!" One or two of the councilors nodded enthusiastically and a couple of others looked smug.

"Very generous of you," Wiz said smoothly. Actually he was more puzzled than gratified. The mayor didn't seem like the sort to be impressed by the morning's activities, much less the kind who'd be moved to sudden acts of generosity. Still . . .

The mayor beckoned and a large, tough-looking man dressed mostly in black stepped forward.

"This is Sheriff Beorn Beornsdorf," Mayor Hendrick said. "He will show you to your new home."

Wiz smiled and acknowledged his recent captor with a nod. The sheriff's neck bent a fraction of an inch in reply but he still looked like he was wishing Wiz and Malkin back into jail.

Wiz looked over at Malkin and jerked his head toward the mayor.

Malkin strolled over, still looking back at Wiz, and walked right into Mayor Hasselhof. She bounced off his ample stomach, apologized profusely, brushing off the front and shoulders of his tunic while she did so.

"Dust speck," Malkin said and stepped away to join Wiz. The mayor eyed her oddly then looked down and seemed to realize his chain of office was back around his neck. He frowned, opened his mouth, then shut it firmly.

The house turned out to be a substantial structure of the town's usual stone-and-timber construction just off one of the town's smaller squares. It was narrow but at least four stories high, with a front right on the street and a small, neglected garden in the back.

The garden wasn't the only thing neglected. As they stood on the stoop Wiz could see that the windows were dirty and laced with cobwebs on the inside. There were streaks of rust running down from the door hinges and the brass lock plate was green with corrosion. Even with the door unlocked, Wiz had to put his shoulder to it to force it open. The unoiled hinges creaked and screamed like damned souls as the door swung to.

The hall inside was equally bad, musty smelling and deep in dust and cobwebs. There were doors opening off to either side and a large staircase leading up. Past the stairs was another door that probably led to the kitchen.

Wiz sniffed the stale air. It obviously hadn't been opened in a while but he didn't detect the odor of damp or rot. "This place doesn't look like anyone's been here in years."

"Not in two years," Malkin told him. "Not since Widder Hackett died."

"Still," Wiz said as he looked around, "it seems like a nice place. I can't imagine why anyone would leave a house like this empty. In the middle of town and all."

Malkin shrugged. "She didn't leave any kin. Besides, it's supposed to be haunted."

"Haunted," Wiz said faintly.

"Probably just rats running around the place."

"Rats," Wiz echoed more faintly.

Malkin considered. "But you never can tell. Old Lady Hackett was a sour sort and that's a fact. If she could come back and haunt the place, like as not she would." She paused. "Maybe she could, too, seeing as how she was a witch and all."

"A witch," Wiz echoed more faintly yet.

"But don't you worry," Malkin finished brightly, "it's probably just rats."

Wiz decided rats were definitely his first choice. "Well anyway, it's home for now so we'll have to get this place cleaned up."

Malkin looked around. "Take a heap of cleaning."

"Oh, I don't know. Sweep it out, scrub down the worst of it and it will be fine. Heck, it'll be a hundred percent better if you just scrub the grime off the windows."

"I don't do windows," Malkin said haughtily.

"I had a 386 system like that once."

She looked at him oddly.

"Okay, I'll do the windows. But we'll need a broom and some rags and stuff."

"I can get those at the market."

"Just be sure you pay for them."

Malkin's face fell. "Where's the fun in that?"

Before Wiz could answer there was a sharp knock at the door. Tugging it open, he found himself face to face with an overdressed, balding little man who looked vaguely familiar.

"I need to talk to you, Wizard," the man snapped. He glared at Malkin. "Alone."

Malkin, who apparently knew him, glared back. "I'll get the stuff," she said to Wiz over the top of the visitor's head. "You and Shorty here have a nice chat." With that she swept out the still-open door, leaving the little man purpling in her wake.

"Jailbird bitch should have gone to The Rock long ago," the man said as Wiz thrust the door closed on its still-protesting hinges. "But who you choose to associate with is your business. We've got other matters to discuss."

"What can I do for you Mr . . .?"

"*Councilor*," the man corrected. "I'm Councilor Dieter Hanwassel and I'm someone to be reckoned with around here."

Wiz looked more closely and saw the man was indeed wearing the heavy gold chain of a city councilman over his elaborately brocaded black-and-silver robe. Where he wasn't going bald Dieter had dark curly hair that fluffed out from his head. Since he was bald from his forehead to the back of his cranium, he looked like he had just had a nasty accident with a lawn mower. The whole effect was comic—until you saw the jut of the jaw, the lips pressed into a tight line and the glitter in his dark eyes. He reminded Wiz of an excited terrier in a too-fancy collar. A terrier who was aching to take a bite out of someone.

"Ah yes, Councilor, I believe we met this morning."

Dieter jerked a nod. "We did. And now that the rest of those ninnies aren't around we can talk seriously."

Wiz put on his blandest expression and nodded. One thing consultants never had to search for was the political factions in an organization. Sooner or later they came searching for you. Usually sooner.

"I'm sorry I can't offer you a seat," Wiz said, "but you see—"

Dieter cut him off. "What you can offer me is your support, since just now you seem to have the council's favor." He eyed Wiz. "I'm a plain man, Wizard, and plain-spoken. We can do a lot together, you and I. And I can do a lot for you."

"You mean you can help me with dragons?"

"Dragons," the councilor snorted. "What do I care about dragons? I'm a practical man and we both know there's nothing you can do about them, eh? No, what I'm interested in is revenues. Do you realize this city hasn't had a revenue increase in near a generation? There's all sort of projects, wonderful projects, just stalled because there's no revenue. Why, there's streets, and fountains, and bridges. All just crying out to be built. And they've gone crying for years because of lack of revenues."

"What do you expect me to do about that? I'm an expert on dragons."

Dieter waved that away. "Tell them you need more money to fight the dragons, that's what. They already agreed to pay you a tenth of the city's revenues. Tell them you need more, and now."

"They'll only pay me if—when—I succeed."

"And you know what they'll do to you if you *don't* succeed, eh?" The Councilman leaned close and glared up at Wiz. "Well, let me tell you, you won't succeed without my help. I have weight on the council and me and my followers, we want those revenues increased."

Wiz wondered how much of those revenues would wind up in the pockets of the councilor and his cronies. Considering what the guy was like he decided a better question would be how much of the money would make it past those pockets.

"Now, I'm not a greedy man, Wizard," Dieter continued in what was obviously supposed to be a placating tone. "When the money flows there'll be help for those as helped us. Sort of finder's fees, you might say."

"It certainly sounds like a worthwhile program. What seems to be the obstacle?"

"The mayor's the obstacle, him and that Rolf who's behind him. All they ever do is cry about 'tax burdens' and 'fiscal responsibility.'" The little man snorted. "'Fiscal responsibility.' What about our responsibility to them as support us I'd like to know?"

Wiz nodded. "It sounds as if you have a very strong case. I can assure you I'll give the matter serious consideration."

"You'll give the matter more than that if you want to stay off The Rock," Dieter said. "I'll be watching you, Wizard. And I'm a man who remembers his enemies as well as his friends."

After his visitor left Wiz spent the next several minutes working the front door back and forth to free up the rusted hinges. The hinges squeaked and groaned in protest and that suited his mood perfectly.

"The runt leave?" Malkin asked when she breezed back in a bit later, her arms loaded with cleaning supplies.

"He's gone. Did you pay for all this stuff?"

"Charged it to the council," she said, dropping everything in the middle of the hall. "Someone will be around later with bedding and stuff. What did the little rat want anyway?"

"My help in raising taxes."

"Figures. Of the whole money-gouging lot Dieter's about the worst." She paused and considered. "Well, anyways the most obnoxious."

"That's a problem for another day," Wiz said as he stooped to pick up a broom. As he stood back up he saw the flash of gold in Malkin's hand. "What's that?"

"Oh, something I picked up in the market," she said breezily, holding up an ornate gold ring with a big green stone. "Do you like it?"

"I thought I told you not to steal anything."

"You told me to pay for the cleaning stuff. And I did—leastways I charged it all legal-like. But this," she said, popping the ring down her bodice, "isn't cleaning stuff."

Tomorrow, Wiz told himself. *I'll worry about this tomorrow.* "Come on, let's try to make this place habitable."

Malkin turned out to be a surprisingly hard worker. She obviously didn't know much more about house cleaning than Wiz did, but she went at it with a will and before long dust was flying in all directions. In a little less than two hours they had the front hall and two of the upstairs bedrooms more or less clean.

"Woof! You don't have any spell to clean this place, do you?" Malkin said as she plopped down on the stair beside Wiz to take a break.

"Not really. Well, I do know one, but it takes everything out of the room." *And sends it off in all directions with roughly the velocity of machine gun bullets.* He remembered the time in the ruined City of Night when he and the others had hacked the spell together to move rubble and how they'd ended up cowering in the dirt from the resulting barrage of missiles. That reminded him of Jerry, Danny and most of all Moira, and sent a pang through him.

"You all right?" Malkin asked, catching his mood.

"Yeah, I'm fine." He focused his attention on her. "Tell me about this widow who used to live here."

"Widder Hackett?" Malkin chuckled. "She was a salty

one, even for a witch. She had a tongue, that one. If you so much as sat down on her stoop she'd come flying out waving a broom and chase you off. Always complaining about dirt and such, she was." The girl looked around the house and shook her head. "What she'd think if she could see this place now! We could clean and polish until the end of time and we'd never get it back to what it was."

"I'll settle for getting it to where it's habitable," Wiz said. "Let's do some more on the upstairs and then knock off for dinner."

"Let's knock off for dinner and then do some more upstairs," Malkin countered. "It's near evening and I haven't eaten today."

"Now that you mention it . . ."

Malkin looked at him. "Well?" she said finally.

"Well what?"

"Well aren't you going to magic us up food?"

"I'm not very good at that—unless the kitchen's got a microwave?"

Malkin snorted. "Fine wizard you are. I don't suppose you can cook either."

"I do all right," Wiz said defensively.

Malkin snorted again. "I know what *that* means, coming from a man. Look here then, I'll go back to the market and get a few things—charge a few things," she amended hastily before Wiz could say anything, "and I'll cook tonight. I don't want food poisoning on top of everything else today. But tomorrow you do the cooking. Now help me get this miserable door open so I can get back to the miserable market before the last of the miserable stalls close."

With Malkin's help he tugged the door open again and he watched her as she disappeared down the street. Then he leaned against the door and pushed it to again as the hinges protested like souls in mortal agony.

The door, Wiz thought. *I've got to do something about that damned door.*

Wiz went down the worn stone steps into the kitchen. It had to be the kitchen, he decided, because private houses don't usually come equipped with torture chambers.

It was a high, narrow room in what he would have thought of as the basement of the house. A couple of thin barred windows high up lit the place dimly. The walls and floors were dank stone and the ceiling was rough beams and planks. There was a huge fireplace with a wicked looking collection of iron hooks and chains hanging under the mantle, plus a contraption of iron spikes and gears and yet more chains off to one side that he vaguely recognized as some kind of spit for roasting meat. There was a stone sink in the opposite wall and in the center of the room a heavy wooden table with a rack full of hooks above it.

Gee, he thought, *clean this place up, light a fire in the fireplace, put some flowers here and there, I'll bet you could brighten it up to, oh, say, dismal.*

Among the pile of supplies Malkin had purchased was a small bottle of oil. Wiz took the oil back upstairs to the door and poured some on the hinges as best he could from the inside. Then he tugged the door open to get them from the outside.

He barely had the door open six inches when a furry gray streak shot through and dashed between his legs.

"Hey!" Wiz yelled, but the streak ignored him. It was halfway up the stairs before it stopped and resolved itself into a cat.

It was a rather bedraggled and quite large cat. A tiger-striped tabby cat, Wiz thought, dredging the terms out of his subconscious. A tiger-striped tabby tomcat, he amended as the cat turned its backside toward him.

The cat sat in the middle of the stairs and looked back over its right shoulder at Wiz.

"What do you think you're doing?" Wiz demanded of the cat. The cat continued to study Wiz with its great yellow eyes as if to say, "I live here. What's your excuse?"

Wiz opened his mouth to say more and then shut it again when he realized there wasn't anything he could say. Not only is arguing with a cat a lost cause, this cat was halfway up the stairs and could easily outrun him if he tried to give chase. Wiz didn't like looking foolish any more than the average cat does, so he decided to leave it for now.

Wiz didn't dislike cats, but from observing his friends who had cats he had arrived at a couple of conclusions. The first was that cats, not being pack animals like dogs or people, do not have consciences. That meant that if you had a cat you were sharing your life with a furry little sociopath.

The second was that every animal had evolved to exploit an ecological niche and in the case of cats that niche was people.

"Well, all right," Wiz told the cat. "But don't get the idea you're staying."

"Who are you shouting at?" asked Malkin as she came in the door with a basket of food.

Wiz nodded toward the stairs. "That."

Malkin studied the cat and the cat studied Malkin. "I think that's Widder Hackett's cat," the tall girl said finally. "Handsome enough."

"So is a leopard, but that doesn't mean I want to share quarters with one."

Malkin grinned at him. "Looks like he's decided to share quarters with you. And if you're planning on catching him to throw him out you can do it yourself. He's a scrapper, that one, and I've no fancy to get myself clawed up to put out an animal that will come right back in every time you open the door."

"Hmmf," Wiz snorted, weighing his ambivalence toward cats against the obvious trouble it would take to get rid of this one. "Does he have a name?"

"Widder Hackett called him Precious, but I think his name is Bobo."

"Bobo, huh? Looks more like Bubba to me." The cat narrowed his yellow eyes and glared at him as if to say "Watch it, bud."

It turned out there was a stove in the kitchen. It was a ceramic tile box next to the fireplace that Wiz had dismissed as a waist-high work counter. There was also a wooden hand pump that drew water into the sink. Malkin got a fire going with the help of a fire-starting spell from Wiz and she quickly threw together a grain-and-vegetable porridge that turned out surprisingly well. They ate in the kitchen under the glow of a magic light globe Wiz conjured up.

The only excitement came when Bobo cornered and caught a rat in the upstairs hallway. He came trotting down the stairs, head high, with the limp furry corpse dangling from his mouth and settled himself under the sink to eat with the humans. Wiz turned his back to the sink and tried to ignore the occasional crunching noises from Bobo's direction.

"Cat's got his uses," Malkin observed.

"Unfortunately I don't have a violin that needs stringing."

"I don't suppose you've got a spell to clean dishes either," Malkin said as she scraped the last of the stew from her bowl.

"I can probably whip one up tomorrow."

"Let it be for tonight then. But one way or another, Wizard, you'll clean those dishes tomorrow. And tomorrow it's your turn to cook."

"Who's the boss in this outfit anyway?"

"Depends," Malkin said lazily, "on who needs who the worst, don't it?"

Tomorrow, Wiz thought. *I'll worry about this tomorrow.*

Actually there was a lot to worry about tommorrow, Wiz admitted to himself as he crawled into bed later that evening. He had to get things set up here so he could work, he had to figure out a way to keep Dieter pacified. And he still didn't have the faintest idea how he was going to solve the village's dragon problem. That last was really beginning to gnaw at him.

Well, Wiz thought as he drifted off to sleep, *it could be worse I suppose.*

"Look at this mess!"

Wiz jerked bolt upright in bed.

"Look at it, I tell you," the voice repeated.

Wiz looked around frantically, but the room was empty.

"**backslash light exe!**" he called out into the darkness. The room filled with the warm yellow glow of a magic globe, but there was still no sign of anyone else in the room.

"I don't suppose you're going to do anything about it, are you?" the voice rasped again. It was a particularly unpleasant voice. It reminded Wiz of a rusty door hinge or slowly pulling an old nail out of a piece of very hard wood.

"What are you carrying on about?" came another voice. Wiz whirled and saw Malkin in the doorway, rubbing sleep from her eyes.

"There's someone in the room. I can hear her but I can't see her."

There was a loud snort from the corner.

"There," Wiz said.

Malkin's eyes narrowed. "I didn't hear anything."

"It was a snort. A definite snort."

"Are you sure you've been getting enough rest?"

"I tell you there's someone here. It sounds like an old woman and she's complaining that the house is dirty."

"Well, look at this place!" the voice came again. "It's a pigsty, an absolute pigsty! And what are you doing about it, I'd like to know? You're sitting there in the dirt and not making a move to clean it up."

"Probably Widder Hackett," Malkin said judiciously. "I guess them as said the place was haunted was right."

"You're taking this awfully calmly."

Malkin shrugged. "So far she's not bothering me."

"Why is it I can hear her and you can't?"

"Because you're the owner, dummy," the old lady's voice grated. "No one but the owner sees or hears the ghost. Them's the rules."

Suddenly things clicked. "When you died without heirs," Wiz said into empty air, "who inherited this place?"

"Why, the council, of course," the voice said. "Not that any of that pack of layabouts lifted a finger to keep my house up. Crooked as a dog's hind leg, every last one of them, and don't think I didn't tell them so!"

Malkin was obviously only hearing half the exchange, but she kept swiveling her head from Wiz to the corner he was looking at, like the spectator at a ping-pong match.

"Which explains why they gave the place to me."

"And what are you going to do about it?" the ghost demanded again.

"Well, this is all kind of new to me," Wiz temporized. "We don't have ghosts where I come from. Except on TV—and you can usually fix those by getting cable."

The ghost of Widder Hackett ignored his sally. "A right uncivilized place, it sounds like. Well, we do things better here. And that means taking care of my house."

Wiz thought about pointing out that death usually severs right of ownership. Then he decided it probably didn't apply here.

"Look, it's the middle of the night. I can't do anything about it right now, can I? I promise you I'll get started on it first thing in the morning."

"I suppose that's the best I can expect from someone like you. All right then, but first thing in the morning, mind."

I couldn't get a ghost that rattles chains or moans, Wiz thought as he tried to get comfortable again in his haunted house. *I've got to get one that nags at 80 dB. I don't suppose there are OSHA noise regulations for ghosts either.*

Wiz finally drifted off to sleep while musing on the most effective kind of hearing protectors to use against ghost noises.

Wiz was having a wonderful dream, about a place with Moira and no dragons, when a rocket went off beside his head. He was bolt upright with the covers off before he realized that what he had heard was a voice and not a particularly violent explosion.

"Well?" came the voice again.

"Well what?" Wiz was not at his best early in the morning and one glance at the rosy hue of sunlight painted on the wall told him it was *very* early morning.

"Well, it's morning," said the voice in a particularly unpleasant tone. "What are you going to do about the house?"

"Ah, the house. Right." He realized he recognized the voice. He also realized he didn't have any caffeine in the house. The third realization, less than thirty seconds later, was that this was not shaping up to be a good day.

True to his word of the night before he fixed breakfast

for himself and Malkin. But Malkin apparently liked to
sleep late as much as Wiz did and since she didn't have
a complaining ghost dogging her footsteps she could
stay in bed. Wiz left a pot of oat porridge on the stove
for her, put down a saucer of milk for Bobo after the
cat jumped in his lap three times trying to get at his
porridge and milk, left the dishes in the sink (over
Widder Hackett's strenuous objections) and dragged his
way upstairs.

Since he still didn't have a handle on the dragon
problem, much less the more immediate stuff, he relied
on routine. Maybe something would come to him while
he worked.

The first order of business, Wiz decided, was to set
up a workroom. In the back of his mind he knew that
a programmer's work space wasn't really appropriate to
someone who was supposed to be a consultant on dragons, but it didn't really matter. It would make the place
more homey and help him think about his real problem—once he figured out which of the mountains of
problems he faced was the real one.

There were two parlors on the ground floor, one on
each side of the entrance hall. Both of them were full
of furniture swathed in dusty sheets and it looked like
it would be a backbreaking job to move it out. Besides,
the front windows were right on the street, which meant
working there would be like working in a department
store window, unless he kept the drapes drawn all the
time, in which case he'd need artificial light. On top
of all that he had a strong suspicion the ghost would
have something to say if he starting moving the furniture around in the parlor—probably quite a lot to say,
in fact.

The second floor, with his and Malkin's bedrooms,
had more possibilities. The upstairs front room had
obviously been some sort of a sitting room rather than

a bedroom. Now it was stark and bare with only a sturdy wooden chair sitting in one corner and a sturdier table against the opposite wall. But light flooded in when Wiz forced open the protesting shutters. It was clearly the best room in the house to serve as his workroom. Without another thought he grabbed one end of the heavy oak table and started to tug it over to the window.

"Don't drag that!" Widder Hackett yelled. "You'll gouge the floor."

The sudden noise made Wiz drop the table. One leg landed on his foot and the other hit the floor with a resounding *thump*. The scream of outrage in his ear almost made him forget the pain in his foot. "You ninny! Look what you've done. That mark will never come out! Oh my beautiful floor."

It was amazing, Wiz thought, that even when he was hopping around holding one foot the ghost's voice seemed to stay right in his ear.

Finally Widder Hackett ran down and the pain in Wiz's foot subsided to a dull throb. Gingerly, favoring his injured foot, Wiz took the table in the middle and heaved it clear of the floor. He delicately staggered across the room and gently lowered it before the window, bending over in a position that put his lower back in dire peril. He straightened to ease the protesting back muscles and reached out to push the table up against the wall. A sharp sound from Widder Hackett stopped him and he ended up carefully lifting the end to slide it into position.

"And be sure you carry the chair too!" the old lady's ghost added.

With the chair and table in place, Wiz sat down to rest his aching foot and to try to get some work done. Even though setting up his magical workstation went smoothly it still wasn't easy. Every couple of minutes Widder Hackett would be back to complain about another outrage to her beloved house and Wiz's lack of action, not to mention morals, character and general deportment. Since the ghost's voice combined the worst features of a foghorn, a screech owl and a table saw ripping lumber full of nails, Wiz was quickly developing a semi-permanent twitch. He had always pictured ghosts as having high, reedy voices that were just on the edge of audibility. Apparently it took more than dying to modulate Widder Hackett's tones.

"I'm surprised they didn't let me out of jail just to give me the house," he muttered as he leaned back to examine the fruits of several hours of not-very-productive work.

"Don't put your feet on the table!" Widder Hackett roared. Wiz jerked his feet back to the floor. "And sit up in that chair. You're putting weight on it wrong and you'll break it like as not."

Wiz had gone to public schools, but he had Catholic friends who had gone to parochial schools. From what they had told him Widder Hackett had a lot in common with the nuns.

Bobo sauntered through the door and jumped up on the table to sniff at Wiz's magical spells. He decided that fiery letters probably weren't good to eat. Then he decided he needed petting and Wiz's hand was just lying on the table not doing anything so Bobo butted his head against it until he got a response.

Wiz sighed and scratched the cat under the chin. "I don't know, Bubba. What do you think I ought to do?"

The cat gazed deep into Wiz's eyes. "Feed me." The thought came crystal sharp into Wiz's mind. Wiz sighed again.

"You know, it's probably a good thing cat lovers don't know what their cats are thinking."

"Feed me now," Bobo's thought came clear again. There was no response except some distracted petting.

The cat gave Wiz a look that clearly indicated he thought Wiz was mentally retarded for not getting the message. Then he jumped down from the table and stalked out the door, tail high.

"And just when are you going to do something about the disgraceful condition of the front parlor?" demanded a now-familiar voice beside his ear.

Wiz sighed again. He had a feeling it was going to be a long, long day.

EIGHT

CALLING HOME

*The problem with being a miracle worker is that
everyone expects you to work miracles.*
                                    —The Consultants' Handbook

Two hours later Wiz started his latest creation running and then let out a long, whooshing sigh.

"You all right?" Malkin asked in a voice that showed
more curiosity than compassion.

"Yeah, fine. But if I'm going to get anything done
around here I'm going to have to hire a housekeeper."

Malkin crossed her arms over her chest. "Good luck.
Not many as will want to work for a strange wizard in
a haunted house."

"Well put an ad in the paper will you? Or have the
town crier announce it or whatever you do here."

"I'll take the news to the market." She looked over
at the rapidly scrolling letters of golden fire above his
desk under the window. "Meanwhile, what's that?"

"It's a workstation. I just built it."

Malkin looked at the gray box and keyboard sitting on
the table and the letters of golden fire hanging above it.

"Built it out of what?"

"Well, actually it's a program, a spell you'd call it. See, we've found that in this world a sufficiently complex program, or spell, produces a physical manifestation, what you'd call a demon."

Malkin regarded the things on the desk. "Don't look like no demon I've ever heard tell of," she said. "But you're the wizard. What's it good for?"

"Well, what you see here is really just a user interface. It virtualizes what I was used to in my world and that makes it easier for me to relate to."

"Seems to me any relations you had with a demon would have to be illegitimate," the tall thief said. "But what's it good for?"

"Just about anything I want it to be. Right now I'm setting up an Internet connection so I can talk to my friends."

"More magic, eh?"

"No, it's technology. I need a machine on the other side," Wiz explained to the uncomprehending but fascinated woman. "So I've created a little dialer demon to troll the net for systems I can set up accounts on."

Malkin cocked an eye at him. "I see. So it's demons and trolls but it's not magic."

"No, it's . . . Okay, have it your way. It's magic."

Just then the system emitted a bell-like tone. "Boy there's luck. Less than five minutes and I've found one. Uh, excuse me will you?" With that he turned back to the console.

"Now what are you doing?" Malkin asked. "Magic aside."

"I guess the easiest way to explain it is to say I'm breaking into something that's locked. Something a good ways from here."

For once the tall thief seemed impressed. "Burglary without being there," Malkin said wonderingly. "Wizard, I think I'd like this world of yours."

Wiz thought about Malkin as a computer criminal. Then he shuddered and turned his attention back to the computer.

Exploiting a hole in the system's security was easy. In a matter of minutes Wiz had two new accounts set up. The final wrinkle was a simple little shell script to take messages from one account and pass them to the other. Anyone who tried to trace him back could only follow him as far as this machine.

"There, that'll give me more protection," he told Malkin as he leaned back from the keyboard. *Not a lot,* he admitted to himself. But until he got Widder Hackett off his back he wasn't going to be able to do much better.

"Protection from who?"

"From anyone at the Wizard's Keep who might want to find me."

His erstwhile assistant regarded him with a look Wiz was coming to know all too well. "These folks are your friends, right?"

"Of course."

"Then I'd think you'd be yelling to them for help instead of hiding from them."

"I can't," Wiz said miserably. "I can't let them find me."

Malkin muttered something about "wizards" and left the room.

The first order of business, Wiz decided, was to tell everyone he was all right. He quickly composed an e-mail message and sent it over the net to **thekeep.org**, the Wizard's Keep's Internet node.

He typed furiously for several minutes, stopping frequently to erase a revealing phrase or to re-read his work to make sure he wasn't giving too much away. Then he spent some time planning the exact path the message would take to reach its destination. At last he hit the final "enter" to send the message on its way and settled back in his chair with a sigh of contentment.

He was promptly jerked erect by Widder Hackett's screech at air-raid-siren intensity.

"Loafing again, are you? The house falling down about your ears and you lolling at your ease. Wizard or not, you are the laziest, most good-for-nothing layabout I have ever seen in all my days."

There was a lot more in that vein.

Over the course of the day Wiz discovered that the person who said you can get used to anything had never met Widder Hackett. The combination of her awful voice and her complaining nearly drove Wiz to distraction. If she had been there all the time he might have gotten used to her. But she would vanish for five or ten or fifteen minutes only to reappear with more demands just as Wiz was settling in to concentrate on what he was doing.

And there was nothing he could do to satisfy her. Even an attempt to sweep and dust the front parlor ended with the ghost shrieking that he was a useless ninny and all he was doing was moving the dirt from one corner of the room to another. Meanwhile, he not only wasn't getting anything done, he wasn't even able to think seriously about what he wanted to do. Worst of all, Wiz discovered that the exorcism spells that laid demons to rest had no effect at all on ghosts.

Fortunately for Wiz, Widder Hackett shut up at about ten o'clock at night—perhaps because old ghosts need their sleep. Be that as it may, Wiz got several hours of uninterrupted work in late that night.

Unfortunately Widder Hackett was back at sunup the next morning, loud as ever and full of new complaints and demands. Even putting a pillow over his head couldn't shut her out, so Wiz was up and about before the cock stopped crowing.

❖   ❖   ❖

Meanwhile Wiz's message was on its way to the Wizard's Keep. It traveled a long and convoluted path through two worlds. First it was injected into the telephone lines by magical interference with a digital switch in a telephone company central office. It traveled over the regular phone network to the modem attached to the system he had cracked. There it slipped by security, thanks to Wiz's handiwork, and was received in one mailbox, transferred to another mailbox and sent out on the Internet. It traveled from computer to computer over the net as each node routed it to a succeeding node moving it closer to its destination. After traveling for several hours and touching every continent, including **penguin.edu** at Ross Station, Antarctica, it reached a node in Cupertino where it was stored until the final node made its daily connection to collect its mail. When **thekeep.org** called, the message was forwarded along with the rest of the day's e-mail down a telephone line to the junction box serving an apartment building—specifically the line leading to the apartment occupied by a programmer and fantasy writer named Judith Connally. There it was magically picked off, translated back to the Wizard's World along with most of the rest of the mail and showed up in Jerry's mailbox in his workstation in the Wizard's Keep.

Since Jerry slept mornings he didn't find it until he came into the workroom about mid-afternoon. He was still yawning over his second mug of blackmoss tea when he sat down at this terminal. He looked over the job he had left running, found it was progressing satisfactorily and punched up a list of his mail.

Jerry called the message up and started reading. By the time he had finished the first screen he was biting his lip.

"Danny! Moira! You'd better come look at this."

Hi Jerry and everyone (especially Moira!):

I can't tell you where I am or what I'm doing, but I'm safe—at least for now.
I don't know how long this job is going to take, but I'll have to stick with it until I'm done.
As to what I'm doing, let's just say I'm taking a lesson from Charlie Bowen.
Say hi to everyone for me and don't worry about me.
Give my love to Moira.

PS: Please don't try to find me. It's very important.

—W

"Who's Charlie Bowen?" Danny asked.

"Someone Wiz used to work with at Seer Software," Jerry told him, abstractedly. "Another programmer."

"A real hotshot, huh?"

"No, that's the funny thing. He was a lousy programmer. He wrote their accounts payable routine and he made a royal mess of it. The module kept fouling up assigning purchase order numbers, choking on invoices and if there was the least little problem in the paperwork, it kicked the thing out and it had to be processed manually. It was taking Seer Software six or eight months to pay even a simple bill and they kept having to explain to everyone it was the software's fault."

Danny took a swig of tea. "So did they fire him?"

"That's the other funny thing," Jerry said. "They promoted him."

Just then Moira came dashing into the room, face flushed and flour up to her elbows. "You've heard from Wiz!" she panted.

Jerry gestured to the message on the screen. She craned forward to read it over Jerry's shoulder. As she read her face fell and then she started to frown, deeper and deeper as she read along. By the time she reached the bottom she was scowling.

"There is something very wrong here. Why didn't he tell us where he is?"

Jerry shrugged. "He said he didn't want us to know."

"He also said he did not want us to worry," Moira said grimly. "Those are mutually exclusive and he knows that."

"Then maybe," Danny said slowly, "he *can't* tell us."

Jerry frowned. "You mean he doesn't know where he is? That's crazy. Wiz's magic could tell him in an instant."

"So maybe he knows and can't tell us," Danny said, groping.

"A geas!" Moira exclaimed. "Of course! He cannot tell us because he is magically forbidden to do so."

"He doesn't sound like anything is stopping him," Jerry objected. "It sounds more like he's being secretive of his own free will."

"That is the problem with a geas," Moira told him. "You do not necessarily know you are under it. Everything seems normal to you and you think you have the best reasons in the world for doing what you do, no matter how badly you want to do the opposite."

Jerry rubbed his chin. "Well, it sure fits with Wiz's behavior. He wants to tell us, so he contacts us. But he can't so he comes in through the net and then won't say where he is."

"Is there any way to trace him?" the hedge witch asked. She gestured at the message header. "Wiz told me once that gives the location of the sender."

"Normally it does," Jerry said. "But take a look at it."

Danny frowned as he ran his finger along the line.

The further he went, the deeper his frown became. "That can't be natural," he said at last.

"It isn't! That isn't a routing path, it's a shaggy dog story."

"Meaning what?" Moira demanded.

"Meaning he deliberately set up this routing to be as difficult and obscure as he could make it," Danny said before Jerry could answer. "See, normally a message is routed automatically by the most efficient path—given the location of the source, location of the destination, topology of the net and the amount of traffic. But you can force the route by using bang paths."

Moira didn't understand much of that, but she was game. "Bang paths?"

"Yeah. Site names separated by bangs." He pointed to an exclamation point between two names. "That's a bang." He studied the list for an instant and pointed at one sequence. "Here he's going from a U.S. site belonging to a Danish industrial concern to the Los Lobos League for Love and Understanding, the sex researchers. So that part of the path is **bang!llulu**."

Jerry groaned. "I wonder how long he searched to come up with that one?" Moira glared at him for the distraction.

"Anyway," Danny went on hastily, "I don't recognize all these site names but from the looks of it this message traveled a couple of times around the planet. Here's a site in Ukraine. That one's in the science city just outside of Tokyo. This one is the Coke machine at Rochester Institute of Technology—they put the Coke machine on the Internet so the computer science majors could find out if there were any sodas in the machine without having to walk all the way to it."

"Personally I always preferred the one at Carnegie-Mellon," Jerry said. "It's the original and it's got a graphical user interface."

Moira wasn't about to let the conversation wander off into a comparison of computerized vending machines. "Well, can you trace him or not?"

Jerry rubbed his chin. "That's hard. See, the path shown on a message isn't completely reliable. You can fake some of it. It's going to be hard to figure out where he's connecting to the net, much less where he is in our world."

"Maybe not," Danny said. "If we can rig up a little perl script and plant it on all these sites we may be able to trace him back to where he's really connecting."

Moira's face lit up. "Can you do that?"

"Well, we're going to have to get into a pile of computers, including that Coke machine, but . . ." His eyes focused on something far away. "Let me think about this and see what I can come up with. But we should be able to do it."

"And then?" Jerry asked.

"Then," said Moira grimly, "we go to his rescue whether he wants it or not."

NINE

A BRACELET, SOME CHICKENS, AND A PRETTY MAID ALL IN A ROW

Don't think of it as a distraction. Look at it as an income opportunity.

—The Consultants' Handbook

Wiz was hard at it again the next morning when Malkin stuck her head into his workroom.

"Someone at the door wants to see you."

The interruption made Wiz lose his place, but by now he was so used to it he just sighed and followed Malkin downstairs. There was a dumpy, middle-aged townswoman snivelling on the doorstep. From her posture and sniffling Wiz figured she was either very upset about something or she was suffering from a really bad allergy. As soon as Wiz appeared she grabbed one of his hands in both of hers.

"O Great Wizard, you see before you a poor woman in great affliction." Whatever it was, it wasn't a problem with her lungs, Wiz thought. Her voice rattled the windowpanes. "Oh, the tragedy," she wailed. "Oh me! Oh me! O Wizard, I beg of you, save me."

78

"Save yourself and put a stopper in it," Widder Hackett snarled in Wiz's ear. "That woman's voice can peel paint and she's got the brains of a titmouse beside."

Wiz had noticed the first and was willing to take the ghost's word for the second. But by this time they were over the threshold and into the hall. Clearly the only way to get rid of their guest now was to hear her out.

"Uh yes, Mrs. ummm . . .?"

"Grimmen," the woman proclaimed, without lowering her voice. "Mrs. Grimmen. I stand before you a vessel of woe, a pitiful shell, a—"

"Yes, but what happened?"

Mrs. Grimmen, her concentration broken, glared at him. "That's what I'm telling you, Wizard. My gold bracelet has been stolen."

"Your bracelet?"

"You heard me. You ain't deaf are you? Oh woe! Oh sorrow! Oh . . .

"Fertilizer!" snapped Widder Hackett—or something very close to that, at any event.

Stolen? Wiz looked back at the stairs where Malkin was standing and raised his eyebrows in unspoken question. The tall woman pinched up her face as if she was insulted by the very thought and shook her head.

"Uh, look Mrs. Grimmen, I'm not really a finder of lost objects. I'm a consultant on dragon problems."

"Well, how do you know a dragon didn't steal it?" the woman demanded. "It was gold after all."

"It was gilded pot metal," Widder Hackett amended.

"Yes, but . . ."

"Oh woe!" Mrs. Grimmen declaimed. "Oh sorrow! Oh alack!"

"Oh tell the ninny to look in the flour barrel," Widder Hackett said. "That's usually where she's hidden it when she can't find it."

"Uh, have you looked in the flour barrel?"

Mrs. Grimmen stopped in mid-wail. "Why would I do a silly thing like that?"

"Well, maybe that's where you left the bracelet."

The woman looked at him like he was crazy. "I didn't leave it anywhere. It was stolen from me. Oh woe! Oh woe!"

"Look, just go home and look in the flour barrel, okay?"

"But it's stolen away, my treasure. Oh woe! Oh woe!"

"Right," said Wiz, taking her by the elbow and gently guiding her toward the door.

"Sheesh! What next?" Wiz muttered as he turned away from the door.

"Chickens, most likely," said Widder Hackett in his ear. Wiz looked out the door and saw a man coming down the street with a live chicken in each hand.

He was scrawny and balding, with a big sharp nose and a receding chin. The way he strutted along with his head thrust forward put Wiz in mind of a chicken as well. Needless to say he stopped at Wiz's front door.

"I'm here to see the wizard," the man announced.

"I'm the wizard," Wiz admitted.

"Kinda young ain't you?"

"I was fast tracked in wizard school. Look, I'm kind of busy right now, so if you don't mind . . ."

"Not so fast, Wizard. I've got a job for you."

"I've already got a job."

Ignoring that the man thrust the chickens in Wiz's face. "Just look at them."

Since the birds were about level with Wiz's nose there wasn't any way to avoid it. From the way they struggled and cackled the chickens weren't any happier about the situation than he was. Aside from that they looked just fine. Of course, Wiz admitted, the only thing he knew about chickens was they came in three kinds: Regular, extra-crispy and spicy Cajun style—plus kung pao if you ordered Chinese.

"What's wrong with them?"

"Well, look at them! They don't lay hardly any eggs and no matter how much I feed them they stay scrawny."

Wiz looked over his shoulder into empty air.

"Don't ask me," Widder Hackett grated. "The old fool's been to every witch and magician for miles around. No one knows what's wrong with those stupid chickens."

"To be honest," Wiz said, "I don't know that this is my kind of problem. I'm really here as a dragon specialist."

"You're the municipal wizard ain't you?" he demanded.

"Actually," Wiz began, "I'm a consultant."

"Wizard, consultant, what's the difference? Point is you're paid out of my taxes to solve our problems. Well, this here," he said, thrusting the protesting chickens forward, "is my problem. So earn your money and solve it!"

"Those aren't dragons," Wiz pointed out.

"Any fool can see that, Mr. Wizard."

"Well, since they're not dragons they are not my problem. I only deal with dragons. Goodbye." Before his visitor could say another word, Wiz put all his weight against the door and forced it closed. Outside, the man made a couple of loud remarks about "uppity employees" and then the sound of his footsteps and the cackling of his chickens receded in the distance.

"Good grief," Wiz muttered weakly.

"Better get used to it," Widder Hackett told him. "There's going to be lots more of them. Word gets around you're a wizard working for the council and you'll have every lamebrain who think's he's got a problem camped out on your doorstep demanding you solve it." She snorted. "And there's lots of lamebrains in this town, I can tell you that."

"But how am I supposed to get any work done if I'm constantly being interrupted by people with lost bracelets and sick chickens?"

"That's nothing. Wait until the love-sick ones start coming to you. Rattle on for hours, they will, and not a word of sense to be found in any of it."

The way she said it left Wiz with a sinking feeling she was speaking from experience.

There was a knock at the door. Wiz whirled and jerked it open.

"I told you I can't do anything about your damned . . . chickens," he finished weakly.

There was an angel on the doorstep. An angel in a drab brown dress.

"I beg your pardon, My Lord," the angel said in an angelic but timid voice. "I, I heard you are looking for a housekeeper."

Wiz realized his angel was actually a girl, perhaps eighteen years old. The plain brown homespun dress concealed a trim figure. Her skin was creamy white with just the right touches of pink. A fringe of wheat-gold curls peeked out from her bonnet. Her eyes were wide and blue as Wedgewood saucers.

Wiz finally managed to get the circuit from his brain to his mouth working again and closed his jaw. "Uh, well, yes," he said. "What's your name?"

"Anna, My Lord."

"Well, I'm Wiz. Wiz Zumwalt. Come in, won't you?" He stepped aside and managed to keep from bowing as the girl ventured over the threshold.

Wiz suddenly realized he had never interviewed anyone for a job other than a programming position and he wasn't quite sure what the etiquette of hiring servants was.

"Ah, nice day isn't it?"

Anna gave him a wide-eyed stare. "Of course, My Lord." The way she said it made him look a little closer. Not only were those eyes as blue as a Wedgewood china plate, Wiz realized, the owner possessed about as much intelligence as a china plate.

"My Lord . . ." Anna ventured tremulously. Then she stopped and gathered her courage. "My Lord, I know I am not very clever, but I will work hard."

"Oh, let her stay," Widder Hackett's voice grated in his ear. "She can't make more of a mess than the pair of you."

Wiz looked at the forlorn beauty and sighed. The first rule of successful housekeeping is you've got to be smarter than the dirt. Looking at her, Wiz figured Anna was probably brighter than the average dust bunny. They'd just have to live with the intellectually superior dust bunnies.

Besides, there weren't any other applicants, and Wiz wasn't going to get anything done with Widder Hackett complaining in his ear.

"All right," he sighed. "You've got the job."

"Oh thank you, My Lord!" Anna's smile made her even more angelically beautiful. "You will not be sorry, I promise you."

"Uh, you're not afraid working for a wizard?"

"Oh no, My Lord," Anna said innocently. "My granny was a witch. I've grown up around the craft, you see."

"That was Old Lady Fressen," Widder Hackett informed Wiz. "Child's her only grandchild and she tried to teach her the Craft." Widder Hackett snorted. "And her with not the sense to come in out of the rain. Not that Old Lady Fressen was any great shakes when it came to brains, mind you." With that the ghost was off on a long, rambling, and none-too-favorable reminiscence about a dead former colleague.

✧   ✧   ✧

In their own ways and in their own times all of the occupants of the house settled in. Even Widder Hackett complained less once Anna set to work.

As if by magic the dirt and dust disappeared from the house. The sheets came off the furniture in the front rooms and light streamed through the newly-washed windows. The wooden floors developed a mellow glow and the odors of dust and age were replaced by the scents of furniture oil and sweet herbs that hung in bunches in all the rooms. The beds were less lumpy and the bedding fresher.

Wiz knew it wasn't magic, of course. The girl worked from morning until night with a fierce concentration and a single-mindedness that he found a little awe-inspiring. If Anna was no mental giant, she knew how to keep house and she had the energy of a dynamo to boot.

Anna even made a difference in the kitchen. Not only was it considerably cleaner after she arrived, it seemed brighter as well. Part of that was that the girl spent an afternoon whitewashing the walls—which earned Wiz an earful of Widder Hackett's complaints about the younger generation and their new-fangled notions—but part of it was simply her personality. New-fangled notions or not, Anna fitted this house far better than Wiz or Malkin did.

Malkin was usually available when Wiz needed her, but the rest of the time she kept to herself. Anna was in awe of the tall thief, but clearly didn't approve of her. Malkin clearly didn't feel any kinship for Anna either. In fact both the women seemed to get along better with Wiz than they did with each other.

The one member of the household who really welcomed Anna was Bobo. For some reason the cat developed an instant bond with the girl and spent hours each day around her or sitting in her lap on the infrequent occasions when she sat down to rest. Considering that Anna also did the cooking and spent much of her time in the kitchen, Wiz reflected, that probably wasn't so odd.

For his part Bobo had made himself at home as only a cat can. Which is to say with total disregard for the rights or feelings of the human inhabitants.

For one thing, Bobo had the typical cat criteria for a place to sleep. To wit, it should be warm, soft and inconvenient. The most inconvenient place of all was Malkin's pillow because she was allergic to cats. After she threw him out several times, learned to keep her door closed always and to search the room before going to bed, Bobo transferred his attentions to Wiz. Since even in his current emaciated state the cat weighed nearly twenty pounds and since his favorite way of getting into bed was to take a running jump and try to land right in the middle of Wiz's stomach, this was a less than ideal arrangement from Wiz's point of view. However it suited Bobo fine and like most cats he had a strong sense of the proper order of the universe.

When Bobo wasn't happy he complained and he had obviously taken voice from his mistress. When he was happy he purred. Since Bobo's purring had the volume and timbre of a Mack truck at idle, happy Bobo wasn't much of an improvement over unhappy Bobo.

For all that, it worked somehow and life settled into a routine.

From the top of the mountain you could see for miles. Myron Pashley couldn't see any further than his computer screen in front of the window.

Special Agent Myron "Clueless" Pashley, FBI, utterly ignored the vista of pine forests stretching down to the tan desert and the blue and purple mountains on the far horizon. Instead he hunched further forward in his swivel chair and ran his finger down the screen. His lips moved silently as he worked the elementary subtraction until he arrived at the final, fatal, number on the last line.

"Whipple, come take a look at this."

Ray Whipple, Pashley's office mate, pulled his head out of the latest copy of *Astrofisicka*. He made a show of reading the journal in the original Russian because he knew it annoyed Pashley.

"Look here," Pashley's finger stabbed down onto the computer screen. Whipple sighed, put the journal down and looked over Pashley's shoulder.

"What happened, get lost in the directory tree again?"

"No, I got something. There's an error in the user accounting."

"So what?"

"What it means," Pashley growled, "is that a hacker's gotten into the system."

"What it means," Ray shot back, "is that the accounting program screwed up again and the roundoff errors are accumulating."

Pashley smiled a superior smile. "Look at the amount of the error. Eighty-seven cents! You read *Cuckoo's Egg* didn't you? You know what that means."

Whipple, who had not only read the book but had helped the author in a small way during his hunt through the Internet for an international spy, couldn't get his jaw back up in time to protest.

"We got us a hacker and we're going to nail him." With that he bent to the computer with a will, punching keys frantically.

Ray retreated to his chair and his journal. He had a sinking feeling he wasn't going to make the deadline for this year's computer Go competition.

Myron Pashley had been born to be an FBI agent,

but he was born too late. He belonged in the Bureau in the days of narrow ties, short haircuts and J. Edgar Hoover; the days when a straight-arrow personality, a gung-ho attitude and a suspicious mind could substitute for intelligence and judgment.

After graduating next-to-last in his class at the FBI academy, Pashley had pictured himself on the streets of urban America, fighting crime that was poisoning the nation's body politic. Instead he was assigned to computer fraud and copyright violations. Not the best use for a technological idiot, his superiors admitted privately, but at least he wasn't likely to get shot or blow an important organized crime investigation. Keep him there for a couple of years, they figured, and eventually he'd get fed up with the Bureau and quit.

His superiors had reckoned without Pashley's zeal. Assigned to combat computer crime, Pashley convinced himself this was the new plague sweeping through America and he threw himself into the battle with the boundless enthusasism—and the brains—of an Irish Setter. He began hanging out on computer bulletin boards, running up huge phone bills as he trawled for the evil "hackers" who were insidiously spreading through the nation's computer networks, committing all sorts of nefarious deeds.

He quickly discovered that hackers were as subtle and devious as they were dangerous. The fact that he could find absolutely no trace of any illegal activities on the bulletin boards he frequented was tangible proof how devilishly clever these "hackers" were.

He would have been more effective if he hadn't needed someone to untangle his electronic screwups on the average of once every fifteen minutes, but he persisted.

Finally his patience was rewarded. On an obscure computer bulletin board in the Southeastern United

States he found his master criminal. The messages Pashley had collected were enough to convince his boss that he really had something and a full-scale investigation was launched.

Three months later a daring and well-coordinated dawn raid on the North Carolina hideaway seized nearly a million dollars' worth of computer equipment plus over fifty firearms. At the press conference that morning Pashley had cheerfully posed in front of tables loaded with seized items while brandishing what he called "a blueprint for techno-terrorism."

That brief shining moment was the high point of Pashley's career.

Unfortunately it was immediately followed by the low point. It turned out his "master hacker" was actually a science fiction novelist who wrote for computer magazines on the side and collected guns as a hobby. Not only were all the weapons the FBI had seized perfectly legal, but the "blueprint for techno-terrorism" turned out to be the notes for the author's latest novel.

Needless to say the author was not happy. He also had a considerable talent for invective and a pen dipped in vitriol which he used to lambaste the Bureau and Special Agent Pashley in several national magazines. For one awful week even Jay Leno had been making jokes about him. Somewhere in that terrible period he had been dubbed "Clueless" Pashley and the name had stuck ever since.

It wasn't as bad as the DEA agent in the gorilla suit, but at least the DEA agent got a solid arrest out of it. All Pashley got was a multi-million-dollar lawsuit, naming him, "John and Jane Does 1 through 999," and the Bureau as defendants.

It hadn't helped matters when Pashley's superiors found he had been rather selective in the bulletin board messages he had shown them. The full message base proved "to anyone but an utter idiot" (in his boss's memo-rable phrase) that the computer bulletin board was merely a way for fans to communicate with their favorite author.

His boss was demoted, his section chief took early retirement and his chief's supervisor was transferred to a job in the Aleutian Islands. But Pashley, whose head should have gone up on a pike over the main entrance to FBI headquarters, wasn't even reprimanded, thanks to the multi-million-dollar lawsuit pending against the Bureau. Instead he was given an "independent assign-ment" and sent to this observatory in the desert south-west to continue his fight against computer crime.

Thus, on this brilliantly sunny afternoon, Pashley was sharing a cubbyhole office with the rather bewildered astrophysicist who had been assigned to "coordinate" with him. After three months in the same office Ray knew all about what Pashley had done, but he still wasn't sure what *he* had done to be punished like this.

For preference Ray Whipple didn't deal with any-thing closer than about five light years. People were especially difficult for him and riding herd on Pashley was straining his skills at interpersonal relations.

Putting the magazine in his lap Ray decided to try one more time. "Look," he protested, "it doesn't work that way."

"You mean you don't know how to make it work that way," Pashley said. "These kids are geniuses."

"But," Ray repeated feebly. "But . . . but . . . but . . ."

"Don't worry. You hold up your end and we'll nail these hackers yet." He hit a few keys and looked at the results on the screen. "Uh, could you get this untangled for me? Computer's screwed up again."

TEN

PROGRESS REPORT I

Never Let Them See You Sweat
—Consultants' Slogan

Normally a consultant presented a proposal in writing. These people preferred a face-to-face approach. *Like making a presentation to the prospective client,* Wiz thought, *only I've already got the job.*

Something over a dozen councilors had assembled in the Mayor's office for the meeting. In addition to Mayor Hasselhof and Dieter there was a distinguished-looking man in a tasteful blue tunic whom Wiz remembered vaguely, one or two other sharp-looking characters and a few old codgers who looked like they had come because they didn't have any place better to be.

Dieter was off to one side with a couple of other council members hanging at his elbows, talking to a slightly taller, younger man who managed to be handsome in a beefy blond sort of way and still look like Dieter. The councilor was punctuating his words with short, sharp hand motions and the other was focusing on him intently and occasionally nodding to show he more or less understood.

As soon as Wiz entered the room Dieter jerked his head around to stare at him and, followed by his entourage, pushed his way through the group over to him.

"Ah, Wizard," the little councilor said just a shade too loudly, "I'd like you to meet my nephew Pieter Halder. My sister's son. Fine boy and my heir." He clapped the young man firmly on the shoulder. Pieter smiled vacantly and nodded.

Dieter fixed Wiz with an eagle's glare. "Have you considered what I told you?"

"Ah, I have the matter under advisement."

"And?" the little man asked sharply.

Out of the corner of his eye Wiz saw that the mayor was watching them. He didn't look any too pleased.

"Well, as you know, this is a serious matter. . . ."

"Serious for you if you go against me, you mean."

"While I'm sure we share many basic objectives . . ." The mayor cut him off by rapping his gavel to call the meeting to order and Dieter and the others retreated to the councilors' benches. Wiz suddenly found himself standing alone in the middle of the room.

"I asked the wizard here to tell us what he's going to do," the mayor announced. "You all know what happened at the Baggot place." There was general muttering and nodding. "Now he's going to explain to us how he's going to fight these dragons."

"Well, actually I wasn't planning on fighting them," Wiz corrected. The temperature in the room seemed to drop ten degrees and the councilors started to mutter among themselves again, this time a low ominous mutter.

Wiz recognized his cue for fancy footwork. He steepled his hands, dropped his voice half an octave and nodded to the council.

"Obviously, to solve a problem of this magnitude it is necessary to grasp the entire solution space by completely reinventing the initial propositions. As you can see this is a major undertaking and to be effective the work flow must be carefully managed."

The councilors were listening intently now, all of them nodding to show their neighbors that they understood perfectly, even if no one else did.

"Now," Wiz went on, "currently we are in the initial definition phase of the project."

"What definition?" Dieter objected. "The problem's dragons and how much money we're going to spend to protect ourselves."

"Money?" another councilor put in. "Who said anything about spending money?"

"Well, there is the wizard's fee . . ." Mayor Hendrick started, but he was drowned out by three other councilors trying to talk at once. He pounded the table with the gavel trying to restore order. Wiz noticed the oak table was dented and battered in front of the mayor's seat.

"As you can see," Wiz said when the mayor finally restored order, "there are some fundamental issues which must be addressed before we can precisely define the problem." Dieter opened his mouth to protest, then snapped it shut and settled for glaring at Wiz.

"We consultants know that before we can address solutions we must quantify the problem."

"Quantify?" asked one of the councilors.

"Reduce it to numbers. We must have something we can measure and count so we will know how much progress we are making."

"Seems like an odd way to go about solving a problem," one of the councilors near Dieter grumbled, "counting things."

"'Specially for them as can't count and ends up with eleven in a dozen," one oldster piped up. That got a chuckle from most of the councilors, a red-faced mumble from the objector and a glare from Dieter.

"There are a number of proven statistical or numerical techniques we could use," Wiz went on. "First we must choose the appropriate one."

"We could count the number of people that get eaten," a councilor suggested.

"No, that's much too insensitive. We need something far more accurate."

"The number of dragons sighted each week?" suggested another.

"Subject to misinterpretation. I propose using a composite index extracted from baseline data which we will collect. By applying appropriate analysis techniques we can reduce the multi-dimensional dataspace to a single, easy-to-understand figure of merit by which to judge our dragon-reduction strategies." *Not to mention being so complicated nobody will be able to figure out what it means*, Wiz thought.

"And what do you propose to do about the dragons while you're gathering all this information?" Dieter's stooge demanded.

"Why nothing at all," Wiz said blandly. "That would invalidate the baseline sample and disturb the entire database."

"Ayup," an old councilor nodded wisely. "Them databases get right testy when they gets disturbed." He continued to nod and stroke his beard. Everyone ignored him.

"And how long is this baseline period going to be?"

"Normally you want at least one year's data. You have to allow for seasonal disturbances you understand." The councilors muttered and shifted in a way that told Wiz he had overplayed his hand.

"But since this is a rush job we will telescope that," he continued smoothly. "Let us say three moons after the program is fully functional."

"And meanwhile we do nothing," Dieter put in.

"No, while we are gathering data we can start an educational campaign to explain to people the dangers of dragons."

"But they all know dragons are dangerous," another councilor protested.

"Yes, but do they know how to avoid dragons? Oh, I'm sure they have some strategies they learned by hook or crook. But we have a responsibility to teach them optimum dragon-avoidance strategies."

"How are we going to do that?"

"Why, with an education campaign, of course. We will prepare pamphlets describing the dangers of dragons and how to avoid them."

"Most of the folks around here are illiterate."

"Quite all right. We will use iconographic representations for the literacy-impaired."

"What did he say?" muttered one of the councilors.

"He means they'll be full of pictures for them as can't read," explained his neighbor, who was quicker on the uptake.

It was a very long meeting.

Well, there's another hurdle crossed, Wiz thought as he stepped out of the town hall into the main square. *Or maybe another bullet dodged.* He wasn't sure he liked the second analogy even though a nasty little voice inside told him it was probably more accurate.

"Ah, Wizard Zumwalt!" came a smooth voice behind him. Wiz came out of his fog and saw the distinguished silver-haired councilor in the blue tunic standing at his elbow.

"Just Wiz, please."

The other smiled and nodded. "Very well, Wiz. And I am Rolf Rannison, head of the cloth merchants' guild and president of the Guild Association." He favored Wiz with an especially sunny smile. "I was hoping you could be my guest for lunch at the Guild Hall."

"Well . . ."

"Please accept," his would-be host urged. "Finest food in town, I can assure you."

Wiz knew he was being hustled, but he also knew that was part of a consultant's job. So he nodded and smiled as best he could. "I'd be honored."

The Guild Hall was a massive stone-and-timber building across the main square from the Town Hall. The private dining room on the second floor was paneled below and decorated with murals above. The paintings showed muscular folk going about the business of commerce in a style that reminded Wiz of WPA post office art.

The table was just a little bit too small so the two were forced close together. Not close enough to be uncomfortable but enough to encourage intimacy. The linen was starched and perfectly pressed, the liveried waiters were expert and unobtrusive and the food was very good, if rich.

It was all so well handled that it took Wiz a while to figure out what it was about the place. It wasn't just that it was old: the room and the Guild Hall felt, well, faded, like some once-great old downtown hotel. The murals were dulled with time and lack of cleaning and the paneling below them showed wormholes here and there. Like a lot of other things in this town, the Guild Hall obviously wasn't what it once was.

By the end of the first course Rolf was on a first-name basis with Wiz. Once or twice in his career in Silicon Valley Wiz had been wooed by some very high-powered headhunters. That was what this meeting with Rolf was like. The man was working on him, trying to bring him around to—what?—and in spite of his cynicism, Wiz found himself responding to the man's charm. If Dieter was born to sell used cars in San Jose, he thought, Rolf could sell bonds on Wall Street. Wiz smiled, pleasantly, tried to enjoy the meal and waited for the shoe to drop.

"I noticed you've already met Dieter," Rolf said casually as they worked their way through a dessert that was mostly berries, whipped cream and some kind of strong liqueur.

"After a fashion. He came to see me the first day."

Rolf smiled knowingly. "He is *dynamic*, isn't he?"

Wiz put down his spoon. "He is also about as subtle as a hand grenade in a barrel of oatmeal."

Rolf chuckled. "I think I understand the reference, but what is a 'hand grenade'?"

Wiz thought about how to explain high explosives to a culture that didn't even have gunpowder. Then he thought about what Moira said about his explanations. "Let's just say it's something that doesn't belong in an oatmeal barrel."

Again that engaging toothpaste smile. "You know one of the things I enjoy so much about you, Wiz? Your outlook is refreshing." He gestured from the wrist. "Like a breath of clean air into a musty closet that has been closed up too long."

Considering his performance this morning a breath of hot air was more like it, Wiz thought. But he made an appropriately modest reply.

"Refreshing nonetheless, Wiz. We have been a backwater for too long. It has narrowed us, cramped our vision." He leaned forward over the table. "Wiz, we need to change and I think you are going to help us make the changes we need so badly."

He used my name twice in two sentences, Wiz thought. *Here it comes.*

"Wiz, that is one of the reasons I hoped we could

meet. I wanted to offer you my support in your program. You're going to do great things for us, I know. In fact I'd go so far as to say your coming marks a new beginning for this town and its people."

Great, Wiz thought. *I am not only supposed to slay dragons, I'm supposed to work bloody miracles.*

"You understand I have a very limited brief. I am a consultant on dragon problems, not a general management consultant."

"Your formal brief, true. But I think you underrate your importance just now. As a wizard of great power, a defeater of dragons and an outsider with new ideas, the whole Council is compelled to listen to you." He paused and cocked an eyebrow. "And very frankly I doubt the present regime will allow you to do much about dragons."

That was so true that Wiz could only nod.

"Where do you fit in all this?"

"Fundamentally I think we want the same things."

Just then what Wiz *really* wanted was to go home to the Wizard's Keep and Moira. But that wasn't one of his options until he got this mess straightened out and he couldn't do that unless he stayed alive. He jerked his attention back to what Rolf was saying.

"You bring us change. But the change has to start at the top. We need new blood on the Council and especially we need a new mayor." He waved a hand in a self-deprecating gesture. "Oh, not necessarily me. But someone with the vision to see the way we must go and the determination to see that we can get there."

"What's wrong with Mayor Hendrick?"

Rolf sighed. "I am afraid he is too much under Dieter's influence. He can see nothing but old solutions to our problems."

"Dieter does have some ideas for doing things differently," Wiz pointed out.

"Dieter's solutions are more of the same old medicine. More taxes to strangle the life out of what little trade we have left." He shook his head. "No, money will not solve our problems. Not without a complete restructuring and a reawakening of civic discipline."

He leaned across the table and touched Wiz's hand. "Wiz, we must—what was your phrase?—reinvent ourselves. Yes, 'reinvent.' A new city, a new culture rising out of the ashes of the old. Why, the possibilities are . . ." Rolf trailed off, seemingly transfixed by something infinitely far off over Wiz's right shoulder. Then his attention snapped back to Wiz and he was all business again. " . . . rather remarkable," he finished smoothly.

A chill ran down Wiz's spine. "Look, I'm flattered that you think so highly of me, but . . ."

Rolf held up a hand. "When someone says they are flattered it means they are preparing to turn you down. Don't, I beg of you. You don't have to say yes, but leave the matter undecided, please."

"I will certainly try to keep an open mind."

Let's see, Wiz thought as he made his way back across the square. *I've been in town less than ten days and I've already made two powerful enemies.* At least Rolf would be his enemy as soon as he figured out that Wiz had no intention of supporting his schemes. Dieter wanted to loot the town. Wiz suspected Rolf's desires ran deeper and more dangerously. The man didn't want money, he wanted power. Probably a lot more power than a mayor had ever had before.

Of the two Rolf was probably the more dangerous. Dieter's hostility was open. With Rolf you'd never see the knife coming until it was buried in your back. You could see Dieter coming, but that didn't mean you could dodge. He touched the ring of protection on his finger.

It would place him in stasis if he was under immediate physical threat. *If the damn spell had any sense I'd have been frozen solid a couple of days ago,* he thought sourly.

Not a living soul was waiting to greet Wiz when he got home. Widder Hackett, however, was.

"Well Mr. Wizard, I hope you enjoyed your stroll around town because there's been the netherworld to pay while you've been gone."

"What's wrong?"

"That demon of yours is holding the girl prisoner up in the upstairs parlor," Widder Hackett said. "What the fiend has planned for her," the ghost continued virtuously, "I wouldn't want to guess.

"It's what comes from consorting with them low-class demons," Widder Hackett added as Wiz pounded up the stairs to rescue Anna.

He came into the room and found a hysterical maid facing off with a very determined scaly green demon.

"What's going on here?"

"I, I was just trying to . . . and it, it . . ." Anna was hyperventilating and for a minute Wiz thought she was going to faint on him.

Wiz recognized the demon. It was the one he had set to guard his desk and it manifested if anyone tried to touch his papers or equipment. Apparently Anna, not knowing better, had tried to clean off the desk.

He put his arm around her shoulders to comfort her, and to catch her if she did faint. Anna was trembling like a leaf and she pressed her face into his shoulder so she wouldn't have to look at the demon.

"Hey, it's all right. He won't hurt you if you don't try to touch anything on the desk."

"But he won't let me leave!"

Wiz looked around and realized that to get to the door they would have to pass the desk. The demon wouldn't attack unless someone tried to touch the things on the desk but it would certainly come alert if anyone but Wiz got close. *I'll have to turn the sensitivity down on the spell,* he thought.

Malkin stuck her head in the door to see what the commotion was, saw Wiz and Anna, and disappeared before Wiz could say anything.

"He won't hurt you if you don't touch what's on the desk," he told her. "Look, I'll dismiss him, okay?" A quick gesture and the demon vanished, looking smug. "There, it's fine." He gently pried her face out of his shoulder and turned her toward the desk. "See? No more demon." With his arm still around her shoulder he walked her past the desk to the door.

"Now, you don't have to clean around the desk, all right? That's not part of your job anyway and I'm sorry I didn't tell you that before. Are you okay now?" Anna sniffled and nodded.

Wiz drew a line on the floor in softly glowing blue light. "Look, anything inside this line I will take care of, okay? Just don't touch any of it and I'll make sure the demon doesn't bother you."

Bobo sauntered into the room, looked at the line and sniffed.

"Now just go on down to the kitchen and rest for a while. You'll be okay?"

Anna sniffled and nodded.

"I'm sorry to be so much trouble My Lord, it's just that . . ."

"I know," Wiz said encouragingly, "it wasn't your fault. Now go on."

Still sniffling, Anna made her way downstairs toward the kitchen.

"Malkin," Wiz called, "can you come in here a minute?"

"What's up?" the slender thief asked as she strode

into the room. Malkin showed no fear but Wiz noticed she kept just far enough away from the desk to keep from triggering the demon. For an instant he wondered how she knew the distance so exactly.

"Uh, about what you just saw. It wasn't really what it looked like."

Malkin waved a lazy hand. "Forget about it."

"But I wanted to explain . . ."

"No need," Malkin said. "The child's safe with you."

The way she said it, Wiz wasn't sure whether to be relieved or insulted.

"You'd better be careful though. The little ninny doesn't have the sense to be afraid of magic. She's likely to blunder into something you'd rather she didn't."

"I'll take extra precautions," Wiz assured her. "What about you? Aren't you afraid of being around all this magic?"

Malkin laughed. "Afraid? Not hardly. I respect it is all." The way she said it, and the way she smiled, left Wiz with a slightly uneasy feeling in the bottom of his stomach. He decided at the same time he turned down the demon's sensitivity he was going to increase the protection.

ELEVEN

MEANWHILE, BACK AT THE OBSERVATORY

Just because someone is hard-working and ambitious doesn't mean that person has the least idea what is going on.

—*The Consultants' Handbook*

It was another sunny day in the desert. Of course, it's almost always sunny in the desert, which is why this particular desert mountaintop sprouted telescopes like lawns sprout toadstools. With telescopes come astronomers, naturally, and just now this particular astronomer's mood was anything but sunny.

"You," Ray Whipple said, "have got to do something about that FBI agent."

There was a pause while the observatory director took his artfully scuffed ostrich-skin cowboy boots off the corner of his desk. "What's the problem?" he asked mildly. Actually he had a pretty good idea what the problem was and he was only surprised it had taken this long to happen.

"He found a seventy-four-cent error in someone's

account and now he's convinced he's on the trail of the mother of all conspiracies."

The director made a show of lighting his pipe. "That's his job after all."

"But the man's an idiot!" Ray protested.

"I know. So does his supervisor. She asked us to keep him here as a 'special favor' to the Bureau."

"He's chasing all over the net looking for some imaginary 'hacker' he thinks he's found and he's dragging me with him!"

"He's not breaking down any doors or shooting people, is he? It's safer for everyone if he stays here where he's out of the way and mostly harmless."

"But I've got to deal with him," Ray groaned.

"Look," the director said sympathetically, "I know this is hard on you. I'll tell you what. When this is over I'll make it up to you. How would you like some extra observing time? How would you like to get your project up on Hubble next year?"

Ray's eyes widened. Time on the Hubble Space Telescope was somewhat more precious than gold in the astronomical community. "You could do that?"

"Just keep our agent happy and keep him out of everyone's hair."

In the event, Clueless Pashley kept himself out of everyone's hair for the next three days. He was so busy tramping through the Internet in pursuit of his master hacker and screwing up his account that he was only an electronic pest for everyone but Whipple.

Pashley's performance on the Internet was reminiscent of the old saw about a thousand monkeys at a thousand typewriters, which is to say it was nearly random and mostly produced garbage. However, as in the case of the monkeys, there is always the element of blind chance and sheer, dumb luck. Pashley's original error was, as his office-mate surmised, an accounting glitch. But in the course of his thrashing around, Special Agent Myron Pashley stumbled and fell face-first into a heap of gold.

Not surprisingly it started with a total disaster.

Like most astronomers, Ray Whipple was used to working at night and sleeping during the day. Even though his current job was "temporary system administrator for administrative support services" (or, as he put it, "computer janitor") he saw no reason to change his habits.

Pashley, on the other hand was an early-to-bed, early-to-rise type who was in the office religiously at 7 A.M. This particular day he managed to be in the office all of thirty minutes before he did something especially stupid and crashed the entire system. Which of course resulted in Ray having to drag himself out of bed and drive back up the mountain at an ungodly-o-clock in the morning to fix what Pashley had done.

To add insult to injury, Whipple had to listen to Pashley the entire time he was trying to bring the system back up.

"I almost had him," Pashley kept insisting. "I was onto something and the hacker crashed the system to cover his tracks."

Ray knew damn well what had caused the crash almost as soon as he sat down at his terminal, but yelling at Pashley wouldn't get him any closer to time on the Hubble. To try to shut out his officemate, he kept his attention glued to the screen as the system booted back up.

Because he was concentrating so intently on his workstation he actually read the list of demon processes as it scrolled up. The last one was one he didn't recognize.

Whipple frowned. He should have known all the demons on the system and here was one he'd never seen. He called it up and found it was a perl script that scanned for incoming traffic with a particular name in the "from" field and forwarded information about it to a site he'd never heard of, **thekeep.org**.

This was getting stranger and stranger. A quick check of the mail queue showed a couple of messages with the right name in the "from" field that hadn't yet been forwarded when the system went down. He called one of those up and scanned through it. Then he came to the routing.

"What the hell?" he exclaimed.

"What?" demanded Pashley, hurrying over to peer over his shoulder. "What did you find?"

The routing was absurd. It looked as if the message touched every continent, including Antarctica, and was routed through the weirdest collection of sites he had ever seen.

This was completely lost on Pashley, but he did pick up on something else.

"Look at the name," Pashley said, jabbing his finger at the screen so it blocked most of Ray Whipple's view. "**Thekeep**. One of those fantasy names is a sure tipoff that it's a hacker site. I'll bet we'll find this is a major hacker nexus."

Whipple, who had played D&D until he got into graduate school, kept quiet. He had learned that arguing with Pashley on one of these subjects was useless.

"Whatever it is, someone got into our system," Whipple said.

"YES!" Pashley shouted in his ear. "I told you we had a hacker on the loose."

Ray Whipple gritted his teeth. "It looks like you're right."

Meanwhile the programmers at **thekeep.org** pursued their own search for Pashley's "hacker." It was slow, tedious work. There were a lot of systems on Wiz's routing list and not all of them were easy to plant a search demon in. A few were flat impossible so the programmers had to resort to other shifts. Fortunately Wiz was so homesick he e-mailed a message almost every day. Unfortunately it still took inordinate amounts of time and work.

"You know what I really resent?" Danny said one evening as the pair was hard at work. "All that work we put into dragon-slaying spells that we'll probably never have the chance to use."

"That is a consequence to be sought rather than mourned," Bal-Simba rumbled from his extra-large chair where he sat reviewing a scroll with Moira and Arianne.

"Well, yeah," Danny agreed. Then he added disconsolately, "But I've got such a *good* one."

"I was even hoping to learn something," Jerry said. "I have this theory about the black-body temperature of dragons."

"Most dragons are not black," Moira told him. "Why you should be interested in just the black ones, I do not know. Much less their temperature."

"No, you don't understand. See, a black body temperature is a physical property of all things, even dragons, no matter what their color. And . . ."

"My Lord, if this is another one of your explanations I am in no mood to hear it."

"But," Jerry said plaintively, "it's such an *interesting* question."

"The only question I am interested in regarding dragons is how to get Wiz back," Moira told him firmly.

Ray Whipple had an easier time of it. Being a legitimate system administrator at a legitimate site, not to mention being actually in this world and being able to invoke the name of the FBI, Whipple had resources Danny and Jerry didn't. By using them and calling in a few favors, Ray was able to trace Wiz back to the system he had broken into very much faster than the people at the Wizard's Keep.

In a matter of days he had a result to show the FBI agent.

"Cute," Ray said as he displayed his find. "It's a cutout using two mailboxes. Incoming mail goes into one, the script automatically transfers it to the other one and then it gets forwarded out of there. But if you trace it back the trail ends at this mailbox."

"Cutouts huh? That's an intelligence trick. And you thought it wasn't spies."

"A lot of people know how to do that," Ray muttered into the screen.

"Now, how do we track him from here?"

"That's going to take a little more work," Ray said, ignoring the "we." "But what I can do is modify his script so that we can see his traffic." The keys rattled under his fingers. "There. Now the script makes an extra copy of all messages that go through that mailbox and sends one to you."

"Hot dog!" Pashley breathed, visions of reinstatement dancing before him, "I told you we'd get this hacker." He stopped. "But wouldn't it be simpler just to ask the people at that site to track where the other side mailbox leads to?"

"I tried that," Whipple told him. "But I didn't get anywhere. I think there's something funny about that site."

TWELVE

BUREAU-CRATIC COMPLICATIONS

If you can delay solving a problem long enough, one of three things will happen: The problem will become so large that it destroys the organization, everyone gets so used to living with the problem that it ceases to be a problem, or the problem solves itself. In cases two and three you win. Meanwhile you don't make enemies by rocking the boat.
—The Consultants' Handbook

It was a bright muggy morning in Washington D.C. The kind of morning that finds legions of bureaucrats hard at work in their air-conditioned offices and trying not to think about what the drive home will be like.

The director of the Federal Bureau of Investigation was hard at work in her air-conditioned office, but she wasn't worried about the drive home. For one thing she probably wouldn't go home until well after sundown. For another she was deep in a review of industrial espionage activities in the United States, trying to decide how much of the report represented a legitimate danger and how much was eager beavers pumping for a bigger share of the department budget.

The Phone rang.

Not just any phone, The Phone. Popular legend to the contrary it was not red. It was a very ordinary looking tan telephone with a funny mouthpiece and an unusually thick cord connecting the handset to the base. It was the director's main link to the White House and the higher echelons of the Justice Department and the national security apparatus.

The director eyed The Phone. Not even the President normally used that telephone to contact her. It rang again and she picked it up.

"Director, do you recognize my voice?"

The director pulled what looked like a cheap pocket calculator out of the top drawer of her desk, checked the date and time and punched in a highly improbable mathematical calculation. "Give me confirmation."

"Alpha," The Voice said, "gamma rho woodchuck three-four."

"Confirmed. I recognize you."

Actually the director had no idea who the person on the other end of the phone was. She only knew he represented No Such Agency, the officially non-existent organization charged with communications and cipher security. The outfit was a couple of rungs up the intelligence food chain from the FBI.

"We have a domestic security problem," The Voice said. "Someone has been using one of our accounts on the computer network. A rather sensitive account. I am afraid we need your cooperation on this one." There was real regret in The Voice.

"We'll be happy to assist you," the director said, trying to keep the excitement out of her own voice. A favor like this to No Such Agency could be worth a lot in the barter market that made official Washington tick. "We can have a team ready to meet with you inside of an hour."

"I understand one of your people is already working on this from the other end, Special Agent Pashley."

"Pashley?" she asked in a voice that didn't betray anything.

The director was trying to quit smoking, but she groped in her desk for the crumpled remnants of her last pack and lit a slightly bent Camel.

"Yes. He apparently found evidence of the penetration at another site and has been tracing it back."

"I'm sure he doesn't realize the significance. I'll put a team of specialists on it instead."

"We think that would be inadvisable just now," The Voice said. "Perhaps it would be better if we worked with this Agent Pashley alone."

"Of course we'll need a small group to liase," the director said hastily.

"Of course," The Voice agreed. "Have your people contact ours at a suitable level and keep us informed of anything Pashley turns up."

After The Voice hung up the director ground out her cigarette and glared at the phone. *Damn that man. And damn Pashley!* Somehow that moron had stumbled into something.

The Bureau had teams of computer experts who could handle this. Real experts, not street agents who had been through a two-week course at the academy. No matter what No Such Agency wanted, she'd get them on the case and pull Pashley and . . .

Her hand stopped halfway to the phone. She *couldn't* pull Pashley. The Bureau's whole defense in the lawsuit depended on the fiction that Pashley was a competent, trusted agent. The Justice Department attorneys had explained to her that, on paper at least, she didn't dare do anything to suggest the Bureau had less than full faith in the turkey.

All right, she'd compromise—on paper. Pashley

would stay on the case, conducting an independent investigation from his damn mountaintop. Meanwhile she'd put together a tiger team to work with No Such Agency.

Wiz was staring at the screen when he heard a peremptory knock at the front door. Since he was staring at the screen because he was fresh out of ideas, he pushed his chair back from the desk and went out on the landing to see who it was. *I really ought to write a screen saver for that thing, just to give me something to look at,* he thought.

He got to the stairs just in time to see Anna opening the door for Dieter Hanwassel. The councilor was flanked by his nephew Pieter and a gawky young man Wiz didn't recognize who was clutching a rather grimy roll of parchment.

Anna had been scrubbing the front hall. She was wearing an apron over her brown dress and a kerchief over her golden curls. A pail of soapy water stood halfway down the hall and she still had the scrub brush in her other hand. As the three entered she realized she was still holding the brush and blushed crimson.

"Good afternoon, gentlemen," Wiz said in his best snow-the-suits manner as he descended. "What can I do for you?"

Even in tights and velvet bathrobes, these guys were suits.

Suit or not, Dieter wasn't snowed. "I want to talk to you, Wizard. On business."

"Of course."

"You know my nephew Pieter. This is Alfred Alfesbern. He's a brilliant young man and he's got the solution to your problem."

"Well . . ." Wiz began.

"We'll talk in your office. Come along Pieter."

"Do I have to?" Pieter whined, looking over Dieter's

shoulder to where Anna had gone back to scrubbing the floor.

"All right," Dieter snapped. "Wait here then. But be ready when we're ready to go." The other nodded, his eyes never leaving the maid.

Somewhat uneasily Wiz led his guests up the stairs and into his workroom. There weren't any chairs for visitors and Wiz didn't want to encourage these visitors to stay anyway.

"Now what can I do for you gentlemen?"

"It's what we can do for you," Dieter said. "We can solve your problem for you. Show him Alfred."

"I call it the Dragon-Stopper," the lanky man said, unrolling the scroll.

Wiz peered over his arm. "It looks like a town with a wall around it."

"It is a town with a wall around it," Dieter put in. "This town."

"You see," Alfred continued, "I have determined that dragons cannot pass through solid material. So if we interpose solid material between the town and the dragons, they cannot reach us." He stood up and beamed triumphantly. "And our problem is solved!"

"But dragons can fly right over a wall."

"Not if we build it high enough," Alfred said. "We just extend the wall up until it is beyond the dragons' ability to fly over it."

Wiz wondered what the altitude ceiling on a dragon was. Even if they couldn't do any better than a Piper Cub that still meant a 10,000 foot wall.

"That's going to be an awfully high wall."

"Details," snapped Dieter. "Quibbling. This will solve the problem and we'll be done with it."

"How are you going to build a wall that high?"

"The same way you build a low one," Dieter said. "What's the matter? Have you gone stupid?"

"No, I mean how are you going to get the work done?"

"We'll hire a good contractor. I know one or two."

I'll bet you do, Wiz thought.

"Gentlemen, I'm not sure this is practical."

"It's perfectly practical," Dieter said. "You're the one being impractical here."

"We've built lots of walls," Alfred put in. "It's a well-known technology." Dieter glared at him and the young man shut up.

"Look here, Wizard," the councilman said, "you can't say absolutely, positively this won't work, can you? So what's the harm in trying? It will put people to work, get money flowing and revive the economy. Besides," he added slyly, "there'll be something in it for you."

"Gentlemen, I really don't think . . ." Before he could finish there was a feminine shriek from downstairs followed by a male bellow of pain.

Down in the hall Pieter Halder was doubled over clutching his groin. Anna was standing with her back against the wall, her face scarlet and her skirt rumpled up against her petticoat. She looked up, saw Wiz and Dieter standing at the top of the stairs, turned and fled sobbing to the kitchen.

Wiz glared at Dieter and the little man backed partway down the stairs under the force of his gaze.

"Get out. All of you. Now."

"She's lying," Pieter gasped, still clutching himself. "I didn't do anything."

"Tried to put his hand up her dress is all," came Widder Hackett's voice out of thin air. "Oh, if only I was alive and still had me magic!"

Wiz faced Dieter again. "You are here as my guests." He bit each word off hard and sharp, advancing as he spoke so Dieter and Alfred kept backing down the stairs. "That will protect you for precisely ten heartbeats more.

If you are still here you will be trespassers and I will deal with you accordingly."

Dieter paled. "You can't treat me this way," he yelled.

"Five heartbeats," Wiz said. "Four, three . . ."

By then all three of them were out the door, Dieter in the lead and Pieter limping doubled over behind.

"You haven't heard the last of this," Dieter shouted as Wiz slammed the door on them. "You'll pay for this! I'll make you pay for it!"

With a final glare at the door, Wiz turned and went down to the kitchen.

Anna was slumped over the kitchen table weeping. She raised her head as Wiz came down the stairs and wiped her reddened eyes.

"I'm sorry, My Lord, but he . . . And I didn't do anything to provoke him. I swear I didn't."

Seeing her shame and misery, Wiz was very glad Pieter and the others were out of his reach.

"I know you didn't," he said gently. "No, you did exactly the right thing. I'm only sorry you didn't hit him harder."

Anna looked up and sniffled. "My granmama told me to do that whenever a man got, got too . . . forward."

Wiz stepped toward her to comfort her and then stopped. The last thing she needed just now was to be touched by a man.

"You're a very brave girl," he said. "And your grandmother was a wise woman. Go on and pull yourself together. Take your time, and if you want to go up to your room and lie down, go ahead."

Anna sniffled again and tried to smile up at him. "Thank you, My Lord, but I need to get dinner started."

"You don't have to."

"Please, My Lord. I'll be all right. Really I will."

Wiz left her in the kitchen and came back up to his workroom. All the while Widder Hackett carried on a monologue about young Halder's moral shortcomings. Clearly it wasn't the first time something like this had happened and apparently Widder Hackett had made a hobby of collecting gossip about his misdeeds.

He had barely gotten settled when Malkin came striding in. "I met the shrimp and a couple of his flunkies on the street," she said. "He was in a worse mood than usual and that miserable nephew of his was walking like he'd run into a banister."

"It wasn't a banister. It was Anna's knee."

"Like that, eh?" the tall woman shrugged. "Serves the copulating little swine right. She's not the first skirt he's tried to lift unwilling."

"So Widder Hackett has been telling me."

Malkin nodded. "Aye, she'd know. The old cow was the biggest gossip in the town. She must have kept records of everything everyone did."

"You thieving little strumpet!" Widder Hackett rasped.

"Careful," Wiz said to Malkin.

"She was an old busybody and I'd tell her so to her face."

Wiz looked around the room. "I think you just did."

Malkin snorted. "So what? She's dead and she can't touch me."

"Why you little guttersnipe!" Widder Hackett roared. "You're a fine one to talk, what with . . ."

The ghost went on for some time and in some detail. In the middle of it Wiz discovered that putting his hands over his ears did absolutely nothing to block out her voice. Malkin watched his antics with some amusement.

"Anyways," she went on when Widder Hackett finally ran down into a mumble, "you've got bigger things to worry about. That half-firkin councilman is going to hold it against you no matter how much provocation his pig nephew gave the girl."

"He's unhappy with me already. Just before Anna kneed Pieter I told him I wouldn't support his latest graft opportunity disguised as a public works project disguised as a dragon defense."

"In that case you've probably made yourself a mortal enemy. Dieter may dote on that little swine but he truly loves the chance to get money out of someone else's pocket."

"Well, it was inevitable anyway," Wiz sighed, "once he figured out I wouldn't go along with his scheme to get his hand into the public treasury up to the armpit."

Malkin nodded and turned to go out. She paused in the doorway. "There's another thing you'd better think about, Wizard. Young Halder's not the only one who's going to come sniffing about after Anna."

"She seems to handle them pretty well."

"Oh, aye. She'll protect herself. If she understands what's about in time. Problem is she's as cow-witted as she is pretty and she might not see the danger. Not all men are as easily discouraged as Pieter Halder. That's why she needs protection."

Wiz sighed. *Another responsibility I don't need.* "Look, go down there and comfort her, will you?"

"Me? What do I know about comforting hysterical females? You do it. You've got the knack and she looks up to you."

"I'm not what she needs just now. Besides I think she'd take it better if a woman told her she did the right thing."

"All right then. I'll look in on her."

"Malkin?"

"Yes?"

"Do you suppose people will get the wrong idea about you and Anna living here with me?"

"Oh, there'll be talk. Always is. But you're a powerful wizard and you're expected to be strange and mysterious in your ways. Besides, no one except chronic gossips are going to believe that you'd take advantage of the girl." She eyed him. "I don't know if you're too married, under a spell or—Fortuna aid me!—a gentleman. But it's obvious you're not going to do her any harm."

"What about you?"

Malkin threw back her head and laughed. "Me? Fortuna, I've got no reputation to lose, being a thief and all. And you could do better than a long stick like me in any establishment in town." She sobered slightly. "Besides, men want women they can look down on and that's a fact."

Wiz started to protest that he found Malkin attractive and then decided this wasn't the time. It was true about her height, Wiz realized. Malkin was easily the tallest woman he'd ever seen in this world. She was over six feet and her slenderness made her appear taller.

By the time he got all this together in his head, Malkin was gone.

THIRTEEN
CHAT MODE

*While ignorance and stupidity may debar a person
from solving a problem, it is no handicap at all
when it comes to screwing up someone else's
solution.*

—The Consultants' Handbook

Wiz was bored, restless and, most of all, homesick
for Moira and the Wizard's Keep. E-Mail was wonderful but it was no substitute for being there. It wasn't
even a substitute for talking on the phone.

He toyed with the idea of trying to set up a telephone
call to the Wizard's Keep, but hooking into the other
world's phone system was really Danny's area of exper-
tise. Wiz wasn't sure he could establish a voice connection and still keep his location hidden

On the other hand, he thought, *I can do something
almost as good.*

Computer chatting would give a much more immediate connection and he knew a way to make that secure.
What's more, he knew where he could find what he
needed to do it.

He spun back to his workstation and started connecting to the Internet.

Danny was bored. As often happened when he got bored he was surfing the Internet, hanging out on his favorite talk channel. As usual it was barely controlled chaos, with perhaps a half dozen conversations going on at once, like a printout of a cocktail party.

FREEKER: Anyone got any good codez?
DRAINO: So he says 'first assume a spherical chicken'
PILGRIM: The P-153 is a piece of shit. Use a canopener.
RINGO: Does anyone have the DTMF codes to do that?
DEATHMASTER: Hahaha
A.NONY.MOUS: Look in the last issue of 2600.
WIZ: Hey Danny how are things at the Keep?

The message scrolled by so quickly he almost missed it. Then he called up the buffer, read it again and goggled.

"DRAINO: Wiz," Danny typed, "is that you? Where are you? Are you all right?"

"Fine," the answer traced out on Danny's screen. "Maybe we'd better go to a private channel."

"Jerry, Moira come here!" Danny yelled over his shoulder. "It's Wiz."

"Well, they've had a problem all right," Special Agent Marty Conklin told the FBI director. In the corner Conklin's boss nodded approvingly. "They've got their butts in a sling so they want us to pull a rabbit out of the hat to save their bacon."

The director winced at the mixed metaphors. She wasn't sure she approved of Conklin either. He was obviously pushing the Bureau's weight restrictions hard and the director had a strong suspicion he couldn't pass the annual physical training test either.

But in Conklin's case the title "special agent" was especially appropriate. He was the FBI's brightest, if arguably weirdest, specialist on computer and telecommunications crime. His boss had managed to make him look halfway presentable in a rumpled gray suit, but he had still come along just in case his prize charge got too far out of hand.

The director lit another cigarette and blew smoke out her nose. *I've got to quit these—as soon as this business is settled,* she thought. "What exactly happened?"

"They left a back door ajar at a black site and now they've got newts in the firewall."

"Can you put that in English?"

Conklin paused to do a mental translation. "Okay, they have a site that's physically highly secure. Everything's guarded and under lock and key. For some reason they need Internet access from the site, but obviously they don't want the next net newt who comes along to take the system home with him."

"Don't want a what?"

"A net newt—slimy little uglies that you find under rocks."

The director nodded. "Oh, you mean hackers."

"No, I mean system breakers, computer criminals." Conklin was about to launch into his canned lecture on how most hackers are not criminals, but his boss cleared his throat meaningfully.

"Well, anyway, what you do in a case like that is set up a firewall. That's a computer that connects to the net on one side and to your secure system on the other.

All it does is pass messages back and forth. It acts as a barrier to keep out the net . . . uh, the bad guys.

"Now normally a firewall doesn't have any user accounts on it. It is strictly there as a gateway to the main system. But in this case someone did something real dumb."

Conklin smiled broadly at having caught the nation's top communications security agency in an error. "When a computer comes from the factory there's a standard password installed, something like 'password' or 'administrator,' something the field engineers can use to set the system up. Anyone using that password has superuser privileges on the system—they can do anything, because you need that kind of access to get the system up and running. Of course, since the password is the same on all machines of that kind it's a major security hole and you're supposed to erase it as soon as the system's set up."

Now the director was smiling too. "And they didn't?"

"No ma'am they did not. So some slimy little newt comes along, uses the password to set up his own accounts and starts helping himself to all the free computer time he can carry. Now they've found it, they're embarrassed and they're scared it's a major security breach so they want us to nail the little sucker."

The director was still smiling. Bureaucratically this was better and better. Not only did No Such Agency need a favor—it didn't have law enforcement powers and couldn't arrest the system breaker even if it could find him—but the problem was the result of a bone-headed blunder by their people. When the FBI cleaned up this mess No Such Agency would owe them big time.

"In fairness to them," Conklin's boss broke in, "it was an easy thing to overlook. The system has only been operational a few weeks and since the firewall doesn't

have any users there was no reason to check the password file."

The director shook her head. She wasn't interested
in being fair to No Such Agency, she was interested in
milking this for all it was worth. Unless . . .

"Is this really a national security problem? I mean
is there a possibility the main system was penetrated
by an outside agency?"

Conklin shook his head. "That's what No Such Agency
is afraid of, but that's a bunch of professional paranoids
playing Cover Your Ass. Fundamentally this was a dumb
stunt, the sort of thing a fourteen-year-old kid would
do from his Macintosh. There's no sign of any other tam-
pering with the system or of any attempt to get from
the firewall back to the main system. I'm ninety-nine
percent sure it's a run-of-the-mill newt."

"But not one hundred percent sure? Then of course
we need to pursue it." *And put those arrogant SOBs
even further in our debt,* she thought. "What are the
chances we can catch this, uh, 'newt'?"

"If he keeps using those accounts, about a hundred
percent. That's why No Such Agency hasn't canceled
them. We're watching, waiting and tracing him back."

"I don't understand," Moira said. "If Wiz is talking
to us 'real-time,' as you say, why is it harder to track
him in chat than when he sends us messages?"

Moira was sitting with the programmers in their
workroom. She tried to spend as little time there as
possible to let them work in peace. So she only popped
in a dozen or so times a day. Jerry had rigged a panic
button to summon her and any of them who weren't
in the room if they got a message from Wiz, but Moira
still checked constantly.

Danny shook his head and compressed his lips into
a tight line. "It shouldn't be, but Wiz got real clever.

He's using a program called IRC to chat and he's connecting through the freenet in Cleveland. Dialing in on the phone system to one of the freenet's numbers and using their IRC facility."

"But you said if you could get back to the telephones in your world you could easily find where he is tapping in from our world," Moira said plaintively.

"And normally we could. We can use the software built into a digital phone switch to let us trace someone's connection point in about three seconds." He made a face. "Problem is, Wiz knows it too."

Jerry nodded. "It's as if he's deliberately making this as hard as he can."

Moira's mouth quirked up in something that wasn't quite a smile. "Most likely he is. If the geas commands that he keep his location secret then he will bend all his efforts to that end. He cannot deliberately go against the geas."

"Anyway," Danny said, "Wiz always said he didn't know much about how we tapped into the phone system."

"That's because he didn't want to know," Jerry said. "The whole thing's blatantly illegal."

"So what are they going to do? Send the FBI to arrest us?"

"His conscience bothered him."

Danny shrugged. "Anyway, he must have understood more than I thought. See, we can use the automatic trace facility in the switch to find him, provided he's coming in through a digital switch. Digital phone switches are just about universal in the United States so I took that as a given."

"And it is not?"

Danny made a face. "His first link is to the local phone company. The next one is into the private phone system of a major oil company, where normal trace facilities don't go. Okay, we got that one. But the next link is via the oil company's leased lines to its satellite link to one of its exploration offices in Ulan Bator, Outer Mongolia. Needless to say, that is not a digital switch."

"Oh," Moira said in a small voice.

"It gets better. The next link is from the Ulan Bator switch to a switchboard someplace else in Outer Mongolia. We think it's in a yurt. Anyway, that one is not only not digital, it's still run by a human operator." Danny made an even worse face. "Currently we are trying to figure out how to get through that one. Then we'll see what other surprises he has in store for us."

"It does not sound hopeful then," Moira said.

"There's one more complication you should know about. Even once we slog through all that we will have to run a trace from the switch he is using to his connection point back in this world. That will take a couple or three hours from the time we locate the right switch."

"Needless to say," Jerry added, "we are still pursuing the e-mail link as well." He reached out and patted Moira's hand. "Don't worry, we'll find him whether he wants to be found or not."

"Is this place secure?" the FBI director asked, looking around the conference room deep in the bowels of the FBI building.

"As secure as we can make it," the staffer at the foot of the table told her. His name was Wilkins and he was in charge of such things.

The director grunted and pulled a package of cigarettes out of her purse. The room was supposed to be a no-smoking area but no one objected.

She lit up, inhaled and blew smoke out through her nostrils. "Before we get to the regular business we have a non-agenda item."

Everyone leaned forward expectantly. If it was too

sensitive to go on the agenda it was very sensitive indeed.

"Moron Pashley," the director said, taking obvious relish in mangling the name. "He's still making trouble."

Everyone leaned back. Several staffers stared down at the papers before them. One or two looked up at the ceiling, as if hoping to find the answer written there. No one in the room had to be told who Pashley was. He wasn't at all important in the grand scheme of things, but since the call from the head of No Such Agency he had become a major burr under the director's saddle. As a result, the top echelon of the FBI spent an inordinate amount of time trying to keep him discreetly under control.

"How?" asked Paul J. Rutherford, her special assistant and troubleshooter. "He's stuck out in the middle of the desert."

"He's less than two hours from a major airport and he wants to go investigate this new hacker case personally."

"That could be tricky," said James Hampton, her legal adviser. "We'd need a very good reason to forbid him."

"If we can't forbid him we can sure as hell transfer him," the director said. "Send him to some place *really* remote."

"Well, there is a site in Antarctica," Rutherford said. The director brightened visibly.

"Won't work," Hampton put in. "It's outside the U.S. and we're legally forbidden to operate anywhere else."

"Well, what can we find *inside* the U.S.?" The director asked. "There's gotta be a deep, dark hole somewhere we can stick this clown."

"Just any hole won't do," Hampton reminded her. "It's got to have a major computer link to the outside world so we can maintain Pashley is working on computer crime."

"The Aleutians!" someone further down the table said. "There are a couple of places out on those islands with major computer links and nothing else but fog, seagulls and Kodiak bears."

The director thought of Pashley meeting a giant bear in the fog. She brightened again.

"Won't work," Rutherford said glumly. "Those computers are too important. If he screws them up we've got major problems, national-security-wise."

"But the Cold War is over," the director protested. "We're not worried about the Russians any more."

"We use them to eavesdrop on the Japanese and Koreans," Hampton said apologetically.

The director ground out her cigarette and muttered a highly politically incorrect phrase from her childhood. One that used "mother" as an adjective three times.

"All right, this clown wants to go to San Francisco 'to pursue a hot lead.' Any suggestions?"

For a long moment no one at the table said anything. Then Hampton voiced the inevitable. "Since it's a legitimate national security case I don't think we dare stop him," he said apologetically.

The director used the phrase again.

Well, Ray Whipple thought, *at least I'm getting some time in San Francisco out of this.* Ray liked San Francisco, especially when it was summer in the desert, but he wasn't looking forward to this trip at all.

He looked around the office to make sure he hadn't forgotten anything—and to keep his mind off what the rest of today was going to be like.

For one thing it involved a ninety-minute automobile ride with Myron Pashley, followed by a wait in an airport and a two-hour flight with the man. That was a lot more than the Recommended Daily Allowance of Pashley and damn close to the LD-50.

Which was the other thing. The man would *not* shut up about this system breaker he was tracking. Since most of what he had to say was palpable nonsense and he seemed utterly immune to anything he didn't want to hear, his chatter was like fingernails on a blackboard to the astronomer. Ray was taking his Walkman and a selection of his favorite Bach tapes in the hope he could drown Pashley out. He suspected strongly the FBI agent wouldn't take the hint.

Look on the bright side, Whipple thought. *When we get to Silicon Valley he's someone else's problem.*

Finally, Ray turned on his vacation demon and logged his terminal off the system. The vacation program would automatically respond to any e-mail messages with an electronic form letter telling the sender he would be gone for a while. He looked around the office for the last time and realized Pashley's terminal was still active and connected. *Idiot!* Ray Whipple thought. As a final gesture he turned on the vacation demon on Pashley's system as well.

Unfortunately Ray was distracted and didn't think it through. The vacation demon didn't think at all. It just did what it was programmed to do.

It was mid-morning when Wiz came into his workroom. Since Anna had started working here he was actually able to sleep in most mornings and he enjoyed the sensation immensely.

Just because he slept late didn't mean others did. Anna was usually up at first light of dawn and even Malkin didn't often sleep later than he did.

This morning both of them were in his workroom staring at the screen saver he had finished the night before. Anna was standing carefully behind the blue line on the floor, broom in hand, obviously interrupted at her work. She was staring at the display like a child seeing her first Christmas tree. Malkin was just behind her, also watching the ever-changing patterns.

Anna saw him and blushed. "Oh, I'm sorry, My Lord, I didn't mean to . . . It's just that it's so beautiful."

"It's a screen saver," Wiz told her. "Although there's really no screen there to save."

Malkin examined the glowing pattern and grunted. "What does it do?"

"Well, it doesn't really do anything." Wiz looked back at the swirl of color. "You know, if they had invented those things back in the sixties when everyone was dropping LSD the intellectual history of the Western World would have been considerably different."

Malkin grunted again and turned away.

"If you'll excuse me, My Lord," Anna said tentatively. "I'll leave this room until later." With that she turned and hurried out.

Wiz watched her go and shook his head. He was no more immune to physical beauty than most men, but like a lot of men he rated other things higher than looks when it came to female attractiveness. Intelligence, for instance—which definitely put Anna out of the running. Besides, the girl's vulnerability triggered his protective instincts.

And always and above all there was Moira. He sighed at the thought and set to work.

As usual, the first thing Wiz did was to check his mail.

The very first message was from a net id he didn't recognize. *Spam or junk mail?* he thought as he called it up.

Special Agent Myron Pashley will be out of the office and unavailable for the next two weeks. Please forward any urgent messages to fbi@fbi.gov

Myron Pashley,
Special Agent, FBI

Wiz went cold. They were on to him! Someone must have found his mailboxes on the broken system and called in the Feds. He recognized the form of the message as a vacation demon. It was just sheer blind luck that the FBI agent who had been getting copies of his messages had gone on vacation and hadn't bothered to exclude his drop from the demon's reply list.

Wiz slammed his hand to his forehead and damned himself as an utter idiot. He had been stupid to use that mailbox setup for so long! It was only a matter of time before someone traced him back, found the cutout and caught him.

But in spite of the danger he needed that e-mail link to the Wizard's Keep. He'd have to come up with something to make it secure from snoopers in both worlds.

System breaking had never been Wiz's idea of hacking. Danny could probably have come up with a much more sophisticated way of hiding while using the net. But you can't become intimately familiar with systems without learning things that are useful in less-than-legal ways.

Wiz thought hard for a couple of minutes and then he smiled. Yeah, there was a way. Something that would be just about untraceable unless they figured out the trick—and drive them nuts if they tried to trace it.

A few minutes work at the keyboard and a net of purple and green lines flashed into being above his work table. Several more key clicks and a few of the intersections burned fiery red. Wiz looked at the glowing orange letters next to the red points of light. Each red dot indicated a computer on the Internet that doubled as a router. *Not bad. The only question is which one to use?*

"Yes!" he whispered. Even Jerry would never think that the system might be lying to him. If he was careful, they'd never have any reason to suspect at the Wizard's Keep.

That first line of defense would be tough, but it was

simple enough that he could put it into effect almost immediately. That would buy him some more time while he added extra layers of security behind it.

Wiz bent to the magical workstation with a will, his fingers flying over the keys. *Just a few more hours,* he thought. *Give me just a few hours and I'll be damn near invulnerable.*

Joshua Weinberg felt like hell. His throat was raw, his cough was worse and he felt like someone was sitting on his chest even when he was standing up. If he hadn't had a damn good reason to come in this morning he would have stayed home in bed, maybe even called the doctor the way Dorothy had been nagging him to do.

But as head of the Silicon Valley office of the FBI, he had responsibilities. Just now he was standing next to one of them.

"It's an honor to have you, Agent Pashley," he said as he led his guest into the main office. He said it loudly enough to set off another coughing fit, but he was sure at least some of the agents in the bull pen heard him.

Privately he was much less impressed. The guy was certainly living up to his advance billing. But as he introduced him to his other agents Weinberg was careful not to betray by so much as the twitch of a muscle that Myron Pashley was anything other than an out-of-town expert on computer crime.

Weinberg knew all about Pashley. He had gotten a personal telephone call from the director of the FBI explaining about Pashley at some length. In fact she had called him at home at 4 A.M. to make sure the call didn't appear on the office phone logs.

Cooperate. Treat him like he knows what he's doing. And watch him every minute.

As soon as Bill Janovsky, his second-in-command, got

back he'd take him aside and explain about their guest and how he was to be handled. Just now Janovsky was up in San Francisco conferring with the U.S. Attorney about a technology transfer case. Their talk would have to wait until this afternoon.

Weinberg wished devoutly he was still chasing Soviet agents around the semiconductor plants. He felt like hell.

In the event, Weinberg didn't get to talk to Janovsky that day. Janovsky was delayed in San Francisco until after 5 P.M. and Weinberg felt so awful he went home sick before Janovsky got back. He felt worse the next morning and stayed home all that day and the next day. By Thursday his wife took him to the doctor and the doctor called an ambulance to take him to the hospital.

One consequence of Weinberg's illness was that it took somewhat longer than usual to get things squared away on Pashley's hacker investigation.

There were a couple of less obvious consequences. For one thing Weinberg hadn't had a chance to tell Janovsky or anyone else about his conversation with the director. His people had seen their boss acting as if Pashley was a big gun expert so naturally they assumed he was.

For another, no one bothered to tell the director that Weinberg was out of commission. There was no reason why they should, after all, since no one in the office knew about her interest in Pashley.

Ray Whipple could have told them a lot about Pashley, but Whipple had gone off to visit some colleagues at Cal Berkeley's Leuschner Observatory to get a first-hand look at some anomalous data collected by the Kuiper Airborne Observatory. Pashley had assured him he would call him when needed and Whipple figured the FBI could do a better job of restraining Pashley than he could.

The net result was that Clueless Pashley was loose in Silicon Valley with the full force of the Federal Bureau of Investigation behind him.

FOURTEEN

RAIDING ON THE PARADE

*Expert: Anyone more than 100 miles from home
carrying a briefcase.*

—The Consultants' Handbook

It is a truism well-known to lawyers that while the
law may be uniform, all judges are not alike. It is a
corollary equally well known to prosecutors that some
judges are easier than others when it comes to search
warrants and such. In San Francisco District Court,
Judge David Faraday was what the local federal prosecutors privately—very privately—called a patsy. A law-
and-order Nixon appointee, he could be counted on to
grant search warrants on nearly any grounds.

So it was hardly surprising that FBI Special Agent
George Arnold showed up in Judge Faraday's office with
Special Agent Clueless Pashley in tow to seek warrants
to raid Judith's apartment.

"And this person has been breaking into government
computers?" Judge Faraday asked after looking over the
papers Pashley and Arnold presented to him.

"Highly sensitive government computers," Pashley

amended. "Your honor this is a major national security case."

Arnold nodded. "Your honor, if need be, we have a civilian expert on computer networks and security waiting outside who can testify to the importance of this warrant." Actually it was Ray Whipple cooling his heels in the outer office, but he was an expert in Pashley's eyes and Arnold was following the lead of the bureau's out-of-town "expert."

"I know about computer crime, Mr. Arnold," Judge Faraday said mildly. "I saw that movie, *War Games*." The judge scanned down through the pile of affidavits.

"Search warrant for subject's apartment, wiretap on subject's telephone, electronic surveillance of premises. Well, this seems in order," he said as he reached for his pen. "Very well, gentlemen, the warrants are granted."

Pashley managed not to cheer.

"Did you get it?" Ray Whipple asked as Pashley and Arnold emerged from the judge's chambers. Pashley tapped his breast pocket significantly, even though the warrant was really in Arnold's briefcase.

"When are you going to serve it?" Ray asked as soon as they were out in the corridor.

"I'd like to hold off on the search warrant for a week or so," Arnold said. "We'll put the wiretap in place immediately and get a snooping van in the parking lot tonight to start executing the surveillance. That van can pick up the electromagnetic emissions from ordinary computers and decode them from five hundred feet away."

The astronomer gave a low whistle. "That's scary."

"Oh, we've got our methods," Pashley assured him jauntily, missing the expression on Whipple's face.

"We can lift information right out of a computer

without the user knowing it," Arnold added. "If we listen for a few days we may get to watch this hacker in action before the bust goes down."

"When's she going to do something?" Myron Pashley wondered aloud for roughly the eighth time that evening.

George Arnold squirmed around to get a better view of the readout. "So far she's still watching television."

Pashley and Arnold were crammed into the surveillance van along with the regular operator and several racks of equipment. "Cramped" was too generous a word for conditions in the van. "Badly ventilated" didn't really cover the subject either, especially since Pashley had found a Yemeni restaurant near the hotel and dined on a vegetarian dish that was mostly chickpeas and garlic. So far they had been sitting almost in each other's laps for almost three hours and even Pashley was getting tired of it.

The directional antenna hidden in the van's roof rack was pointed at Judith Connally's apartment less than three hundred feet away. At that distance it could easily pick up electronic emanations from Judith's apartment.

"Wait a minute," the technician said. "The television's just gone off. Hold it, okay, she's starting to work on the computer."

"Here we go!" Pashley crowed. For an awful instant Arnold thought Pashley was going to hug him.

"What's she doing?"

"Looks like loading a program," the tech said, keeping his eyes fixed on the displays. "Okay, she's just put a file up on the screen. I got it now."

Pashley, Arnold and the technician wriggled around until they could all see the display screen.

```
# include <iostream.h>

template <int T>
struct A{A(){A<T>>1>B;cout<<T%2;}};
struct A<0>{};
void main(){A<99>();}
```

"It's screwed up," Arnold complained.

The tech checked the instruments. "No, that's what's on her screen all right."

"What do you make of this stuff?" Arnold asked.

"Code," Pashley assured him. "This is all in code. When we raid the place we'll probably find a code book that translates all these code words."

Neither Pashley nor Arnold knew it, but it was indeed code they were looking at, although not in the sense they meant. Inside her apartment Judith was settling down to work on one of her private programming projects. Since for preference Judith used C and since her C style was both idiosyncratic and highly personal, it was hardly surprising that the FBI agents couldn't make sense of it. Since the particular program Judith was laboring over was her entry in this year's Obfuscated C++ Contest it was to be expected. Since one of the utilities Judith had developed to help her was an uglyprinter, which turned even the best-structured C code into an utter muddle, it was inevitable.

Judith Connally was playing relativistic Tetris when the knock came at the door.

"Damn!" she muttered as the distraction made her miss an especially intricate maneuver in the time direction. The rest of her carefully constructed edifice came tumbling down even before she was out of the chair to answer the door.

Judith had never met Myron Pashley, but as soon as she opened the door she knew what he was. For one thing he was wearing that dark-suit-narrow-tie-white-shirt outfit no one wore anymore but government agents and EDS employees. And EDS employees weren't allowed to wear wrap-around sunglasses.

"Special Agent Pashley, FBI," the man announced, holding out his identification. "We have a warrant to search these premises." He thrust a paper into Judith's hands and pushed her aside. "Stand out of the way, please."

He was followed into the apartment by six other men and a woman, all dressed in the same style if not the same clothing. Since Judith's apartment was not large, it was suddenly very crowded. Judith found herself crammed back against a book case.

One of the agents sat down at her computer and started calling up directories. Others fanned out through the apartment.

After a quick run-through of her more recent sins, Judith relaxed. There was nothing in the apartment which was the least bit incriminating. Then she looked at the search warrant and nearly burst out laughing. A national security case? Get real!

Then she stopped laughing and started worrying. She hadn't done anything, but what had the people in the other world been up to? Wiz was apparently in some kind of trouble and you never knew what Danny was going to do. There wasn't anything illegal here, but the laws didn't anticipate contact with alternate worlds where magic worked. If someone halfway competent had even a hint of a suspicion something like that was going on, the stuff in this apartment would be enough to blow it sky high. Whether that would mean jail or years in protective custody as a "vital resource" she didn't know, but she wasn't eager to find out.

Pashley moved to her desk and Judith's heart caught in her throat. There, lying on top of the stack of unpaid bills and unanswered mail, was her documentation for the magic compiler for Wiz's world. With its mixture of programming and magic that book alone would be enough to give the whole show away.

"What's this?" Pashley demanded, hefting the book.

"That's the design document for magic in my novels," Judith told him as blandly as she could. "Do you want it?"

Pashley knew all about seizing writer's notes after his experiences in North Carolina. "That won't be necessary." He turned to put the document back on the desk and missed seeing Judith slump in relief.

The agents went through the apartment like a polite hurricane. They always said "please" and called Judith "m'aam," but they were relentless and unstoppable. After turning the place upside down, taking her computer, boxing up all her disks and tapes, photographing everything (including the dishes in the kitchen sink and the bra hanging on the bedroom doorknob), giving her a carefully itemized receipt with serial numbers, and making an appointment with Judith to come in for questioning "with your attorney present if you desire," the agents finally left.

"Hit me," Wiz said glumly to the demon crouched on his work table.

The demon in the green eyeshade, gaiters and violently checked vest gave Wiz a toothy grin before flipping down a ten. That made twenty-three and Wiz was busted out. The demon gathered the cards in and shuffled them. Then he cocked an eyebrow at Wiz, waiting for the signal to deal again.

Wiz slumped back in his chair and sighed. It was still early afternoon, but it was not a good day. Not that that was unusual. The townfolk had learned by now that "their" wizard wasn't available before noon, but as soon as noon arrived there was a small line of them on his doorstep, demanding to see him.

He had tried refusing to see anyone, but that meant either being a prisoner in his house or being stopped on every street corner by someone with a long, incomprehensible tale of woe. So he had gone back to seeing a few people every morning, even though there was nothing he could do for most of them.

This morning's crowd had included a farmer who wanted him to find the pot of gold his grandfather was supposed to have buried on the farm, a lovesick young man who wanted his beloved to notice him and a nervous middle-aged woman who apparently expected him to guess what she wanted since she never did get around to telling him.

Meanwhile, in spite of the building urgency he was at a complete and utter standstill on the dragon problem. He tried to tell himself he was too overcome with distractions to focus on it, but the fact he was playing blackjack rather than working told him how accurate that was. The truth was he didn't have even a notion of how to begin.

Wiz knew from experience there was a hierarchy to working on a software problem. There was hacking, there was programming, there was playing, there was doodling and there was what a British friend of his rather inelegantly described as "code wanking." He had been reduced to code wanking days ago and now he had lost his enthusiasm even for that.

He sighed and looked over at the demon. The demon leered back and riffled the cards suggestively.

"Busy, I see." Wiz turned to see Malkin standing in the doorway.

"Not really. What's up?"

"Message from Ol' Droopy. He wants to know how you're coming."

It took Wiz an instant to identify "Ol' Droopy" as the mayor and somewhat longer to formulate an answer.

"Tell him things are progressing at a satisfactory pace."

"So I see. Anyway, you can tell him yourself. I'm not your messenger. He just stopped me on the way back here."

As she moved Wiz noticed a slight bulge in her tunic.

"Wait a minute! Did you steal his chain of office again?"

"Naw. Did that once, didn't I?" She reached into her tunic and produced a wide leather belt with an ornate gemmed buckle. "I do wonder how far he'll get before his breeches fall down, though."

Wiz groaned. "One of these days you're going to get us all thrown right back in jail."

"That's all right," Malkin said cheerfully. "I've still got the keys hidden away."

Wiz groaned again.

"Besides, you're a fine one to talk. With your messing about with dragons and the Council you're likely to get us staked out on The Rock."

"Well, why do you stay, then?"

Malkin smiled in a peculiarly sunny fashion. "I want to see what's going to happen next. Hanging around here is more fun than a mummer's show. Besides, it gives me a base of operations, so to speak."

Wiz thought about what that last meant. Then he decided he didn't want to know. He also remembered why he had never had roommates. Then he thought of the rats in the psych lab. The more he thought about them the more sympathy he felt.

"Of course, if you want me to leave . . ."

"No, no. I need you for background resource. But try to be a little more discreet, will you?"

Malkin draped the belt over her shoulder, buckle

resting on her breast. Wiz noticed it hung nearly down to her knees behind. "Oh, I'm always careful," Malkin said cheerfully. "You have to be in my business."

With that she was gone. Wiz sighed again and turned back to the demon, who raised a pair of scaly eyebrows and riffled the cards. Wiz dismissed him with a gesture. Somehow he'd lost all his taste for taking chances—any more chances.

Judith wasn't the only one upset by the FBI raid. If she was annoyed, the mood in the Wizard's Keep verged on panic.

Bal-Simba frowned when a breathless Jerry and Danny told him, in alternating choruses, what had happened.

"How serious is this?" the big wizard asked when his visitors finally reached a stopping place.

"Pretty serious," Jerry told him. "If **thekeep.org** goes off line we lose our communication link to Wiz." *And probably all chance of finding him,* he thought. But he saw the look on Moira's face and he didn't say that.

"Is Judith in any danger?" Moira asked.

"Danger? No. She's probably not even in trouble, well not much. She's not doing anything illegal. Wiz might be in trouble if they could catch him, but there's not much chance of that."

"The Sparrow told me once that you keep records on these devices," Bal-Simba said. "Is there anything there which would arouse their ire?"

Danny grinned. "There aren't any records on that machine. We keep all that at this end, just in case. As far as the domain is concerned, Judith's system isn't much more than a dumb terminal, even though it's officially listed as the main server."

"That was Judith's idea," Jerry reminded his younger colleague. "After she saw some of the stuff you'd been up to she didn't want any record of it on her system."

"Anyway it was a pretty smart move," Danny said. "There's no way they can pin anything on her. There's even a complete set of domain software on her system."

"We've also got a backup way to reach Judith. We're setting up a modem link over a regular telephone line. She just calls a phone number we give her and logs in."

"Can we give that number to Wiz?"

Danny frowned. "That's going to be trickier. You can bet the FBI has a wiretap on the connection to **thekeep.org**. If we use the current Internet connection to tell Wiz about the new number we'll be telling the FBI too. Since we, ah, weren't completely aboveboard in getting that number it wouldn't do to have them tapping that line too. We may be able to rig up a code or something, but it will take more time."

"Then how do we tell Judith about the number?"

"Easy. We call her, preferably at a friend's house."

"Is this like the number we gave Major Gilligan when we sent him back to your World?"

"Not exactly. That was an 800 number." Danny made a face. "Big mistake. I found out the hard way they monitor those real close. They found us and shut us down in just a couple of weeks. According to some of the people I've been talking to on the net they're not as careful about local numbers, especially the ones that don't show long-distance charges."

"Meaning you've been hanging around with the phone phreakers again," Jerry said.

"Be glad I was," Danny shot back. "Otherwise we'd have worse problems."

Jerry didn't have a good answer for that one, so he let it slide.

"But can they sever the link?" Moira persisted.

"They may think they have already since they don't know we're tapped into her line."

"Can they cut it entirely?"

"Yeah, by disconnecting the line. But they probably won't do that. There's no reason for them to do it." He sighed. "You know there was a time when government agents were pretty dumb about these things. I understand they've gotten smarter."

"But they still might cut us off from Wiz?"

"Theoretically," Jerry said. "But don't worry. It would take an absolute idiot to do something like that."

It was not a good day for Special Agent Pashley. He had spent the morning interviewing Judith Connally with her lawyer present and he felt he was further behind than ever. After two hours of questioning and several very pointed inquiries by Judith's lawyer as to the exact charge, he had turned her loose. The results from the examination of Judith's computer and related material hadn't helped any.

"Technicalities," he grumbled into his coffee cup. "Tied in knots by damn technicalities."

"I told you it was a mailbox," Ray Whipple told him.

"It's a top secret government mailbox and these hackers are breaking into it!"

"Look," Ray said slowly and carefully, as if explaining something to a child. "We only know that some messages from that mailbox passed through her system. The messages we have were addressed to other accounts on that domain, she says she never got any messages from that account, there's no sign of any such messages on her system and she doesn't know where to find the people the messages were sent to."

"Yeah, but someone had to send the message in the first place and that person had to break into the mailbox."

"But she didn't send mail to herself," the astronomer said patiently. "The messages weren't for her and she didn't know that address was some sort of government secret. Hell, she claims she didn't even know those accounts were on her machine. That makes her as much a victim as the government. You can't arrest her for that. Especially since the thing's so secret you can't admit it's a secret in the first place."

"Hah!" Pashley said.

Whipple shrugged. "You can't prove otherwise."

"Technicalities," Pashley repeated. "Picky little technicalities. They're what's ruining this country."

"Myron, she's innocent."

Pashley snorted. "With a record like hers? She disappears, right out of a locked hospital ward, and no one knows where she's gone, and she's innocent?"

"She had a head injury. The hospital screwed up when she came out of the coma, she wandered around for a while before they found her. The hospital admitted they were wrong by settling with her, didn't they?"

"For all we know she was kidnapped by aliens for experiments or something," Pashley retorted.

Actually Pashley was closer to the mark than Whipple, although neither of them would have believed the real story. Judith had been taken to Wiz's World as part of the battle against computer criminal magicians at Caer Mort. She had been healed there and returned to our world when the situation was stabilized.

Suddenly Pashley brightened. "A brain probe! Maybe she's jacked into the net directly through her brain. We can find out with an X-ray or MRI or something." He stood up and strode out into the main office. "Hey John," he called, "have we got an X-ray machine around here?"

Ray Whipple put his head in his hands and groaned.

By mutual consent, the programmers and Judith Connally kept word of the FBI raid from Wiz. So naturally Wiz kept sending e-mail and chatting with **thekeep.org** as if it was still there.

Which it was, of course. In spite of what it said in the paperwork, the real server for the domain had always been in the Wizard's Keep in another world. True, there was now no computer in Judith's apartment, but that didn't matter to the signal. It was tapped off magically between the junction box and the apartment. First, however, it traveled through the local telephone office, where the FBI was monitoring the line.

Clueless Pashley looked at the surveillance report and slammed it down on the table. "We didn't get it," he said disgustedly. "Someone's still using that computer link."

"But that's impossible," Arnold protested. "We got her computer."

"Well, she's still on-line. Look at this. She must have another computer in there."

The other FBI agent went over the transcript and shook his head.

"But we got all the computer equipment in the apartment."

"Then it's got to be disguised as something else." He riffled through the sheaf of pictures of Judith's apartment. "What about that wall of electronic stuff?"

"That was a stereo system."

"Are you sure? You can disguise a computer to look like anything. These hackers are diabolical. Come on, let's go back to the judge."

This time the agents carried off a complete stereo system, a big-screen television complete with video game console, and anything else in the apartment that looked electronic, including a clock radio. Again they gave Judith an itemized receipt with serial numbers. Then they departed as quickly and officiously as they came.

"This," Judith said to the bare wall where her stereo had been, "is bloody ridiculous."

FIFTEEN

COMPETITION

Utter incompetence never kept anyone from under-bidding and over-promising to get the job.
— *The Consultants' Handbook*

Wiz was having another lousy morning. He had left the house to escape the usual flow of people who wanted him to solve their problems only to run into the mayor at the town hall, who wanted to know how the dragon program was coming, and by the way did he have anything for a head cold? Wiz barely got out of that when he encountered Dieter Hanwassel and a couple of his council flunkies in the square.

"There you are, Wizard." Dieter made it sound like an accusation.

"Here I am," Wiz agreed glumly. Then he waited.

"I'm giving you one last chance, Wizard," Dieter said at last. "You can see things our way or suffer the consequences."

"Gentlemen, I have already told you I will give your position all the consideration it deserves."

"You mean you'll try to stall us," Dieter said. "Well, we won't be stalled. You'll either cooperate or else."

"I wonder how the rest of the council would take it if they knew what you were proposing?" Wiz asked with a slight smile. "I understand they are not all in favor of increasing taxes."

The little man turned purple. "Defy me, will you!" Then with a visible effort he controlled himself. "Well, we'll see." He turned and stalked up the steps into the town hall. His hangers-on followed. "I've a trick that's worth two of you," he said to his cronies as they drifted out of earshot. Wiz wasn't sure whether he was supposed to hear that or not.

Wiz spent another hour or so wandering around town, looking at things and fending off a couple of requests for magical help. Malkin was waiting for him when he got home.

"Messenger came from the council for you just a few minutes ago," she told him as soon as he walked in the door. "Ol' Droopy and some of the others want to see you in the mayor's office right away."

"Great. I just came from there. Now what?"

The tall woman shrugged. "Nothing good, I'll warrant."

There was a group gathered in the mayor's office by the time Wiz arrived. Dieter, the mayor, Rolf and several others were talking to a blond young man Wiz didn't recognize. The stranger's back was to the door but Dieter's wasn't. As soon as Wiz walked into the room he peered around the young man's shoulder and smiled at Wiz, not at all pleasantly.

"We have found another magician," Dieter said, gesturing to the young man. "Llewllyn here is skilled in the new magic."

On that cue the young man turned and swept a deep bow in Wiz's direction. The newcomer was undeniably handsome. Blond hair fell in ringlets to broad shoulders. Pearly teeth peeked between ruby lips as he smiled and his blue eyes sparkled. He was only a little shorter than Wiz, not as heavily built, which made him decidedly slender—but elegant rather than skinny. Handsome, personable and utterly devoid of sincerity. He reminded Wiz of every used car salesman and mortician he had ever met. Instinctively Wiz looked for the white belt and shoes. Then the significance of what Dieter had just said sunk in.

"The, ah, new magic?"

The young man inclined his head in assent. "Yes, the powerful new magic of the south. I am a direct disciple of the Sparrow, the mightiest of all the southern wizards. It was he who taught me personally."

"That's very interesting," Wiz said noncommittally.

"We are like brothers, the Sparrow and I. Why he even calls me the Eagle—just a joke between us, of course."

With an effort Wiz managed to keep his mouth closed. To almost everyone in the lands of the North, Wiz Zumwalt was known as the Sparrow, a name Bal-Simba had given him when he first arrived. Apparently this joker not only hadn't met Wiz, he had never talked to anyone who knew him.

Part of Wiz's mission had been to teach magic to more than just wizards. Wizards and apprentices were now teaching the system to hedge witches and others. Obviously this guy had learned the new magic at third or fourth remove—assuming he knew it at all, which Wiz wasn't willing to grant without proof.

Over Llewllyn's shoulder Wiz saw Dieter nodding approvingly. The mayor looked worried. Rolf simply smiled benignly. The implication was clear. This guy was competition and some of the council would love to dump Wiz and sign on Llewllyn. Dieter because he hated Wiz, and Rolf because he saw the young man as easier to manipulate.

Wiz gritted his teeth. His first instinct was to expose the phony. But he remembered the consultants he had seen in his world and how they dealt with these situations. He could always expose Llewllyn, but Dieter could always find another stooge. Maybe there was a more effective way.

Llewllyn, recognizing an opportunity, made a small gesture with his right hand. A sparkle of rainbow light flashed from his finger tips. Several of the councilors gasped and he smiled like a toothpaste commercial.

"There," said Dieter triumphantly. "You see?"

"Oh it's all very well, I suppose," Wiz said carelessly. "Quite remarkable, really, considering."

"You can, of course, do better?" Dieter shot back.

Wiz smiled at the venomous little man. "Well, since you ask . . ." He thought quickly. Most of the magic he knew either wasn't spectacular or was much too powerful. But there was a spell he had come up with to amuse Danny's son, Ian. He tilted his head back and took a deep breath. Then he blew multi-colored bubbles that rose gently to the ceiling and burst into points of rainbow light.

"A conjurer's trick," Dieter snorted. He looked expectantly at Llewllyn. The young man glared at Wiz with what was obviously intended to be an intimidating stare. However Llewllyn was too young and too pretty to intimidate much of anyone. Wiz smiled back.

"May I suggest a compromise?" Rolf put in smoothly.

"What?" the mayor asked suspiciously.

"Why not a competition?"

"Here?" Wiz asked. "Now?"

Dieter smiled. "Here and now. Why not?"

Wiz, who knew a good deal more about wizards' duels, could have given him a couple of good reasons. First, a wizards' duel usually started with lightning bolts and moved quickly to earthquakes. After that they tended to get *really* destructive. That's why wizards generally had it out on mountain tops or blasted heaths or other pieces of low-value real estate. Setting up an indoor wizards' duel was like trying to get ringside seats for a hand grenade fight in a broom closet.

The other reason was that wizards' duels were almost always to the death. That might not have bothered Dieter or Rolf, but Wiz didn't want to kill Llewllyn just because he was a charlatan.

Llewllyn, sensing he had an advantage, decided to push it. "Behold," he cried, "the power of the new magic!"

He moved his lips as he mumbled a word and letters of glowing rainbow fire appeared in the air between them. Dieter and the others gasped at the display and Mayor Hendrick looked worried. The new magician paused, obviously enjoying the sensation he had created.

Wiz was considerably less impressed but intently interested. All Llewllyn had done was list out the spell. A nice effect, but anyone who understood Wiz's magic language could read the listing and see how the spell worked.

As Wiz ran through it he was even less impressed. It was really one very simple spell, dressed up by some subroutines. Further, Llewllyn didn't have the thing written to respond to one command. He had to issue a series of commands and that meant there were opportunities for another magician to interfere. Wiz smiled politely and worked out a couple of lines of code in his head.

Llewllyn smiled at his appreciative audience and made the listing vanish with a flashy swipe of his hand.

"Beozar!" Llewllyn declaimed. "Cautich!" he added. Wiz watched intently, his lips barely moving. "Deodarin." Llewllyn's voice rose to a crescendo and he threw wide his arms. "Behold!"

There was a weak *pop* and then a fizzling sound like a lightbulb burning out.

Llewllyn went pale. "Beozar! Cautich!" He thundered out again. "Deodarin!" and flung his arms out. "Behold!"

This time the fizzle was accompanied by a dim reddish spark that died with the sound.

Dieter shifted uncomfortably and the Mayor frowned.

"Maybe if we drew the curtains to darken the room," Wiz said helpfully.

Llewllyn had gone pale and he was mumbling, but he didn't try the spell a third time.

"I'm sure it's just a temporary problem," Wiz said. "Why don't you take off and work on it a little. I'm sure it will be better in the morning."

"Ah, yes, of course," Llewllyn said to his now visibly unimpressed audience. "This far north one must allow for the effects of the different stars. Tomorrow would be more propitious." The mayor and Dieter both scowled at him. "Or maybe even a little later today," the young man added hastily. "Yes. Now if you'll excuse me." As he bowed quickly and turned toward the door the mayor nodded to the guardsman lounging there.

"See that our guest doesn't wander off," the mayor commanded. "Meanwhile we will decide what to do with him."

The guard followed Llewllyn out and there was a strained silence in the room.

"I'm sure he's quite good, actually." Wiz sighed for effect. "But magic is tricky, after all, and it is so hard to really master beyond the merely superficial."

"He ought to be sent to The Rock for impersonating a magician," Dieter said venomously.

The last thing Wiz wanted was to be responsible for the man's death. "Oh, surely that's somewhat extreme," he said hastily. "After all he was only, ah, 'overly enthusiastic' about his skill at magic."

"He's a liar and he ought to go to The Rock for trying to fool the council," Dieter replied.

"Wiz is right," Rolf put in. "No harm was done. Surely the council can show mercy in this instance."

"Then what?" Dieter snapped. "Is he going to hang around here and steal chickens?"

Mentioning chickens seemed to have an unusual impact on the councilors, as if they knew something Wiz didn't.

"Well, I could take him on as a junior assistant," Wiz said. "He could probably handle some of the minor details, under careful supervision, of course. Naturally I'd need an office on the square here."

"I don't know that we need two wizards now," Mayor Hendrick said.

"Consultants, please," Wiz corrected. "And it would have certain advantages." *Like keeping this guy where I can watch him.* If Llewllyn stayed around he was likely to be trouble and he obviously intended to stick around.

The mayor rubbed his chin. "Still . . ."

"I say let's put it to a vote," Dieter snapped.

Obviously the hassle of another council vote didn't appeal to the mayor. "Oh, all right, but only under the wizard's supervision."

Wiz nodded. "Naturally."

Dieter looked at him suspiciously, but he only nodded. "Now there is the matter of the fee."

The mayor frowned. "I thought we settled that."

"For the basic dragon situation, yes. However, on closer inspection it has become obvious that job will require services not covered in the original contract."

"I don't remember us signing any contract," Dieter said sourly.

Wiz smiled a superior smile. "Oh, you don't *sign* a contract with a wizard. It is implicitly made manifest. Here, let me show you." He made a sweeping gesture at the wall and under his breath muttered **list apl.man exe**. The wall was covered with fiery letters as the command list for Jerry's version of APL appeared. The reflected light cast a sickly pallor on the mayor, Dieter and the others. Surreptitiously one or two of the council members made signs to ward off evil.

"Now here in section three, paragraph five, sub-paragraph C, item three, you can clearly see . . ."

"All right wizard, I see," the mayor said hastily. Dieter and the others didn't seem disposed to argue the point, so Wiz gestured again and the "contract" disappeared.

"I think under the circumstances an additional four gold pieces a week would be reasonable, don't you?" he said blandly.

The mayor obviously didn't think it was all that reasonable, but he nodded nonetheless.

"Very good. Now if you gentlemen will excuse me I need to go find my new assistant."

Wiz found Llewllyn in the hall looking like he couldn't decide whether to bolt or brazen it out.

"How did you do that?" Llewllyn asked. "Interfere with my spell, I mean."

Wiz just smiled.

"Come now. Fellow professionals and all that."

Wiz thought that Llewllyn's racket had more in common with a bunco game than magic. Then he remembered what line of work he was in just now. "Oh it's quite simple really. I guess the Sparrow forgot to tell you that."

The young man's eyes widened. "You know the Sparrow?"

"Well enough," Wiz told him.

"Oh," he said in a small voice, eyes shifting left and right. Then he straightened and his voice firmed. "I wonder that I never met you when I was with him," Llewllyn said. "But you must tell me about him some-time—ah, about your experiences with him, I mean."

"Oh, it wasn't very interesting," Wiz said. "You know the Sparrow. Dull as dishwater, really."

"Well, yes, of course, but . . ."

"That wasn't what I wanted to talk to you about. I'm afraid your performance just now offended several rather powerful members of the council."

Llewllyn looked even more apprehensive. "Oh but surely . . ."

"I know you didn't intend to, of course. But, you know how clients, ah, councilors are. So very, very petty about things like results.

"Now," Wiz went on, "in spite of that I managed to convince them that you have potential. That given super-vision and a little guidance you could be an asset to the operation here. So as an alternative I got them to agree to let me take you on as a junior assistant."

Llewllyn was more apprehensive than ever. "Alter-native?" he asked faintly.

Wiz smiled. "Why dwell on unpleasantness? Espe-cially when it need never happen?"

"Of course. Assistant you say?"

"*Junior* assistant, but still a consultant with all the rights, privileges and duties thereof." He smiled even more broadly. "I'm sure the Sparrow would advise you to take it, were he here."

The young man's eyes widened. "You don't mean he is likely to come here, do you?"

"Llewllyn," Wiz said sincerely, "I can guarantee the Sparrow will never get any closer to this place than he is right now."

"Oh." The young man sighed. "I mean, what a pity."

"I know what you meant," Wiz said. "Now let's get on with it, shall we?"

"Uh, a moment, My Lord. What about my renumeration?"

Wiz did a quick calculation in his head, based on what junior consultants in his world made versus what the consulting companies charged. "Okay," he said, "I'll pay you one gold piece a week. You'll work in the office here under my supervision. Your primary job will be client contact and low-level problem solving. Be in the office for at least four day-tenths a day, five days a week. You can set your own office hours, but keep them."

Llewllyn's nose wrinkled. "That sounds like a clerk, not a magician."

"It's a consultant. And the less magic you use the better."

"I don't know . . ."

Wiz shrugged. "Consider the alternative."

Llewllyn's face fell. "The alternative?"

"Dieter thinks you sold him a bill of goods. As my assistant you are under my protection. Otherwise . . ." Again the shrug.

Llewllyn swept a graceful bow to Wiz. "My Lord," he said grandly, "you have a new assistant."

Wiz tried to look happy.

Anna was upstairs cleaning when Wiz got back, but Malkin was in the kitchen, brewing a pot of herb tea.

"What do you know about a magician named Llewllyn?"

"Never heard of him," the tall woman said cheerfully, cocking one leg over the corner of the table and sitting on the freshly scrubbed surface.

"Slender, long blond hair, really white teeth. Handsome and a born con man."

"Oh, *him*." Malkin said. "He's from around here. Used to hold himself out as a bard but I never heard of anyone who paid him for his singing. I'm kind of surprised he showed his face in these parts. Here, you want some of this? It's a mixture Anna made up."

"Thanks," Wiz said and poured himself a mug of the tea. It was mostly peppermint with a lemony-orangey overtone. A little weak but not bad, he decided. "I take it he had a good reason for leaving."

The thief gave a snort of laughter. "Only a due regard for his own skin. Seems he'd been stealing old man Colbach's chickens and bouncing his daughter at the same time." She grinned and shook her head. "I don't know which made him the madder."

Wiz took another sip of tea. "I'm surprised he came back at all."

"Well, thinking on it, he's safe enough. The girl's married respectable now and the first child looked like her husband, so no one much cares on that score. Farmer Colbach probably still harbors a grudge about the chickens but he don't come to town much. Besides, he's not likely to push it because it would just remind folks about his daughter." She took another sip from her cup. "I guess you ran into him."

"Actually I hired him as my assistant."

Malkin looked down at him hard. "Then you've got mighty strange tastes in your assistants."

Wiz looked back very deliberately. "I know," he said.

SIXTEEN
BLACK BAG JOB

Forget what you read in the papers. These are not very bright guys.
   —Deep Throat to Woodward, *All The President's Men*

Another morning, another surveillance report. By now Pashley was beside himself.

"Look at this!" he shouted. "She's still on the net."

"Take it easy," Arnold said. "Just simmer down and let's think." Pashley paused and took a deep breath. His face turned a lighter shade of red.

"Now, how is she doing it? We got every piece of electronic equipment in the place."

"You're sure she hasn't brought a computer back in?" Ray Whipple asked. He was spending a lot more time than he liked at the FBI office and was even discovering he had common interests with some of the agents.

"No way," Arnold said. "We've been watching."

"What has the van turned up?"

"Absolutely nothing. If there's a computer in there it's got Tempest-class emissions security. We know there's no computer in there."

Pashley was frantically thumbing through the eight-by-ten glossy color photographs of Judith's apartment the agents had taken on the first raid. Suddenly his head snapped up.

"Wait a minute! There is another computer in here." He stood up so fast he nearly knocked the chair over. "Come on, let's go back to the judge."

"You want a warrant to seize *what*?" Judge David Faraday said in an utterly bewildered voice.

"A toaster," Special Agent Pashley repeated confidently. "We believe it is a vital piece of evidence in this hacker case."

"But it's a toaster!" Judge Faraday almost wailed.

"Yes, Your Honor but there's a computer hidden inside." He stepped up to the desk and held out a repair manual. "As you can see here there is a micro-controller—that's a computer—in the toaster. Further," he pulled out a couple of clippings, "this is the exact make and model which hackers at a hackers convention actually connected to a communications network, like a telephone system."

"This happened in 1990," Judge Faraday said as he glanced at the clipping.

"Yes, sir, at a secret hackers' convention called InterOp which was held not far from here."

"This clipping is from the *San Jose Mercury*."

"Yes, sir."

"So this secret convention of," he ran his finger down the clipping, "ten thousand or so computer criminals was covered by the local newspapers."

Pashley was oblivious to the change in Judge Faraday's voice. "Yes, sir. There were some television stories, but we couldn't get the tape as evidence. But you can see it talks about the toaster oven right here."

"Mr. Pashley," Judge Faraday said mildly.

"Yes, sir?"

"Get out of my sight." The judge's voice rose. "Get out of this courthouse!" His face got red and a vein began to throb in his temple. *"Don't ever let me see you again. On anything."* Judge Faraday was screaming now. *"IS THAT CLEAR?"*

"But do we get the warrant?" Pashley asked over his shoulder as Arnold hustled him out of the judge's office.

Ray Whipple shifted nervously on the chill vinyl seat. There was something going on here but he wasn't sure what.

Uncharacteristically, Pashley had sought him out to offer him a lift back to the hotel. Instead of driving him nuts with innane chatter while he drove, Pashley wasn't saying anything. Whipple didn't find that to be much of an improvement.

Ray's knowledge of the city was minimal and his sense of direction useless for finding anything smaller than a star, but eventually even he realized they were heading in the wrong direction.

"Where are we going?"

Pashley didn't take his eyes off the road. "I've got a little errand to run."

Two more turns in quick succession brought them into a neighborhood the astrophysicist recognized vaguely. Then another turn and Whipple went cold as he realized where they were. By that time Pashley had turned off the headlights and pulled over to the curb less than a block away from Judith's apartment.

"What are we doing here?"

"We're here to get that toaster," Pashley said.

Whipple went even colder. "I thought the judge denied the warrant."

Pashley thrust out his jaw and gave the astronomer

a steely stare. "There are issues of national security at stake. I'm not going to let a technicality stop me."

"That's burglary!"

"No sweat. It's what we call a 'black bag job' in the FBI."

It occurred to Ray that that was also what the Watergate Plumbers called it at the Nixon White House.

"What if she's home?"

"She isn't. She's off playing games with some friends. You just wait here and if you see her coming honk the horn, okay?"

"I dunno about this."

"Look," Pashley said in the voice exasperated mothers use on small children, "just sit here and blow the horn if she comes. Nice and simple. What can go wrong?"

Ray's suddenly overheated imagination came up with dozens of possibilities. "Leave the keys in the ignition, okay?"

Pashley shook his head. "Sorry. You're not a government employee. You can't legally drive this car."

Whipple decided to pass on that. "I don't want to drive it, I just want to be able to honk the horn."

Pashley tossed the keys on the seat. "All right then, but don't go anywhere." He got out of the car and started up the sidewalk, his trench coat flapping against his knees.

"I wonder how big the astrophysical library is at Folsom Prison," Whipple muttered and settled in to wait.

Clueless Pashley was muttering too as he turned into the apartment complex. "Damn pissants and their technicalities! Ruin the damn country."

There was another problem Pashley hadn't mentioned to Whipple. Since Judge Faraday had turned him down for the warrant the mood at the local FBI office had turned decidedly chilly. The surveillance team had been withdrawn and the electronic listening van was back in the government garage. Pashley suspected it had something to do with the fact that AIC Weinberg was almost ready to come back to work. For some reason Weinberg didn't seem to like this investigation.

Actually the incident with Judge Faraday had pushed Janovsky to visit Weinberg in the hospital and tell him what Pashley had been up to. Weinberg hadn't been able to fully brief his second-in-command on Pashley because he was still hooked up to a cardiac monitor when Janovsky told his story, and the monitor thought Weinberg was having a heart attack. The emergency team hustled Janovsky out of the room before Weinberg could get out anything coherent, but Janovsky got the drift.

Pashley skulked by the gate for a couple of minutes, oblivious to the way the street lights highlighted him. It wasn't quite 10 P.M. but the court was deserted and most of the porch lights were off. The apartments had their drapes drawn tightly against the chill evening and he could faintly hear the sound of a television yammering out some game show at the top of its electronic lungs.

Judith's apartment was on the ground floor about halfway back. Her porch light was on but the tall bushes to either side of the door gave him some cover. With a final look around Pashley dropped to one knee and produced a black vinyl case containing a dozen lock picks. He selected one, put the tension wrench in the keyhole and went to work.

If Pashley wasn't smart, he was clever with his hands. He also knew how to pick locks. Unfortunately lock picking is not like riding a bicycle. You need to keep doing it to keep in practice and Pashley hadn't practiced for a couple of years. It took him longer than he expected to tickle the tumblers and get the lock to turn.

❖   ❖   ❖

Meanwhile Ray Whipple was getting more nervous by the minute. "Think about the Hubble," he breathed, like an acolyte reciting a mantra. "Think about time on the Hubble." He thought about it. He thought hard about that observing time. Then he thought about doing time—three-to-five as an accessory to burglary. Somehow he thought about that time more than he thought about the time on the Hubble Space Telescope.

Judith's drapes were drawn and her apartment was dark. Pashley had forgotten a flashlight, so he groped blindly toward the kitchen. The first thing he found was a coffee table loaded with magazines. He found it by tripping on it and knocking the coffee table completely over, making an unholy racket in the process. His further progress was somewhat impeded because he kept stepping on magazines and nearly slipping on their slick pages.

After a few more bumps and stumbles Pashley found the doorway to the kitchen. He made his way through, kicking over the trash can and strewing garbage all over the floor. He felt his way along the counter and after knocking off a box of corn flakes, a stack of dirty dishes and two glass canisters, he finally found the toaster. He yanked the cord out of the wall, sending an array of cans, jars and bottles crashing to the floor and made for the door with his prize.

The police car at the end of the block made Ray Whipple's heart pound. Then a helicopter came over, low and without lights. Ray knew a losing cause when he saw one. With a twinge of regret he silently bid farewell to time on the Hubble. Then he started the car and slowly, carefully drove away.

❖   ❖   ❖

Pashley saw the policemen as soon as they saw him, which was as soon as he stepped out of Judith's apartment. They were just coming in the front gate so he whirled and ran for the back gate, toaster tucked in the crook of his elbow like a quarterback running for daylight and the policemen pounding after him.

Without breaking stride Pashley straight-armed the gate, knocking it open, and sprinted into the apartment parking lot. He was nearly blinded by the sudden glare of the police helicopter's spotlight, but he ran on, dodging between parked cars. There was a six-foot concrete block wall at the back of the parking lot and Pashley scrambled over, almost into the arms of two more policemen.

"Drop that toaster!" Pashley whirled and found himself with his back to the wall facing two cops with drawn guns. Reluctantly he set the toaster down and raised his hands.

"You don't understand," Pashley shouted over the noise of the helicopter. "I'm an FBI agent on a secret mission."

One of the cops was short, chunky and Asian. The other cop was tall, lean and black. Neither of them looked the least bit friendly. "Turn around, spread your legs and put your hands against the wall." As Pashley complied the black cop moved toward him cautiously, well to one side and out of his partner's line of fire. Keeping his eye on Pashley he nudged the toaster away with his foot.

"Be careful with that. It's vital evidence in a national security matter."

The cops just looked at each other.

"Man," the Asian muttered to his partner, "these designer drugs are bad stuff."

Things got a little complicated once they got Pashley back to the station. While the police definitely had him on burglary, the dwelling was unoccupied. That bumped the offense down to something one step above a misdemeanor. The value of the toaster was less than a hundred dollars so it didn't even qualify as grand theft. For a while the police thought they had Pashley on a charge of impersonating an FBI agent. Then they found out he *was* an FBI agent. Pashley's urgent insistence that the toaster was vital evidence in a national security case didn't help.

True to his word, the mayor found an office for Wiz and Llewllyn in the town hall. Granted, the room was so small the rough trestle table practically formed a barricade across it, but it was conveniently located just inside the main entrance. Both the location and the row of pegs for hanging cloaks and hats hinted at its former use. With Llewllyn sitting in the rickety chair and Wiz standing beside him the place was decidedly claustrophobic. Still, it would do.

Word had obviously spread about the new consulting service. A man was waiting for them when they arrived that morning. Wiz had wanted to spend a few minutes briefing Llewllyn, but obviously he wasn't going to get the chance.

Llewllyn, however, seemed to have no doubts at all. "Come in," he called to the man waiting in the hall. "Never mind my associate here," he said, with a dismissive wave of his hand at Wiz. "What is the nature of your problem?"

"I've been hexed is my problem," the man declared. "Werner the Butcher, he put a curse on me."

It took Wiz a minute to realize that "butcher" was the hexer's occupation, not a nickname.

"How do you know?" he asked.

The man looked at Llewllyn and he nodded for him to answer Wiz's question.

"Me business is gone to blazes, that's how I know. Hardly a customer since that black-hearted miscreant cursed me. Worse, I can't get to sleep no more. I toss and turn through the night. I want that curse lifted."

"When did you notice you were having trouble sleeping?" Wiz asked.

"After I was cursed, of course!" The man looked at Llewllyn. "He simple or something?"

"No," Llewllyn assured him, "merely an assistant."

Wiz cleared his throat.

"Ah, associate actually," the sometime bard amended hastily. "A specialist in another area, but quite competent I assure you."

The man snorted and turned his attention completely to Llewllyn.

"Ah, yes," the young man said, "it so happens I have a special amulet, hewn from the heart of the black oak that grows by the Southern Swamp, prepared by the great wizard Actantos himself. A sure cure. And I can let you have it for just . . ."

Wiz cleared his throat more forcefully.

"But I'm sure you don't need anything so powerful," he finished hurriedly. "Now suppose you tell me what led up to the cursing."

"Will this really help?" The man sounded skeptical.

"Magic is a matter of information," Llewllyn assured him. "The more information the more effective the magic."

"Well, Werner's a surly one. Got his skill in magic from his gran on his momma's side. She was a first cousin once removed of Old Lady Fressen, and . . ."

Llewllyn cut short his reminiscences. "On the other hand, there is such a thing as too much information. Perhaps you can skip ahead to the day the curse was laid."

"That was nigh on two week ago, when I caught Werner picking my whiffleberries."

"He was in your orchard?"

"No, no. The whiffleberry bush is right by the garden wall and some of it hangs over into his garden. Well, since time immemorial there's been an agreement that what's on his side of the wall belongs to him. But I look out this afternoon and here's Werner poaching. He had a whole limb pulled over to his side, he did and he was clearly taking berries that were on my side of the wall."

"And you confronted the, ah, miscreant?"

"Of course I confronted him! I'll not stand for anyone taking what's mine. Well, he denied it, he did, claimed the berries were on his side of the wall and never mind my pointing out the branch near broken off where he'd pulled on it so hard. He protested he wasn't poaching and I pointed out to him that a man'd put his thumb on the scales when folks was buying, as everyone knows he does, mind you, why a man like that couldn't be trusted nohow."

To Wiz it sounded like both parties needed a good talking to and he couldn't for the life of him see what whiffleberries had to do with magic or curses. Of course, he admitted, he'd never heard of whiffleberries before and maybe they had some magic property and . . . Then something Llewllyn said, or rather the way he said it, jerked his attention back to the conversation.

"So you expected him to steal the berries when you weren't looking?" Llewllyn asked in a carefully neutral voice.

"Stayed in the back of the house the whole day to watch the bush," their client confirmed. "Only came into the shop in front when a customer called. Even watched most of that first night, expecting him to come sneaking over the wall."

"And you still think he will plunder your whiffleberry bush?" Llewllyn prompted in the same tone.

"The berries are still there, ain't they? As soon as his miserable curse has me worn down I expect he'll come creeping over the wall some night and make off with the whole lot of them."

"Hmm," Llewllyn said, and rubbed his chin. "Hmm," he said again.

Their client leaned forward anxiously. "Can you help me?"

"Oh, of course," Llewllyn said with an airy wave of his hand. "Not that it is not a difficult problem, mind you, but you have come to the right place. I have the perfect answer for you." He leaned over the table toward the man.

"First, I shall place a curse on the whiffleberries. By magic or by stealth the thief may make off with them, but they will do him no good. For if he should partake of the stolen fruit, his bowels shall loosen, his intestines shall bloat and he shall pass the night in the most intense suffering. Fear not, for your berries shall be guarded by the most puissant magic."

Llewllyn held up a finger. "But understand, such curses are most powerful. To protect yourself you must not go into your garden, nay, even look into your garden for the next fortnight."

The man shifted uneasily. "That might be hard. The privy's back there."

"Oh, for that, of course. But do not linger and do not so much as look out your back window at the whiffleberry bush for fourteen days, you understand? I'd suggest you spend your time in your shop as much as you can. Fear not, business will pick up as soon as I lift the curse."

The man nodded.

"Now as for the curse on you, I must lift it gradually

lest the powers invoked rend you limb from limb." The man went slightly pale and nodded again.

"You must stuff your pillow with catnip and place a sprig of tansy under it. This evening I will perform certain mystical operations to banish the invisible demons which are plaguing you. You must drink a cup of wine each night and go to bed at your accustomed time. Over the next two or three nights the curse will dissipate."

"That's all?"

"For you, yes. My part will be much more difficult, but never fear, it will be accomplished."

The man stood and reached for the purse on his belt. "Wonderful! What do I owe you?"

Wiz cleared his throat again.

"Oh, nothing," Llewllyn told him. "Our fees are paid by the town council."

"Then may Fortuna smile upon the honorable council!" the man exclaimed and hurried out.

"Okay," Wiz said after the man was out of earshot. "I understand about the pillow. Catnip's good for helping you sleep. I understand why you told him to spend time in his shop, to get his business back, and I understand why you told him not to keep watching that bush, to relieve his anxiety . . ."

Llewllyn arched an eyebrow. "Do you not believe in the Sparrow's magic?"

"What I just saw was another branch of magic, what I call applied psychology—which by the way you have a talent for —" Llewllyn acknowledged the compliment with a gracious nod, "— but what was that business about a curse on anyone who steals those whiffleberries? The bloating, suffering and stuff?"

"Those are the usual effects of eating green whiffleberries," Llewllyn said dryly. "And if you were from these parts, and if you were not distracted by some stupid neighborhood feud, you would know that whiffleberries will not ripen for another moon or so."

Wiz looked at his assistant. "You may have more talent for this than I thought."

Next, not at all to Wiz's surprise, was the chicken man. He strutted through the door, neck out like a bantam rooster, and two chickens clutched in his skinny hand. He nodded to the two consultants and plunked the two birds down on the table. The birds squawked and shifted and tried to stand up, something they couldn't quite manage with their feet tied together. So they settled for sitting on the table and complaining in an undertone.

"I'm here about my chickens," he announced. "They still won't lay eggs." He jabbed a bony finger at Wiz, "And don't give me none of your lip about dragons, boy, the mayor hisself says you're to help me."

I'll bet the mayor loved having someone to palm you off on, Wiz thought, but he only nodded pleasantly. "I wouldn't dream of it now that the council has renegotiated the contract. My associate here will take care of your problem."

The man scowled at Llewllyn. "He's younger than you are," he grumbled. "Prettier too."

Llewllyn simply nodded and picked up one of the chickens. "Hmm," he said stroking the bird's feathers. He prodded the fowl gently. "Ah, yess." Then he studied the bird's eyes. "Quite so," he said, lifting the chicken higher to study its feet. "Uh huh."

By this point the chicken was thoroughly confused by these goings-on, and Wiz and the bird's owner weren't much better.

"Yes," Llewllyn said at last, "I see the problem clearly."

"If you can do that you're better than the rest of them so-called magicians," the chicken man said. "But what are you going to do about it? That's what I want to know."

The bard put the chicken down on the table. "Why

my good man, I'm going to solve your problem. That's what we wizards, ah, consultants, are here for. Now this is a difficult case. The causes are obviously complex and subtle. I will not go into the boring details, but suffice it to say that the cure is straightforward. Simply pluck a sprig of tansy and place it above the door to your henhouse."

"That's it? That's all?"

Llewllyn smiled a superior smile. "The secret is in knowing the cure, not in performing it." Then he leaned over the clucking chickens and waggled his finger under the man's nose. "But this is most important. Do not go into the hen house until the moon has waned and waxed again. Feed and water your chickens outside the coop but otherwise do not go near them."

"Why?"

"Because during this delicate period it would not be safe. You might contract the dread—" his voice lowered to a near whisper "—chicken pox."

"Oh, right. Of course. I'll do just as you say. Thank you sir. Thank you." With that the man gathered his chickens and strutted out.

"Chicken pox, huh?" Wiz said when the man had left, birds dangling.

Llewllyn shrugged. "Not my most inspired invention, I will admit, but it should suffice."

"And tansy?"

"The stuff's a roadside weed around here and it stinks. The smell makes them think it's powerful. Like putting alum in medicine so it will taste bad."

"What do you think he's going to do if his chickens don't improve?"

"Oh, they will improve." Llewllyn's face screwed up as if he was thinking of something unpleasant. "My Lord, I have a certain experience with chickens. The only thing wrong with those birds is that he is pestering them to

death. If he leaves them alone they will settle down and
all will be well. And if not—" Again the shrug. "I will
simply tell him he must obtain a coal black cock without a speck of white upon him. That should occupy him
for a few moons."

Their next client was a heavyset young woman with
a bad complexion and a red nose. She ventured through
the door as if she was afraid that the two men would
bite her. In one plump hand she held a handkerchief
which looked as if it had seen recent use. Wiz decided
that was a bad sign.

Llewllyn didn't seem to notice. He rose and made a
sweeping bow to their client. "Come in young lady.
Please sit and tell us what has brought you to us."

The young woman twisted her hanky and bit her lip.
"I don't know," she said in an undertone. "It's such a
small thing, really."

Llewllyn's smile grew even brighter. "There is no
problem too small for us, dear lady. We are here to serve
your every wish. Please be seated and tell us about it."

Thus encouraged the girl eased herself down into the
chair.

"Well, I, I hardly know where to begin."

"Begin wherever you feel like, dear lady," Llewllyn
said gently. "The magic will tell me the rest."

"There is the young man," the girl said in a low voice.

"Ah," Llewllyn nodded. "A special young man? Perhaps one who does not notice you?"

"How did you know?" the girl asked.

"Magic tells me many things. But do go on."

"Well," the girl relaxed in her chair, "he's our neighbor you see . . ."

By the time Wiz left fifteen minutes later Llewllyn
and the girl were head-to-head across the table. He
hadn't given her any advice that Wiz could see, just a
lot of encouragement, but she seemed to think he had

the answer to everything from her love life to the riddle of Dark Matter—or she would have if she'd known what Dark Matter was, Wiz thought.

Obviously his new assistant had a future in this end of the business. Now if Wiz could just keep him from bilking the customers or trying to practice unauthorized magic, he'd have one less thing to worry about.

That morning the director of the FBI had a *lot* of things to worry about. As her assistants filled her in on Clueless Pashley's latest exploit, she stubbed out her cigarette and lit a new one. She was back up to a pack-and-a-half a day and headed rapidly for two packs. Her fingers were stained, her breath stank, she had burn holes in her clothes and twice she had nearly set her desk on fire when she missed an ash tray.

"Where is this clown now?" she asked Paul Rutherford when he finished his report.

"The local office bailed him out," her assistant said. "They've got him stashed in a safe house to keep him away from the newspapers."

This was a public relations disaster.

"Senator Halliburton's office called this morning. His committee wants to hold hearings on violating civil rights in national security cases. This Judith Connally and the science fiction writer are going to be his star witnesses."

A public relations disaster and a political nightmare, the director amended. "Could this get any worse?"

"Only if Pashley gets back out on the street," Rutherford ventured. The director glared at him and he wilted. "Uh, no ma'am, I don't think it's likely to get much worse."

Unbidden a snatch of a country song came into the director's head. *You gotta know when to hold'em, and know when to fold 'em.* She hated country music.

"All right." She mashed out the half-smoked cigarette. "Settle!"

"Settle?"

"That writer's case against us. Tell the Justice Department to settle with him. And settle with this Connally woman. Make apologies, blame it on a rogue agent. But settle."

"Ma'am," Rutherford said carefully, "that sets a very bad precedent."

"It will set a worse precedent if the director of the FBI murders an agent," she growled. "Just pay whatever it takes.

SEVENTEEN

INVITATION TO AN AUTO-DE-FE

At ——— Bullshit Is Our Most Important Product
    —graffiti on the lavatory wall at a major consultantcy

Wiz got home just after noon to find the mayor sniffling on his doorstep. At first Wiz thought someone had died. Then His Honor produced a well-used handkerchief from his sleeve and blew his nose again.

Wiz invited the man in. As they crossed the threshold Malkin was just coming up from the kitchen. They eyed each other with mutual distaste for a moment and the mayor put a protective hand on his chain of office.

"You wanted to see me, Your Honor?" Wiz asked, as much to break the tension as anything else.

"I came to warn you, Wizard." He stopped, his face screwed up and he sneezed thunderously.

"What? That it's pollen season?"

The mayor sniffled and wiped his watering eyes. "No, it's Dieter. He's moving against you in the council. At our next meeting, two days from today, he plans to call for your resignation."

There was nothing Wiz would have liked better than to resign. But since his resignation would doubtless be followed immediately by his condemnation to The Rock, it didn't seem like a good idea to follow his desires.

The mayor looked even more like a basset hound than usual. "He's gathering votes on the council. I'll support you, of course, but it will be close, I'll tell you that."

"What do you want me to do?"

"Could you perhaps be at the meeting? You know, talk to them the way you did before."

"Of course. Can you get me some time on the agenda before the vote?"

After the mayor departed, sniffling and mumbling, Malkin looked at her boss. "Well, oh great Wizard, what are you going to do now?"

"I am going to do what any consultant does when he gets into trouble," Wiz said. "I am going to give a presentation."

Malkin snorted. "If I was you I'd give a thought to a quick escape. You heard the mayor. Dieter's got enough votes on the council to have your guts for garters."

"Maybe now he does. But the council will have to take a formal vote and they won't do that until they hear me out because there's always the chance I'll come up with a miracle. A successful presentation doesn't just impart information. It changes attitudes."

"Look," Malkin said slowly and carefully, as if explaining something to a small and none-too-bright child, "Dieter wants to be cock of this dungheap and get more money from taxes. Ol' Droopy wants to stay cock of the dungheap and he doesn't want more taxes. Cross either one of them and you're a dragon's breakfast. Now how in blazes is this presentation of yours going to change any of that?"

"Presentations don't change things," Wiz said airily, "they just change perceptions."

"And just how do they do that?" she demanded.

"Generally by confusing the issue."

The tall girl chewed on that for a while. "Well," she said at last, "if you're set on this, I want to be there when you make this presentation of yours."

Wiz quirked a smile. "An expression of loyalty?"

"No, I want to see which way it goes so I can get out of here while they're still busy tearing you to pieces."

"Oh, it won't come to that," Wiz assured her. *I hope!* "Before this is over I'll have them eating out of my hand."

Malkin eyed him under raised brows. "Maybe, but my question is how many fingers you're going to have left on that hand."

Bright colors and pretty pictures, Wiz thought. *That's the essence of a successful presentation.* He looked at the code taking shape in glowing characters above his desk and sighed. *Especially when you don't have any content.*

The conventional wisdom was that the more images, graphically displayed numbers and visual tricks you packed into a presentation, the more effective the presentation. Of course the logical implication of that is that the average executive has the attention span of a three-year-old and the analytical skills of a magpie. Normally Wiz would have found that a very depressing reflection. Just now it was comforting. The only thing standing between him and doom in an utterly impossible situation was his ability to sling creative bullshit.

It would certainly be well-illustrated bullshit. Using the spell Danny had developed so long ago and far away, he had set up an Internet connection back to what he still thought of as the "real world" and set an ftp demon to downloading graphics files from sites all around the world. He already had a library of hundreds of images and they were still coming in.

Even so, it was slow going. Wiz was the sort of programmer who had always preferred substance to form.

Here the substance was that he had to use form to cover
the fact that he had no substance. That meant writing
a bunch of new tools. With the council meeting the day
after tomorrow Wiz was going to have to bust his butt
to save his neck.

Well, that worked too. As a programmer he was no
stranger to all-nighters to meet tight deadlines. This was
just one more all-nighter. He tried not to think about
the stakes.

The day turned to evening and evening shaded into
night and still Wiz toiled away, developing the routines
to give a presentation that would knock the Council's
eyes out.

Anna brought him sandwiches and tea along about
dinner time, but otherwise he worked undisturbed until
well into the evening.

"Get your head out of your spells, Wizard," the ghost
of Widder Hackett rasped in his ear. "You've got a problem."

"It's a tight schedule, but that's not a problem," Wiz
said without turning to look at his invisible kibitzer.

"Oh, no?" Widder Hackett grated. "Just you look at
that window." Wiz moved to open the shutter.

"No, you dummy!" the voice rasped in his ear. "Don't
want him to see you. Look through the crack."

Putting his eye to the crack between the shutters and
peering out into the moonlit street Wiz saw they had a
visitor. Or more precisely, he realized, they had a watcher.
One of the Watch, the tall skinny one, was leaning against
the house on the other side of the street.

"What's he doing there?"

"Watching is what," Widder Hackett snapped.
"There's another behind and two more at each end of
the street. My own house watched by the police like
some common den of thieves. I never thought in all my
living days . . . I never!"

Wiz forbore to mention that Widder Hackett's living days had ended some time before. "I'm going down there to find out what this is all about."

Widder Hackett snorted. "What makes you think he'll tell you anything?"

"If he won't the council will."

Subtlety wasn't Wiz's strong point and he was both too curious and too angry to be circumspect. As soon as he opened the front door the guardsman stepped back into the shadows.

light exe Wiz commanded and a sphere of brilliant white light appeared over his shoulder. The light was behind Wiz, but it shone right into the eyes of the now-revealed watcher, who squinted and turned his head away. Without a word Wiz strode across the street. The globe of light floated right with him.

"Good evening," Wiz said crisply.

"Evening, My Lord," the guard said, trying to shield his eyes with his hands "Uh, would you mind . . ."

"Sorry I can't turn it off," Wiz lied. "Now, what are you doing here?"

"Well, I'm ah, watching, My Lord. So so speak."

"Watching for what?"

"Criminals, begging My Lord's pardon. We've had criminals around here in this neighborhood and we thought . . ."

"'We' being the council? Is that it?" *Meaning Dieter*, Wiz thought. *But why?*

"Well, ah, as to that, My Lord, I really couldn't say. All I know is I'm supposed to keep watch here until the thieves are apprehended."

Thieves, eh? Suddenly it fell into place. "I appreciate your concern, but it isn't necessary. Tell the sheriff I can guard my own property."

"That's as may be," the guardsman said stolidly, "but I have my orders, My Lord."

"Oh well, if you want to watch, I'm sure you may. But I will tell you now you won't find anything."

"That's as may be, My Lord."

Wiz nodded and returned to his house. He left the light globe on until he was back inside.

"Where's Malkin?" he demanded into thin air as soon as the door closed behind him.

"How would I know?" Widder Hackett rasped. "Out tarting it up I have no doubt."

"She didn't go out the door. I would have known."

"She usually doesn't," Widder Hackett said with obvious satisfaction.

With that there was nothing to do but wait until Malkin got back. Wiz went back to his programming, pausing every so often to peer through the crack in the shutters at his watchers.

It wasn't a terribly productive evening. Between fuming over the watch, worrying about Malkin and starting at every squeak of a floorboard or rattle of a windowpane, Wiz didn't do nearly the amount of work he had planned. Since it was well after midnight when he heard Malkin on the stairs he lost most of the night's work.

When Wiz confronted her in the hallway she was dressed in dark trousers, dark soft boots and a dark pullover. Her dark hair was stuffed up under a dark knit cap and there was a dark burlap sack over her shoulder.

"Where have you been?"

"Oh, out and about," Malkin said nonchalantly. She set the sack on the floor with an audible clank. "Sightseeing, you might say."

"And the stuff in the bag is souvenirs, right? In case you don't know it, lady, there is a cop across the street watching this place and two more at each end of the block."

"And two more on the street behind," Malkin added. "But they never watch the roofs. Half of them's too fat to climb and the rest is scared of heights."

"So you've been coming and going over the roofs."

"Sometimes. The sewer's good too, if you don't mind a few rats."

"Are you trying to get us all killed? The cops are on to you, the place is being watched, half the council is looking for an excuse to put me away—and you with me. Lady, we are just one small slip from disaster here."

Malkin's eyes glowed. "I know," she said breathlessly. "Isn't it exciting?"

"An adrenaline junkie," Wiz groaned. "I had to get hooked up with a kleptomaniac adrenaline junkie."

"Serves you right for hiring folks out of jail."

Wiz growled in frustration.

"Besides, I don't see what you're so worried about. I got in safe with the stuff didn't I? They never saw me."

"Did it ever occur to you that their next logical move is going to be to search the house?"

"Law says they can't search no private home held freehold without a warrant signed by the mayor upon presentation of probable cause. Said probable cause to be solely within the discretion of the mayor. They gave you this place so you have it freehold." She grinned. "And you think the mayor's going to issue a warrant to search this place? You being his ally and all? Old Iron Pants will have to wait a month of blue moons before that happens."

As it happened the month of blue moons ended at about seven o'clock the next morning. Wiz was pulled groggily awake by the sound of a thunderous pounding on the door. Stumbling downstairs he found Anna confronting a gang of armed ruffians. When he looked a little closer he realized that the lead ruffian was the sheriff and that he was brandishing a piece of paper as if it were a shield before him.

"Stand aside, Wizard," he announced before Wiz was even off the stairs. "We're here to search the place for stolen goods. Got a warrant."

Wiz's brain was at best severely challenged at this time of the morning, especially when his blood caffeine level was low, but that woke him up and sent his mind into high gear.

"The mayor signed a search warrant?"

The sheriff grinned nastily. "Mayor's home with a cold. A real bad cold that's got him incapacitated. So this was signed by three council members like the law provides. All legal and proper."

Meaning Dieter, Wiz thought, a sinking feeling in the pit of his stomach.

"Well, I can't stop you from searching," he said standing aside from the door. "But I can't protect you either," he added as the sheriff and his men pushed into the hall. "This is a wizard's house, you know," he shouted to their backs as they thundered up the stairs.

For the next two hours the sheriff's men went over the house eaves to cellars. They found a notebook Wiz had lost, an old copper pan that had belonged to Widder Hackett, a number of rats and an indignant pigeon who was trying to nest in the attic, but not one bit of stolen property.

The only excitement came when Bobo decided that for some inexplicable reason the sheriff's highly polished boots belonged to him, and proceeded to mark his property in the time-honored tomcat fashion. Luckily for Bobo he was a good deal faster than the sheriff or any of his men.

Meanwhile Malkin stood around looking smug, Anna was wide-eyed with terror and Widder Hackett hurled abuse at the searchers at the top of her nonexistent lungs.

Unfortunately the searchers couldn't hear her. Even more unfortunately Wiz could. By the time the sheriff's men finished, Wiz was a nervous wreck.

"Well?" the sheriff demanded as he strode into Wiz's workroom. "Are you done in here?"

The two guards who had been tapping the floor for loose boards nodded in unison and stood up. "Every place but this table," the guard in front said. "You want us to dig up the garden next?"

"What's wrong with this table?" demanded the sheriff.

"Looks as if it's magic like."

"That's my desk," Wiz added. "You'd better not touch it."

"Bah!" barked the sheriff.

"Hey, I won't be responsible . . ." Wiz began, but the sheriff was already reaching for the pile of parchments.

No one but the very brave, the very skilled or the very foolish messes with a wizard's working equipment. The sheriff might have been brave but he was certainly not at all skilled.

As soon as his hand moved over the top of the table there was a twisting in the air and a small green demon materialized below the glowing letters. A small green demon with a very large mouth. Lined with large, pointed and very sharp teeth. Before the sheriff could react the creature chomped down hard on the proferred hand.

The sheriff yelped and jerked his arm away. On the back of his hand in a neat semicircle were eight round puncture marks. "It bit me!" he screamed.

"Actually there are eight of them, so that's a byte," Wiz said, examining the wounds.

The sheriff pulled his hand back. "That's what I said!" He pointed toward the table with his good hand. "Arrest that thing!" he commanded.

The demon crouched on the edge of the table and grinned at them. It had an unusually large grin that showed off its pearly white and pointy teeth to excellent advantage. All three rows of them.

The guards shifted back and forth but made no move toward the grinning entity crouched on the table.

"I dunno," the first one demurred.

"Law says we're only supposed to arrest people," the second one said. "Don't say nothing about things like that."

"You can arrest strayed livestock," the sheriff retorted. "Well, impound them anyway." He gestured at the demon again. "*Impound* that thing."

"Don't know that it's rightly livestock," the first guard said.

"Don't think it's strayed either," his companion added.

"It's right where it's supposed to be," Wiz added helpfully.

"Well, then," said the second guard.

The sheriff was nearly beside himself with fury. "This is an outrage! A complete outrage against the majesty of the law." He was bouncing up and down and his face was so red Wiz was afraid he was going to have a stroke. He decided it was time to pour some oil on the water.

"Look sheriff, you can see there's nothing on that desk but papers. No stolen property, right? Now I'm sorry the demon hurt you, but I'm sure he won't do it again. Why don't you and your men go down into the kitchen and Anna will see to your wound."

"But, but, but . . ."

"It looks nasty, sheriff. The only cure for a demon byte is to have it flushed by a beautiful woman. I'm sure she can find some ale for you and your men while she tends to it."

The sheriff glared at the demon, who glared back. He glared at Wiz, who smiled. Then he glared at his two subordinates. Without a word he turned and stalked out of the room with the guards close on his heels.

Wiz collapsed against the wall and let his breath out in a great *whoosh*.

"Don't know what you're so worried about," Widder Hackett's voice rasped in his ear. "Malkin had the stuff out of the house before they got in the door."

"What'd she do with it?"

"Buried it in the garden."

"The garden?" Wiz yelped. "Didn't you hear them say they were going to dig up the garden?"

"I didn't say *our* garden," the Widder Hackett said gleefully. "Old Trescott's garden next door." She cackled so hard she went into a coughing fit. "Oh, I'd love to see the look on Mrs. High-and-Mighty's face if they was to dig up the loot under her cherry tree. Say, why don't you . . ."

"Uh, let's save that for an emergency, shall we?" Wiz said hastily.

EIGHTEEN
PRESENTATION

*Any sufficiently advanced technology is
indistinguishable from magic.*

—Clarke's Law

*Any sufficiently advanced magic is
indistinguishable from technology.*
—Anderson's Reformulation of Clarke's Law

*Any sufficiently advanced anything is
indistinguishable from utter nonsense.*
—Digby's Generalization of Clarke's Law

*Especially if it is sufficiently advanced
nonsense to begin with.*
—Zumwalt's Corollary to
Digby's Generalization of Clarke's Law

The council kept Wiz and Malkin waiting for over
an hour. While Wiz fidgeted in a too-hard chair in the
hall and Malkin ostentatiously checked the place for
escape routes, the councilors met behind closed doors.
Every so often the sound of shouting or an especially

ringing bit of oratory would penetrate through the thick
carved doors. Wiz fiddled with his notes and tried not
to think about the corners he had to cut.

Some of the pieces, such as the buzzword generator, were beautiful. But other details he had been forced
to leave to demons because of the time he lost to the
sheriff and his searchers.

True to his word, the sheriff had spent most of the
rest of the day digging up the garden. Or, more cor-
rectly, the sheriff lounged under a tree while his men
dug holes more or less at random in the garden. They
didn't find anything but they didn't quit until nearly
sundown. Wiz was on pins and needles all day, afraid
there was something Malkin had overlooked. But in
her own way Malkin was as thoroughly professional as
Wiz. There was nothing and the sheriff left empty-
handed.

At last the doors swung open and the usher beckoned them within. The expression on the man's face did
nothing for Wiz's confidence.

The council was seated around a long U-shaped table.
Their mood was a cross between a lynch mob and the
crowd at a formal execution. Which is to say some of
them were looking forward to what they were going to
do, some of them would reluctantly do their duty and
some of them were there for the show.

Wiz started talking before he even reached the center
of the U. "Gentlemen, I cannot tell you what a pleasure it is to come before you today," he said as he strode
into the room. His confidence was of a piece with his
sincerity, but so far they seemed to be buying it.

He gestured grandly and the daylight streaming in
through the windows dimmed to twilight. Another gesture and a demon appeared at the back of the room
with a slide projector. The projector was already on and
a slide flashed on the wall bearing the words "Success

And Prosperity" in vivid red and yellow on a bright blue background—a combination carefully chosen to be arresting without quite giving the viewers a headache. There was a brief murmur from the council and Wiz charged on before they could recover.

"My research has shown that you face a unique set of opportunities. To meet them I propose a dynamic, proactive reinvention of the organization to empower the teams using 60-second skills to address for success the strategic planning requirements in light of the Theory Z competitive strategy in time to produce a win-win-win situation."

Maybe I shouldn't have spent so much time on the buzzword generator, Wiz thought. But damn! The output was lovely. If the slide picking demon had done its job nearly as well, they just might, *might* get out of this with a whole skin.

All the while the demon was flashing slides on the wall, medieval streets crammed with modern tourists, waving fields of grain, several interior shots of the Cloisters medieval museum in New York City. Happy children. Wiz thought he glimpsed a shot of Mickey Mouse at Disneyland but he wasn't sure.

The torrent of words and pictures had the desired effect. Everyone was so stunned no one thought to ask about dragons.

"Clearly," Wiz continued, "what is called for is to install a reorganization that promotes a new strategic vision, a tightly focused vision that energizes the new tomorrow.

"While continuing the traditions of the past—" the mayor smiled and nodded "—we must meet the challenges of the future—" it was Dieter's turn to smile "—and provide bold new approaches to the organization's needs." That brought a nod from Rolf.

"We must empower ourselves to consistently use our

organizational resources to install this vision. This means using team management-focused techniques to create the need to change and to produce organizational systems which reinforce the vision.".

The picture on the screen showed a USDA map of the United States with the dates of the average last frosts marked.

"That doesn't look like anything around here," one of the more alert councilmen put in.

"Those are magical isoclines," Wiz said hastily.

"Still don't look like the country around here."

"It's a transmorphic projection. Maybe we'd better come back to this later. Next."

The next slide was a pie chart, showing sales of Sara Lee pies for 1993.

The trouble with trusting a demon's judgment, Wiz realized belatedly, is that it doesn't have any. He was damn glad none of his audience could read English.

Wiz smiled brightly. "By now you are doubtless interested in the specifics of my recommended action plan. As soon as I have finished, my assistant," a nod to Malkin, "will distribute copies of the white paper emphasizing the highlights. Meanwhile, let us examine the critical challenges we must meet to empower our vision of empowerment."

The demon flashed up a slide showing someone going over Niagara Falls in a barrel.

"The first challenge is organizational. The traditional organization emphasizes musty, sterile parlimentarianism at the expense of action which would clearly reflect the true makeup of the council." That brought nods from the mayor, Dieter and Rolf, all of whom were absolutely convinced the council was really behind them.

"This means your present decision-making process is diffuse and suboptimal. We must proactively react to counteract this tendency with a broader vision which is only available at the top." The mayor beamed and Dieter frowned.

"However, given the present organization this is clearly impossible because of the workload such a top-down environment imposes on the mayor. Therefore the key to repositioning the products and services to build a corporate advantage is install an action-direction vision by creatively teaming together. To that end, we create an Office of the Mayor to actualize the latency by creative teaming. Working directly with the mayor on this critical team will be innovation powerhouses representing the major resources within the present council. While the mayor will clearly be the team leader he will benefit from the synergy and creative flow of ideas from the team structure."

Again smiles from the critical three. The mayor saw it as a way to subordinate his main rivals to him and the other two saw it as giving them a power base close to the top. That alone should guarantee absolute gridlock, Wiz thought as he paused for breath.

That was a mistake. "What about the rest of the council?" demanded one of the councilmen off to the side. "What about money?" demanded another.

"Yes, money. What about money? What about taxes?" several other voices chimed in.

"I'm glad you raised that critical point," Wiz said brightly. "That is the second platform of my recommendations, but perhaps we can deal with it out of turn.

"The important fiscal consideration is to provide revenue enhancement without increasing taxes. In fact, as you can see clearly from this revenue elasticity chart—" up went a phase diagram of the melting point of lead-tin-antimony solder alloys "—the projected revenue needs can be met with a decrease in current taxes.

"Clearly what is needed is a proactive, projective infrastructure investment of the revenue stream."

"There ain't no revenue," one of the councilors objected.

"That is precisely why you apply the revenues projectively," Wiz assured him. "As you can see from this next chart—" up flashed a bar chart showing the amount of track laid by the Indian railways from 1850 to 1900 "—the revenues can be applied to development in a fashion which will encourage and develop the trade."

That produced an approving mutter from Dieter's faction. The mayor's people sat in puzzled silence and Rolf's followers looked to their leader for their cue.

"Let us go back to the organization for a moment," Rolf said smoothly. "I believe there is more."

"There is indeed," Wiz said, relieved that he didn't have to do his New Age Bugaloo around the difference between "revenue enhancement" and "tax increase."

Up on the screen flashed an organizational chart of the Supreme Soviet.

"Now this," Wiz said, gesturing with his pointer, "is your present structure. I'm sure all of you can see the inefficiencies and conflict potential implied here so I won't dwell on them. Next slide," he commanded before anyone could object.

Up on the screen flashed the current Miss July, blond, pneumatic and airbrushed to perfection.

Wiz closed his jaw with an audible snap. "Uh, that was just to make sure you were awake. Next slide."

Up came an even more baroque organizational chart. Glancing at the legend Wiz saw it was for General Motors circa 1965.

"Here is my recommendation. A more modern, teaming approach to today's challenges. Rather than concentrating the burdens, it spreads them throughout the organization to make management more effective.

"As you can see, this emphasizes creative teaming to empower all the members of the council to make the crucial decisions needed to create tomorrow. By establishing internal task forces, the Office of the Mayor can be freed from the day to day detail of running operations to concentrate on developing an action-directed migration plan to create tomorrow. These teams will prioritize opportunities for infrastructure enhancements using the new revenue stream as it comes on line." That got a stir of approval as the council members considered the opportunities for graft. "Naturally, every council member will have several team assignments to fully tap into the organization's creative resources. I won't bore you with the details of these teams," *mainly because I didn't have time to work them out*, "but I would like to point out the compensation committee, which will determine remuneration for the council members."

"You mean we'll get paid for sitting on the council?" someone asked.

"It seems only fair," Wiz said blandly.

"And just who's going to be on this compensation committee?" demanded a voice from the side of the room.

Wiz tapped the image at random with his pointer. "That is up to the personnel committee, here."

"And who's on the personnel committee?"

"That is the responsibility of the organizational committee. As a consultant it would be unethical of me to advise you on the makeup of these committees. I'm sure you will be able to work out these details among yourselves."

A quick glance from the mayor to Dieter to Rolf showed them all deep in thought. Rolf was smiling benignly, Dieter was looking sideways at the other two and the mayor was rubbing his chin and nodding.

"Gentlemen, the tide has turned." Up came a tidal

chart for New Bedford, MA. "Opportunity awaits us. Fortune favors the brave."

Up came the GM organizational chart once more.

"More importantly we must team together to form an empowerment matrix which will reinvent the corporation, uh, organization, in an entrepreneurial model to reach beyond the present to grasp the opportunities of the future!"

They didn't quite give him a standing ovation, but there were one or two tentative claps from the back of the room.

Wiz let out his breath with what he hoped was a not-too-audible sigh. "Very well. Are there any questions?"

"Can we go back to that last-but-two slide?" came a tremulous voice from the back of the room.

Malkin didn't have much to say on the way home. That was fine with Wiz. He was weak with relief and completely exhausted from everything that had happened in the last three days. What he wanted now was sleep, not conversation.

However, Malkin did have one observation. "I don't know if you're the greatest wizard I've ever met," she told him as soon as they came through the front door, "but you are sure the luckiest." With that she turned and went up the stairs.

Wiz started to reply, but then he realized that she was right and that left him with nothing to say.

After a minute he also realized he was hungry. He vaguely remembered eating something after the sheriff's men got through searching the house, but he wasn't sure if he'd had anything since then. Rather than going upstairs to bed, he went downstairs to the kitchen.

Down in the kitchen his assistant wizard was enchanting his maid.

" . . . so we escaped before the bandits even realized what had happened."

"That's so exciting," Anna breathed.

Llewllyn waved a hand dismissively. "Oh tut. All in a day's work for a journeying wizard."

He had a wonderful rich voice and talked enchantingly with hand gestures, smiles and just the right amount of eye contact. If you treated the content as some kind of fairy tale, it was great.

Anna obviously thought it was great. She sat at the table with her chin in both hands, her pale blue eyes fastened rapturously on his face. He didn't have his arm around her waist yet but things were definitely moving in that direction.

Wiz cleared his throat. Both of them started and turned toward the door. Anna blushed and for an instant Llewllyn looked flustered. "Ah, My Lord, how was the meeting with the Council?" he asked before Wiz could say anything.

"Productive. Very productive." *Produced more confusion than anything I've seen since the last Total Quality Management seminar.* "Can I see you upstairs Llewllyn?"

The young man turned and bowed to the still-blushing Anna. "Forgive me my lady, but duty calls."

"Okay," Wiz said as soon as they were in the front room, "the council's going to be reorganizing following a proposal I presented to them. Since you're the one in the office most of the time they'll probably be coming to you with questions. Refer any and all questions to me. Don't try to answer them yourself. The situation's kind of, ah, delicate."

Llewllyn smiled knowingly. "Am I to be permitted to know the nature of this plan?"

"Malkin's got copies of the materials I gave the council. You can get one from her."

"Very good, My Lord. Is there aught else?"

"Yes. One other thing." Wiz thrust his face very close to Llewllyn's. "If you mistreat Anna in any way I will personally break you in two."

The younger man's eyes widened. "By magic?"

Wiz flexed his muscles. "That wouldn't be nearly as much fun."

"And you think that I . . . ? For shame."

"Spare me the speeches. Just don't, okay?"

With that he turned on his heel and went upstairs to his workroom.

Wiz ran into Malkin in the upstairs hall. "Our favorite house pest was in the kitchen," Wiz told her. "I filled him in and he's probably going to ask you for a copy of that presentation. Give it to him, but don't let him get any ideas about doing anything on his own, especially answering questions."

The tall woman nodded

"Oh yeah, one other thing. Llewllyn seems to me making a play for Anna."

Malkin snorted. "You finally noticed that did you? You may," she said, stressing the word may, "be a mighty wizard, but you're still blind as any other man. Well, you have nothing to worry about on that score."

"I know," Wiz said. "I told him I'd break him in two if I caught him messing with Anna."

Malkin grinned nastily. "I told him I'd have his balls for earrings and do it with a dull butter knife." The grin got broader and nastier. "Slowly. With a red-hot butter knife."

Looking at her expression, Wiz felt a certain tightness in a very sensitive spot. "Oh," he said in a very small voice.

NINETEEN
CONTACT

Networking is a vitally important part of the consultant's craft. Never lose touch with former clients or colleagues.

—The Consultants' Handbook

Danny swore a particularly sulfurous oath just as Moira walked into the programmers' workroom.

"I'm sorry, My Lords," she said and turned to go.

Jerry looked up. "Oh, hi Moira. No, that's all right. We weren't swearing at you. We were swearing at the system."

"More problems?" she asked in the resigned voice Jerry and Danny had come to know all too well since the search for Wiz started.

"I'm afraid so. We've been checking the sites on that wacko routing path of Wiz's and checking them regularly. But now we keep pinging and we keep getting nonsense."

Danny went over the routing list item by item. Then he stopped dead. "Wait a minute! According to this he's going through **shark.vax**."

194

"That's the North Australia Oceanographic Institute. So?"

"So **shark.vax** is down. They had a typhoon or something. There was a message about it on the net."

"Let me see that!" Jerry grabbed the tablet from Danny's hand. He traced down it and frowned. The frown grew deeper as he compared the tablet to the screen.

"Ping **shark.vax**." Danny nodded and typed frantically.

"What is it?" Moira demanded, pressing close.

"I think . . ." Jerry began, but Danny cut him off. "See. **shark.vax** isn't there. But how is he using it if it's not there?"

"Magic?" Moira suggested.

Jerry slammed his hand down on the table so hard a pile of manuscripts slid onto the floor. "No, a gimmicked router table! He got into one of those routers and redid the table."

"Slick. No wonder we couldn't find him."

"Does this help?"

"Yes, it helps a lot. All we've got to do now is find the router he tricked and see where the entries in the table really lead. With that we can find the switch he's using and from there we can trace him back to this world."

"But not quickly?"

Jerry forced a smile. "Oh, it's not automatic, but we'll find him. He can't keep hiding like this for much longer."

TWENTY
THE PRANCING PIG

Good advice is where you find it.
                                   —The Consultants' Handbook

I can't keep going on like this, Wiz Zumwalt thought wearily. It wasn't just that he had lost another solitaire game. He was stuck on the project and stuck fast. Even if he could keep a lid on things with the town council, which was doubtful, he still hadn't made any real progress on protecting humans from dragons.

In fact, he realized, a lot of what he had done since he came here was in the nature of avoiding work on the problem hoping something would bubble up from his subconscious. But his subconscious was as flat as an open can of Coke left on a programmer's desk over the weekend.

Maybe his subconscious didn't have enough to work on. The truth of the matter was that he didn't know much about dragons and he hadn't really learned much about them since he came here.

"Hey, Malkin," he called over his shoulder, at the same time he clicked his mouse to deal another game.

"What?" came a voice in his ear.

Wiz jumped. There was Malkin at his shoulder.

"I wish you wouldn't sneak up on me like that when I'm working."

The tall thief shrugged. "I'm not sneaking. It's my normal way of walking. Kind of a professional asset, you might say."

"You might say sneaking, too," Wiz retorted. "Anyway, I wanted to ask you about dragons."

"Why ask me? You're supposed to be the expert."

"Yeah, but I've noticed the people around here don't talk much about dragons, or even seem to know very much about them."

"They don't know because they don't want to know. As far as most folks hereabouts are concerned the time you learn anything about dragons is usually when someone gets eaten."

"Still, there must be someone."

"Well now, since you mention it, there is one fellow who probably knows more than most."

"I wonder if I can talk to him."

Malkin shrugged. "Easy enough. If you're up for a little walk."

When they left the house they turned away from the main square and the town hall and headed downhill, toward the river. Wiz, who hadn't been this way much, looked around with interest.

"There's a lot I don't understand about the way humans and dragons relate to each other here," he told her.

"It's simple enough. Dragons eat humans when they feel like it."

"Yeah, but beyond that. For instance why haven't the dragons attacked the town?"

In answer Malkin pointed to a stretch of the street before them. The paving bricks were rougher, darker and shinier. Vitrified, Wiz saw, as if fired at too high a heat. Looking further he realized there was more than one such patch on the street or on the sides of buildings.

"Folks salvage what they can when they rebuild," Malkin told him. "Usually there's only bricks and not too many of them."

The tall woman led him further down into the city. Soon he could smell the river and the mud flats that lined it. They must be almost to the end of the town, Wiz thought.

The river flowed under the bridge between mud banks that took up most of the bed. In spring it must be a torrent, but now, in late summer, there was only enough water to fill a narrow channel.

In the failing light Wiz could see that the earth the town sat on wasn't ordinary dirt at all. It was heavily mixed with bits of brick, old paving stones and rubble. Here and there vitrified pieces glinted dully in the light of the setting sun.

Wiz realized the entire hill the town sat on was composed of the remains of earlier towns, like ancient Troy. Except here it wasn't earthquakes and human enemies who had laid down layer after layer of debris to serve as the base for the builders, it was dragons.

"Malkin, look at that."

"What?"

"The river banks. That's not dirt. That's rubble from older towns."

"So?"

"So this place has been destroyed and rebuilt a number of times."

Malkin shrugged and kept walking, unconcerned by her hometown's history.

How many times had the town been destroyed by dragon fire? Wiz wondered as they proceeded across the bridge. How many times had the survivors returned to try to rebuild?

Yet Malkin didn't seem to care. To her it was just a fact of life, even though it could happen again at any time.

That, Wiz decided, was the scariest thing of all.

The stone bridge was wide enough for two wagons abreast, and well-maintained. The town on the other side of it wasn't. Almost as soon as they stepped off the bridge the streets narrowed into muddy lanes and began to twist like the tracks of a herd of drunken cows. The aroma told Wiz they weren't cleaned regularly either. The smell of sun-warmed garbage and ripe raw sewage held a compost-like overtone that suggested they hadn't ever been cleaned.

"Bog Side," Malkin explained as Wiz tried to shut off direct communication between his nose and his gorge. "It's the place to come for entertainment."

The tall tumbledown houses and maze of narrow garbage-strewn byways didn't look like Wiz's definition of Disneyland. The characters who swaggered or skulked or slunk along the streets didn't remind him much of Mickey and Snow White either. In fact, they made the inhabitants of North Beach and Sunset Strip seem innocuous. Wiz found himself pressing close to Malkin for protection.

Malkin swaggered along, ignoring the others or shouldering them out of her way like so many gawking tourists in a shopping mall. A couple of the more flashily dressed women eyed Wiz and a few of the larger men looked him up and down speculatively, but either Wiz's reputation as a powerful wizard had preceded him or they knew Malkin too well to try anything. Except for an occasional hand lightly brushing his belt for the pouch that wasn't there, no one interfered with them.

Malkin led him deeper into the twisty maze of lanes and alleys, between houses that sagged out over the street to support each other like staggering drunks, down

alleys over piles of garbage and through open spaces
where buildings had collapsed into heaps of broken brick
and rotted timbers. Once they passed a long row of substantial brick buildings, sturdy and windowless but
stained with time and marred by graffiti and abuse.

"Almost there," Malkin said as she turned into an alley
even narrower and more noisome than the last. Wiz was
utterly lost, but from the overtone of mud and long-
dead fish permeating the general stench, he thought
they had doubled back toward the river.

The alley suddenly opened out into a square facing
the river and Wiz blinked as he stepped from the gloom
into the mellow light of the setting sun. Not that the
view was much of an improvement. The open space was
small and piled more than head-high with rubble and
garbage. The buildings on either side leaned alarmingly
and one of them had already slumped down into a pile
of brick spilling out into the square. The opposite side
was formed by the burned-out shell of another of the
windowless brick buildings. Looking at the blackened
brick and fire-damaged mortar Wiz wondered how much
longer it would stay standing.

Halfway down the square, Malkin turned suddenly
and ducked into a low doorway. Hanging out over the
door was a carved wooden sign depicting a rampant and
wildly concupiscent pig, its head turned sideways and
its tongue thrust out. The hooves, tongue and other parts
were picked out in gold leaf, now faded to a mellow
brown. Whether through lack of skill or excess of it, the
sign carver had turned the conventional heraldic pose
into a gesture of pornographic defiance.

Wiz ducked through the doorway and nearly fell
headfirst down the short flight of uneven stone stairs
that led into the room.

The place was long, narrow and mostly dark. The reek
of old beer and stale urine told Wiz it was a tavern even

before his eyes adjusted well enough to see the barrels stacked along one wall. A few mutton tallow lamps added more stench than light to the scene, and here and there the fading rays of the sun peeked through cracks in the bricks. The three or four patrons scattered around at the rough tables and benches all possessed a mien that did not encourage casual acquaintance and a manner that made Wiz want to stay as far away from them as possible. The only one who paid any attention to the newcomers was the barkeep, a big man in a dirty white smock who looked them up and down and then went back to picking his teeth with a double-edged dagger.

It was definitely not the kind of drinking establishment Wiz was used to. There wasn't a fern in sight, although Wiz thought he detected a smear of moss growing out of a seep of moisture on one wall.

Malkin put her hands on her hips, looked around and breathed a deep, contented sigh. She plopped herself down on the nearest bench and bellowed for the barkeep.

"Hi, Cully! Jacks of your best for me and the wizard here." The big man grunted acknowledgement and turned to his barrels. It seemed Malkin was known, if not welcomed, in this place.

"Come here often?" Wiz asked casually.

"Often enough. The Prancing Pig's the place to be if you want to meet folks in the Bog Side."

Glancing around, Wiz couldn't imagine going up to anyone in this place and asking him his sign.

Cully slapped down two leather mugs before them. From the stuff that slopped on the table Wiz could see the contents were beer. He picked his up and took a sip. It was thick, potent and flavored with some kind of bitter herb besides hops. The pine pitch used to seal the leather gave it a resiny aftertaste. Wiz was no judge of beer, but the stuff wasn't bad.

"This is the real city," Malkin said. "The folks down here don't put on airs and there's none of that social scramble and bicker, bicker, bicker you get on the other side of the bridge. Folks in the Bog Side stick together."

"When they're not slitting each others' throats you mean."

Malkin shrugged. "That's in the way of business." She took a long pull on her mug and slapped it down with a lusty sigh.

Wiz followed with a smaller pull on his tankard. "That reminds me. Those big buildings on this side of the river. Are those warehouses?"

Malkin shrugged. "Some were. A long time ago. Farmers'd bring in wool. Some of it would be spun and woven here and more would be traded downriver as it was."

"What happened?"

Malkin looked at him as if he was a touch slow. "Dragons is what happened. You can't grow much wool when there's dragons using your flocks as a lunch counter, not to mention snapping up the crew of a riverboat or two. The farmers still graze sheep, but there's not so much wool as there used to be. Not so many come to buy, either."

It made sense, Wiz thought as he took another pull on the oddly flavored beer. Dragons matured slowly and few survived to adulthood. But in a place with little natural magic there was nothing to threaten an adult dragon and they lived a very long time. Over the centuries there would be a slow, steady increase in population and that would mean more dragons to bedevil their human neighbors.

"It couldn't have all been one-sided, though. Otherwise people would never have gotten established in the valley. You had to have ways of fighting back."

Malkin snorted into her mug. "Buying peace, more

like. Used to be the council would make a deal with dragons. So many sheep, or cattle, or maidens a year and the dragons would leave the rest alone—mostly."

"But that doesn't work any more?"

"Seems like there's a different dragon every year."

Population pressure again, Wiz thought. Somehow Malthusian economics looked different when you were part of the consumable resource instead of the expanding population. Pretty clearly buying off the dragons wasn't the answer. All that got you was more dragons exploiting the resource.

"You must have had other ways of fighting back."

Malkin thumped down her now-empty mug and considered. "There's children's tales of heroes who could kill dragons. I suppose they're true because there used to be statues to them in half the squares in town."

"Used to be?"

"Dragons didn't like it. They'd swoop down and melt the statues where they stood. Burn down a lot of the town in the process." Again the shrug. "That was a long time ago, too."

It didn't feel like a solution to Wiz, but he persisted. "Still, you could kill dragons."

"A hero could. Had to be a hero who would face a dragon in single combat. Sometimes the dragon'd win and burn the town. Sometimes the human would win and we'd be free of dragons for a bit. But heroing ain't what it used to be. Not so many of them any more and there's more dragons, seems like."

"I understand why you have more dragons, but why aren't there more heroes?"

"'Cause win or lose most of them are only good for one fight." She jerked her head back toward the bar. "Cully here. He's the only one around now."

"Cully fought a dragon?"

Malkin nodded. "He's the one I want you to meet.

Hey, Cully," she called over her shoulder. "The wizard here wants to meet you. And bring us a couple more while you're at it."

As the bartender made his way over with a pitcher of beer Wiz looked at him closely. He was a big man, run to fat now in late middle age and his skin blotchy from sampling too much of his wares. He moved with a pronounced limp with his withered left arm pressed close to his side. For all that he must have been formidable in his youth.

"So you're the wizard, eh?" Cully said as he plopped the pitcher of beer down on the table. Wiz saw he had brought a jack for himself.

"More a consultant just now," Wiz said. "I'm working with the council on their dragon problem."

"Scared a dragon right out of the Baggot Place," Malkin put in. "Frightened him so bad he flew away without harming anyone."

Cully looked Wiz up and down. "So I heard," he said in a tone that wasn't quite a challenge.

"It's a skill," Wiz shrugged. "But you actually fought a dragon and won."

Cully filled his own jack and passed the pitcher to Malkin. "Aye. It's a dragon's treasure that got me this place. And as for winning—" He shrugged his good arm. "Well, I'm here and the dragon ain't."

Wiz leaned forward. "Did you have some kind of special weapon?"

"What's the matter, Wizard? Your own methods not good enough?"

"Oh, my methodology for dragon abatement is perfectly adequate. But like any practitioner I seek to add to my knowledge base."

The big man digested that while he drained most of his tankard.

"Oh, aye, there's all kinds of lore on killing dragons."

Cully grinned. Since half his face was a mass of burn scars the result was not only lopsided, it was something to terrify small children. "Thing is, most of it don't work." He twitched his bad arm and Wiz saw the skin was mostly scar tissue. "That's how I got like this, following some of that advice."

Wiz wondered if the dragons exchanged tips on fighting humans.

"Still, you beat a dragon in a single combat."

Cully's grin grew even more lopsided. "I never said it was a straight-up fight. That's not in the rules, you see."

"There are rules?"

"Of a sort. If you don't follow them the dragon won't fight you. It's his choice, you know, seeing as how he can fly and you can't."

"What are the rules?"

"Only show up at the appointed place at the appointed time, all by yourself. After that anything goes."

"How'd you do it?"

"How do *you* do it, Wizard?" Cully shot back.

"I do what any good consultant does. Mostly I talk them to death."

Cully considered. "That's a new one anyway. I wish you the luck of it." He paused. "As for me, I started by hiding in some rocks and braining him with a boulder. Then?" The big man shrugged. "Then it was just one hell of a fight." He looked over Wiz's shoulder as if seeing something miles away. "One hell of a fight."

The mood held for a long minute as Wiz considered the implications.

"And no one's done it since you?"

Cully's eyes focused back on Wiz. "Not for more than forty years. There's some as have tried. But none with any luck, you see."

"Are the dragons getting smarter?"

"There's them as says that," Cully admitted. "Or maybe those would-be dragon slayers is getting dumber. Or softer." He let out a gusty sigh and drained the last of his beer. "I'll tell you one thing, Wizard. Dragon slaying ain't what it used to be." Then he grinned again. "But then neither's much else."

Again silence as both men sat lost in thought, Cully in his memories and Wiz in the implications of what he had learned. He needed to absorb all this and the heavy beer was going to his head.

"Well," he said, pushing his end of the bench back from the table, "thanks a lot Cully. You've given me a lot to think about."

The big man grinned his terrifying grin. "Any time you need advice on killing dragons, come and see me."

"Thanks, Cully." Wiz turned to go but the tavern keeper cleared his throat.

"You forgot to pay for the beer."

In a sinking instant Wiz realized he didn't have any money with him. But Malkin reached into her belt pouch and flipped a silver coin down on the table.

Cully scooped up the coin, bit it, and nodded. "He's got you paying for him, eh?"

"Wizards don't use money," Malkin said carelessly.

"Yeah?" the big man said skeptically. "What do they use then?"

"Plastic," Wiz blurted. "Ah, little cards, like so," he opened his fingers. "When you want something you just show them your plastic."

Cully looked at him with eyes narrowed and Wiz felt foolish.

"And they take this plastic stuff? Just like that?"

"Well," said Wiz, remembering the times he had gone over his limit, "mostly."

For the first time the big man's face showed respect. "You must be a mighty wizard indeed."

✦   ✦   ✦

"Where'd you get that silver?" Wiz asked as he and Malkin emerged into the cool evening air.

"One of those pickpockets back at the bridge wasn't as good as he thought he was," Malkin said with a radiant smile. "He had money in his pouch too."

"You picked a pickpocket's pocket while he was trying to pick your pocket?"

"It was a challenge."

Wiz just sighed and followed his guide back down the alley, his head full of beer fumes and his mind full of dragons.

So the dragons were getting harder to kill, eh? That made sense too, in a way. The older, more powerful dragons staked out their territories in the center of the Dragon Lands and forced the younger ones to the periphery. That meant that the dragons the humans faced were less powerful and less experienced—less intelligent too, if Griswold was any example. But as population pressure increased bigger, smarter and more dangerous dragons were trying to grab territory on the edge. They'd be harder for human warriors to beat.

He nearly stumbled into a sewage pit and he had to rush to keep up with Malkin.

"Cully is the last of the dragon slayers, huh?"

Malkin nodded. "Far as anyone knows." Her tone changed slightly. "He may be my father too. Big enough anyway."

"You didn't know your father?"

"Nah," Malkin said. "Left or died or something before I was born."

"Didn't your mother tell you anything about him?"

A snort of laughter in the dark. "Barely knew my mother. I was too young to ask questions like that."

"I'm sorry."

"For what? She 'prenticed me to Mother Massiter

when I was bare old enough to walk. I was a slavey there
for a few years. Then I came into some growth, discovered my talent and I've been on my own ever since."

"But don't you ever wonder . . ."

Malkin's voice roughened. "The world's full of won-
dering, Wizard. Now let it be and we'll be home soon
enough."

They walked along in silence, each wrapped in
thought, until they emerged at the foot of the bridge
that led out of the Bog Side. There was but a sliver of
moon and the bridge was dark. Wiz listened to the water
rushing along beneath them and considered what he'd
learned. *No wonder these people need help,* he thought.
*They're losing to the dragons and they don't even know
it yet.*

He never even saw the shadow that detached itself
from the gloom and brought the raised club down on
his head with skull-smashing force.

Wiz never saw the blow coming, nor the four cloaked
figures that came charging out of the dark. He didn't
have to. The protective spell in his ring sensed the danger
and wrapped him in a stasis field, leaving him frozen
in the center of the band of attackers.

The first man's club bounced out of his numbed fingers. Before he could bend to retrieve it, a second,
smaller figure twisted in and struck with the speed of
a cobra. His dagger flashed down, struck the magic field,
skittered off and buried itself in the wielder's thigh. The
man screamed and fell back. The other two stopped their
headlong charge and stared at the motionless figure of
the wizard, considering their next move.

"I'm struck down," wailed the little one with the knife.
"Laid low by a cowardly wizard's blow."

"Ah, it's nothing but a scratch," growled the man with
the club.

"A scratch?" the wounded man yelped. "A scratch?"

His voice went higher and quavered. "It's a Fortuna great wound in me leg, it is. Nigh mortal, I tell you."

"Well, stand away and we'll finish him," said a third man. "All of us striking together." He hefted his cudgel and fitted his actions to his words.

The fourth and last assassin had a sword. The three remaining men struck Wiz simultaneously and in turns. They hit him high. They hit him low. They pounded and hammered and thrust and sliced and hacked and hewed. Wiz just stood there, frozen in time and oblivious to their efforts.

"Doesn't seem to matter what we do," the shortest one gasped at last. "It hurts us worse than it does him." He rubbed his shoulder. "Got me bursitis going again, it has."

"We could set him on fire," the tall one with the sword said speculatively.

"Not likely he'd burn," said the third. "He's an expert on dragons after all."

"Let's throw him in the river then."

"Don't look at me," the aggrieved voice came out of the shadows. "I'm wounded out of commission."

"Three of us can handle him all right. Come on boys."

The men clustered around Wiz and tried to jerk him aloft. But the stasis spell worked in proportion to the applied acceleration and Wiz would not move.

"He's heavy as lead," one of them grunted.

"Let's tip him, then," said the man with the sword. "Maybe we can move him that way."

By slowly tilting the frozen Wiz back on his heels and working him forward inch by painful inch the thugs got Wiz to the stone rail.

"Now," the tall one panted, "how we going to get him over the railing?"

"Maybe we could hoist him up and tip him like?" the one with the sword said dubiously.

"Won't do any good if he lands in the mud bank," the third said, having regained his breath.

The two looked at each other and then leaned over the rail to peer down to the river.

A strong hand grasped each man by the belt and boosted both assassins up and over the rail before they knew what had happened. The third man rushed to the aid of his friends only to be seized and propelled over the stone railing after them. Three splashes from below confirmed that they had indeed been over the river and not the mud bank.

"Now," said Malkin, turning to face the fourth thug.

"No need," the man hobbled to his feet and held out a hand to ward her off. "No need. I'm going." With that he hoisted himself over the stone rail and disappeared into the darkness below.

With the threat vanished, the spell relaxed its grip and time speeded up to normal for Wiz. He blinked as his eyes refocused, realized he was facing in a different direction and then saw Malkin looking over the bridge railing.

"Something happened didn't it?"

Malkin looked at him oddly. "Four Bog Side bullies just tried to kill you is all. I guess that qualifies as 'something'—at least for normal folk."

She strode ahead briskly. "Come on," she said over her shoulder. "Let's get off this bridge before something else happens."

"Who?" said Wiz as he caught up beside her.

"Hired help," Malkin told him. "And not of the best, either. Seems as if someone wants you dead, but they don't want to spend a lot of money on the project."

"Dieter?"

Malkin considered. "Mayhap. But as like Mayor Hendrick. Or one of the others."

"Wait a minute. The mayor's my strongest supporter."

"He's tied his wagon to your star and that's a fact. But mayhap he's afraid your star will fall and wants to hedge his bet. After all, if you die accidental-like, you can't rightly be said to have failed, now can you?"

"Hendrick?"

"Or maybe one of the common folk, who's afraid of dragons."

"Well, if they're afraid of dragons," Wiz said despairingly, "don't they want me to succeed?"

"They're likely afraid you'll stir the dragons up to burn the town again."

"Great. Try to do them a favor and they try to kill you."

Malkin grinned. "You expected gratitude?"

TWENTY-ONE

FANFARE FOR KAZOOS AND DRAGON

Just because it doesn't work the way you expected doesn't mean it's useless.

—*The Consultants' Handbook*

Wiz stewed about the incident on the bridge for the next three days without coming to any kind of conclusion—except that someone here *really* didn't like him. Since he had known that almost from the moment he set foot in town, the information didn't help him any.

He was still stewing when the mayor showed up on his doorstep. He was hoarse and made liberal use of the handkerchief in his sleeve, but he looked better than he had the last time Wiz had seen him.

"What can I do for you, Your Honor?" he asked once they were settled in his workroom.

"It's this new organization," Mayor Hendrick said. "Oh, I'm sure it's wonderful and all that. But it's so, well, complicated, we meet and we meet and we meet and nothing ever seems to get done."

"Reinventing and re-empowering an organization does take some time to get up to speed," Wiz said. "But I'm sure once the initial formalities are out of the way you will find it a vast improvement."

"Maybe, but that's not exactly what I wanted to talk to you about. I need something to help me maintain my position."

Thoughts of a palace coup flashed through Wiz's mind. "Maintain your position?"

"With this new executive committee. I need something to increase my dignity," the mayor said. Wiz thought about suggesting a face-lift and a personality transplant, but he decided against it.

Wiz shrugged. "Well, I'm not much on public speaking."

"Oh, but you handled that presentation wonderfully," the mayor said. "Anyway, I speak well enough as it is. What I need is something more, well, *imposing*, if you know what I mean? Something magical. I was thinking, perhaps, a halo?"

Wiz thought that a halo would make the mayor look more ridiculous than dignified. "Fine for a darkened room, but what about broad daylight?"

Mayor Hastlebone sniffled. "Yes, that is a problem. What do you suggest then?"

"Well, how about some background music?"

"You mean like a fanfare of trumpets?" The mayor brightened. "Yes, that would be just the thing." He waved his hand. "Make it so, Wizard."

"It's not quite that simple. Let me think for a minute. What do you want it to sound like?"

"Oh, something like Ta-daa tum tum tum TAA." The mayor waved his hand in time to the imaginary music. "You know, important."

"I guess so," Wiz said, punching keys on his workstation and watching the fiery letters scroll past. "Can you do that sound again?"

"TA-DAA TUM TUM TUM TAAA." The mayor was louder this time.

"Okay got it. Now . . ."

"You mean you're not going to make a hundred trumpets materialize in the room?" The mayor sounded disappointed.

"No, I've captured the sound and I'll use that. After I juice it up, of course."

Calling up his synthesizer module, Wiz set to work. Eventually he came up with something that combined the theme from *Masterpiece Theater* with the post call from a horse race. Even to Wiz's musically untrained ear it sounded more like a chorus of kazoos than a trumpet call.

The mayor's face fell.

"Needs something more," Wiz said quickly. "How about a three-part echo effect?"

Wiz noticed that the sound of the trumpets had brought Llewllyn to the doorway. He didn't seem awed, but he was very interested.

A few more minutes of fiddling and Wiz tried again. Now it sounded like some of the kazoos had bass voices and they weren't quite playing together. The mayor brightened at the noise.

"Now I just say *fanfare exe*?"

"That's right. Try it."

Mayor Hendrick puffed out his chest and struck a pose as if delivering an oration. **fanfare exe**! Flinging one arm outward he began to address a non-existent crowd.

As soon as he opened his mouth the invisible trumpets brayed. His Honor stood with his mouth open for a minute and then closed it just as the fanfare finished. "My friends," the mayor began and was immediately drowned out by the trumpets.

"Ah, I think this needs a little more work," Wiz said. "Let me play with it some more and perhaps we can do better."

The mayor's reply was drowned out by a volley of trumpets.

"Say 'fanfare cancel exe,'" Wiz shouted through the noise.

"What?" Immediately another round of racket burst on top of the existing one.

"FANFARE CANCEL EXE," Wiz shouted.

"*FANFARE CANCEL EXE?*" the mayor asked. The trumpets cut off in mid-bray.

"This needs a little work," Wiz said into the ringing silence.

"I thought a wizard simply waved his wand, or staff, to make things happen."

"I'm afraid there's a little more to it than that, at least on such complex spells. This may take a couple of days, but I'm sure I can cook something up you'll like."

He had just seen the mayor out the front door, still sniffling, when a noise in the kitchen caught his attention. He went downstairs and found Llewllyn and Anna sitting at the table with a large basket between them. There was a blanket neatly folded on top of the basket.

"You wanted to see me?" he asked Llewllyn.

"Ah, a trifle really. Nothing of any importance I assure you."

Wiz gestured at the blanket and basket. "And this?"

"We're going on a picnic," Anna said brightly. Her face fell. "That's if you don't mind, My Lord. I'll be back in plenty of time to fix dinner and all my work's done, except for washing the walls and I can't do that until the soapmaker finishes her next batch of cleaning soap and that won't be for another two days, so . . ."

"No, it's fine with me." Then he eyed Llewllyn. "Just remember our discussion."

The young man gave his boss a toothpaste smile. "Of course, My Lord."

"Oh, by the way," Wiz said casually to Anna. "Have you seen the butterknife anywhere?" Then he smiled insincerely at Llewllyn, who had suddenly gone a little pale and developed a distinct hunch.

A pleasant way out of town a jumble of rocky spires reared from the countryside. It was a common destination for picnics and other more private affairs, as Llewllyn knew from his previous residence nearby.

Anna had packed a lunch in a wicker basket and neatly covered the provisions with a spare blanket to serve as a tablecloth. She had fixed the lunch herself, but Llewllyn was the one who suggested the blanket.

"My gran would never let me come here," she told Llewllyn as they turned off the road onto the path into the rocks.

"Oh, it's perfectly safe, I can assure you," the putative wizard said carelessly. "I've been here many times."

"Many times?"

"Picnics," Llewllyn added hastily, catching her tone. "I've been here on picnics."

"Oh, this is a lovely spot," the girl said, as they came to a glade in the rocks.

"There's a better one a little ways up. More private— ah—better view." He took her hand and helped her up the steep trail among the pink granite boulders. The path twisted and climbed until it reached a spot just below the top of the main spire. Rocks jutted up around them, forming a natural bowl enclosing a flat spot just large enough for a cozy picnic.

"Here, you see? You can see for miles and no one can see us at all."

"No one?"

"Completely private." He moved closer to her. "And look at the view." He stood behind her and extended one arm over her shoulder to point out the sights. "There's the river, and there's the town over there, you see?" Somehow it was completely natural that Llewllyn's other arm fell around Anna's waist.

"Are you sure we'll be all right?" she asked wide-eyed.

"Never fear," Llewllyn said. "I am here to protect you."

"Oh, Llewllyn," she whispered softly.

He drew her to him and held her in his arms. "You know I would give my last drop of heart's blood for you. I love you more than life itself."

"Oh, Llewllyn."

Anna's eyes were dewy and her lips soft and partly open. Llewllyn bent forward to kiss her.

A shadow passed before the sun.

Anna's eyes grew round and she went rigid in Llewllyn's arms. The wizard wasn't used to getting that kind of response so it took him a second to realize she was looking over his shoulder and not at him. He turned around in time to see a dragon settle down among the crags below them.

Peering around a rock Llewllyn could see the dragon, or part of it, nestled among the rocks below them. It had curled up, blocking the trail.

Anna shrank back against him, cowering in his arms. Llewllyn clasped her tightly to stop his own trembling.

"Be brave, my beloved," he said to her. "I will protect you." She made no sound but clung to him more tightly.

Llewllyn's first instinct was to sneak away. But he knew this place well enough to know there wasn't anyplace to sneak to from here. The only way out was the trail they had come up. They could stay where they were, but sooner or later the dragon was sure to see or smell them. There really wasn't anything else to do, he decided. Especially not with the girl here.

"I will face the monster."

Anna turned even paler. "Oh, but you can't. You'll be killed."

The wizard took her in his arms. "If I am it will be in a good cause. I will gladly offer up my last drop of heart's blood to save you."

"Oh, be careful," Anna breathed. "Come back to me."

He patted her cheek. "Never fear my darling. All will be well."

A quick peek around the rocks showed the dragon was lying down and couldn't see the trail. Llewllyn took a deep breath and moved toward the dragon, dodging from boulder to boulder and sometimes crawling on his belly.

His first thought was that he might be able to find another way down the rocks. Or perhaps, if the dragon was truly asleep, they could sneak by it. By the time he reached the place where the dragon rested he knew both hopes were in vain. The rocks were much too steep and while he could hear the dragon breathing regularly, it was obviously not asleep.

Llewllyn stopped and thought hard. He had scant experience with dragons. But he knew Wiz had handled one by talking to it and if there was one thing Llewllyn was confident of, it was his ability to talk.

No help for it, really, he told himself. Then he stood up, straightened his tunic, brushed the grass out of his blond hair and squared his shoulders. It never hurt to make an impressive entrance.

In fact, he realized, he had a spell of his master's to make the entrance even more impressive. All the trumpets might even make the dragon think he had an army behind him.

fanfare exe! he whispered. Then he took a deep

breath and opened his mouth to go forth and do battle with the dragon.

The dragon, meanwhile, was mostly interested in getting a nice nap. He had fed that morning on a dozen or so sheep at an outlying farmstead and taken light exercise by flying a few dozen leagues. Now he was ready to settle down and digest his meal. The rocks were nicely warm from the sun and the scenery suited his dragonish nature.

He was just relaxing into gentle slumber when the blare of trumpets yanked him awake.

The dragon's head jerked up and he roared in surprise and anger. A lance of flame shot from his jaws directed at nothing in particular but passing over the rock behind which Llewllyn waited. The bard was unharmed but the blast of superheated air cost him what little courage he had remaining.

Unfortunately, when Llewllyn became frightened he stuttered uncontrollably. Every time he tried to get a syllable out it touched off another peal of trumpets. The rocks rang and resounded with the noise of a trumpet fanfare played as a twenty-part round and the dragon's head darted this way and that seeking the source of his torment.

Finally it was too much. With a roar of frustration the dragon leapt into the sky to try to find a quieter place for his nap.

Llewllyn was still watching the dragon go when Anna came running down the trail and into his arms.

"You're all right! I saw the fire and the dragon, and I was afraid." She stopped with her eyes even wider as the significance sank in. "You did it," Anna breathed. "You defeated a dragon."

Llewllyn opened his mouth to say something modest but the trumpet fanfare cut him off.

Anna's eyes grew even wider. "Oh, you are a mighty

wizard! And my hero." Llewllyn just smiled and held Anna tighter. Occasionally, given enough hints, he did know when to shut up.

Winging away from the rocks the dragon came to a somewhat different conclusion. *A pretty pass indeed when you can't even take a nap without being disturbed by these pesky humans and their stupid magical jokes,* he thought. *I'm going to have to do something about them. And this new wizard of theirs.*

TWENTY-TWO
DRAGON TROUBLE

The Consultant's Three Rules of Crisis Management:
1) *When Life Hands You A Lemon, Make Lemonade.*
2) *When Life Hands You A Hemlock, Don't Make Hemlock-ade.*
2a) *Always Know The Difference Between A Lemon and A Hemlock.*

—The Consultants' Handbook

" . . . and then the dragon flew away," Anna told Wiz and Malkin, her blue eyes round as saucers. "And we were saved!"

"Oh, it was nothing really," Llewllyn said modestly from where he stood at her side, his hand resting on her shoulder. Anna reached up and placed her hand over his. Then she beamed up at her savior.

Wiz and Malkin exchanged glances and then stared down at their plates and the remains of dinner. Obviously both of them thought that for once Llewllyn's description of events was more accurate than Anna's.

The pair had been through the incident three times and Wiz still wasn't completely sure what **had** happened. For one thing, the story had grown with each retelling. For another he trusted neither Llewllyn's veracity nor Anna's powers of observation. He was reasonably certain there had been a dragon involved and that the dragon had flown away, perhaps in response to something Llewllyn had done. He suspected from Anna's description of the sound of trumpets that his fanfare spell had been involved as well. Beyond that, he wasn't willing to speculate— except about the reason for the grass stains on the blanket and the dried grass in Anna's hair and the flush on the girl's cheeks.

Obviously something more was called for, so Wiz tried. "Well, I'm glad you're safe."

Anna sighed. "I owe it all to Llewllyn. Isn't he wonderful?"

Malkin kept her eyes on her plate.

"Quite remarkable," Wiz said dryly, rising from the table. "But if you'll excuse me, I have work to do." *Like trying to keep my dinner down,* he thought as he headed up the stairs.

Since Llewllyn had developed the habit of cadging meals with them the scene was repeated at lunch the next day.

Since the mayor had summoned Wiz to discuss the fanfare spell, the scene was prolonged because Llewllyn insisted on accompanying him to the town hall. The young man paused several times to ostentatiously greet important people, keeping Wiz close so he could bask in his reflected glory. Somehow he managed to work the fact that he had defeated a dragon into each conversation, so Wiz had to listen to more or less the same story three or four more times. By the time they reached the street that led to the main square Wiz was thoroughly fed up with his assistant.

"You know that what you did was stupid," Wiz told

him finally. "I mean terminally stupid. Why didn't you just wait for the dragon to leave?"

"Were I by myself I might have," Llewllyn admitted with a disarming smile. "But Anna was there."

"So you risked her life as well as your own to impress her."

"No, to protect her. Better for me to face near-certain death at the fangs and claws of a dragon than for anything to happen to her. Were I slain perhaps the monster would be satisfied and not look further among the rocks."

"Still it was stupid."

Llewllyn nodded, as if to show he was too well bred to argue with his employer. "Perhaps, My Lord. I can only say that love makes a man do strange and wonderful things."

Wiz snorted.

"But I do love her," Llewllyn proclaimed. "Why, I would shed my last drop of heart's blood for her."

"Yeah, but will you marry her?"

"Of course, My Lord, in due time. Do you doubt me?"

"Your record in that department isn't exactly sterling," Wiz said as they turned the corner into the main square.

"Ah, but I was young and callow then, a mere stripling. You see before you not a boy, but a man full-grown, a man redeemed by love."

Wiz thought that what he saw before him was a pompous windbag and he was about to say something to that effect. But just then the world stuttered.

One instant Llewllyn was beside him and the next he was in front and staring open-mouthed. Everyone was running and screaming and there was dust in the air that hadn't been there before.

Wiz started to ask what had happened. Then he saw the brick. No, not a brick, a piece of worked stone. Like part of a cornice. It was lying in the street behind Llewllyn, surrounded by the dust it had raised when it fell. There were several other pieces of freshly broken stone nearby. Looking up he could see that a big chunk of the stonework on the building was missing.

Wiz looked back and saw Llewllyn had progressed to working his jaws, but not far enough to actually make noise. He also saw they had drawn a crowd.

"It, it, it . . . bounced," Llewllyn finally managed. "It just hit you and it split to pieces and it bounced right off the top of your head."

Looking around, Wiz saw that several councilors and the sheriff had joined the excited group.

"Think nothing of it," he said over the rising buzz of conversation. "As a great wizard I am protected by a spell that renders me invulnerable to mortal danger." The conversation grew even louder.

"But you froze. Like a statue," his assistant said.

Wiz had been hoping no one would notice that. "A side effect," he said with a wave of his hand. "So long as the danger lasts I am immobile and invulnerable. Now come. Let us be on our way."

Maybe that will stop people from trying to terminate my contract with extreme prejudice, he thought as the crowd parted before them. *At least it might if I can find someplace to sit down before I get the shakes.*

Wiz didn't see the bald little man with the leather sack of mason's tools lounging at the edge of the crowd and wouldn't have recognized him if he had. Nor would he have attached any special importance to the thoughtful way he rubbed his chin as Wiz and Llewllyn proceeded on their way.

Having a piece of rock dumped on his head may not have hurt Wiz physically, but it sure didn't do anything for his mood. Between Llewllyn's bragging, the mayor's insistence on having the new spell before the next executive committee meeting and being sneered at by Pieter Halder on the town hall steps, he was in a foul mood when he got home that evening.

Anna, however, was still starry-eyed and bubbling. For once Llewllyn wasn't hanging around, so Wiz was spared that, but the maid's innocent prattling about the wonders of her true love was just as hard to take.

" . . . and someday we'll be married," the maid finished up her latest, albeit short, line of thought.

"You hope," Wiz said in an undertone, unable to contain himself further.

Not enough of an undertone, unfortunately. "Why of course we will," Anna said innocently.

"Look Anna, I don't mean to burst your bubble or anything, but are you sure Llewllyn is the marrying kind?"

"My bubble?" Anna said blankly.

"A figure of speech. I mean your illusions about Llewllyn." As soon as he said it, he knew it was the wrong thing to say, but by then it was too late.

"But they're not illusions. They're real. As real as Llewllyn's magic that saved me from the dragon!"

"Uh, yeah, his magic is another thing. I mean . . ."

"Oh, I know what you mean," Anna burst out. "You're jealous of Llewllyn's powers and I think you're awful!" Then she remembered she was talking to her employer and dashed from the room in a flood of tears.

Wiz watched her go and turned back to his tea. "Women!" he snorted.

"Men!" Malkin retorted. "Well, that was nicely done. What do you intend for an encore? Pull the wings off flies?"

"Now wait a minute. You're the one who brought up the dull butter knife."

"Aye, and I would too. But that doesn't excuse being

cruel to the child. That was cruel and all it's likely to accomplish is driving them closer together."

"Little trollop's right," Widder Hackett chimed in. "All you did was hurt her feelings."

"But I was trying to let her down easy. To help her."

"By making her miserable?" Malkin replied.

"Help her my left foot," Widder Hackett grated. "Of all the shoddy, ill-done . . ." There was a lot more.

Wiz looked to either side at the women, one visible and now silent, one invisible and just working up a good head of steam.

"All right have it your way," he snapped. "I'm a miserable failure as a human being. Now if you'll excuse me, I'm going to get some air." With that he stormed out of the kitchen with Widder Hackett still railing in his ear.

Wiz stood on the stoop for an instant, looking out along the dark street. There were no street lights and the moon was only half-full. There wasn't so much as a candle showing in a window, which made the street gloomy and forbidding. It was as if the houses were bombed out and abandoned, he thought. Somewhere several streets over a dog howled, adding to the effect.

He turned and started away from the square, head down and lost in thought.

The truth was, he did feel bad about making Anna cry. But dammit! The girl was his responsibility and he couldn't let her get too mixed up with someone like Llewllyn.

The other truth was he didn't want the responsibility, he admitted as he picked his way along the dark, deserted way. In fact he didn't want any of the responsibilities he had acquired since he got here. Yet he was stuck with them and he was juggling like a madman trying to meet them. That was one of the reasons he'd been so hard on Anna.

Ever since he got here he had been writing checks furiously. Sooner or later some of them were going to come due and he was way overdrawn at the luck bank.

It wasn't just that, this wasn't *fun* any more. In the beginning this had all been a big game, but now the joke was old and not particularly funny.

He couldn't even take pride in his job, like he could writing a good tight module of code in something like COBOL. At heart he just wasn't a con man and playing the role was taking its toll on him. He sucked a breath of the cold night air and sighed gustily. This wasn't working out at all the way he had anticipated.

He was cold and tired and frustrated and a little scared and more than anything else he just wanted to go home.

Wiz never even saw the shadow that separated itself from the wall as he passed. And he never heard the hiss of the blade through the air. The edge landed squarely across his shoulders and as he froze into immobility a sharp whistle rang out from the darkness from whence the shadow had come.

"Ow!" said the shadow. "My wrist."

"I told you not to hit him, didn't I?" retorted a second cloaked man as he emerged from the darkness. He was shorter and for an instant a moonbeam gleamed off his dark pate. "Just tickle him in the ribs, I said. But no, you have to take a mucking great whack at him."

There was a rattling on the cobblestones just around the corner.

"Here comes the cart," said the first one. "Let's get this business over with."

Heaving and straining the three men loaded Wiz's immobile form into the cart. The spell didn't increase Wiz's weight, but it did do funny things to his inertia. The footpads found they could only move him slowly and that made him seem even heavier. It didn't help that one of them had to keep his sword pressed against

Wiz at all times lest the spell break. That left two of them to do most of the work, including burying the frozen wizard under the turnips that made up two-thirds of the cart's load.

It was not a quiet business, especially since all three men had a tendency to curse and mutter at every little bit of work. But not a shutter banged open nor even a light showed at a window, as if these kinds of goings-on were commonplace here.

Finally, with Wiz stowed and covered, the pair mounted the cart and rattled off in the night, leaving the occasional turnip behind to mark their passage.

A few minutes jolting over cobblestones brought them to the city's west gate. It was lit by flaming torches on either side and before it stood a represen-tative of the city's guard. He was tall, gangly, wearing a steel cap and leather-covered jack. In the crook of his bony arm he carried a halberd that had definitely seen better days.

"And where do you think you're going?"

"Out to my granny's," said the tall one. The medium-sized one next to him nodded vigorously and the short one sat twisted on the seat to keep his knife on Wiz's throat under the pile of turnips.

"At this time of night?"

"We had to finish work," the tall one said. "Then we had to eat dinner and harness the cart and load it, and . . ."

The guard peered past the driver. "What have you got in there?"

"Uh, turnips."

"Why are you taking turnips out of the city?" he demanded.

"Granny lost her entire turnip crop," the tall man said smoothly. "Weevils got them, they did."

"Turnip weevils," added the driver helpfully. "Terrible

things, turnip weevils." His companion, who recognized lily-gilding when he heard it, poked him in the ribs to shut up.

The guard had never heard of turnip weevils, but then he was a city boy. More importantly perhaps, in this city the best and brightest did not become city guardsmen and out of that lot, the best and brightest of the not-so-good and not-so-smart weren't assigned to gate duty after curfew. Still, this was irregular and he had the reputation of the city guard to uphold.

"What's the rest of that stuff?"

"Building supplies. We're going to make some repairs on her cottage while we're about it."

"Fixing the fireplace," the man in the back added helpfully.

"It's after curfew. You won't be able to get back in until morning."

"That's all right. We'll stay at my granny's."

The guard still thought the whole thing was extremely fishy, but his orders were more about people and things coming into the city than people and things going out.

"All right. Pass on then. But I'm going to remember the lot of you."

"Well?" said the tall one at last.

"Well what?" the guard replied.

"Aren't you going to open the gate?"

"If you want the gate opened do it yourself. There's three of you."

The driver started to protest, thought better of it and nudged his companion to get down off the seat.

"Takes two to manage. Can you at least help him?"

The guard jerked his chin at the man in the back of the cart. "What's wrong with him? And why's he sitting funny like that?"

"Hurt meself loading the cart," the little one said.

"Set off me lumbago, it did, and sitting any other way hurts." The guard snorted and turned to help the third man open the gate. The cart creaked through and off into the night with Wiz still magically frozen under a load of turnips.

"Hurry up with that cement, will you? My arm's getting tired."

A fire provided light and kept off the chill. A couple of hundred feet away the horse, still hitched to the cart, munched grass placidly. Wiz was standing in a tub half-full of cement, gesturing to empty air. One of the thugs was holding a sword to his throat and the other two were bent over another tub stirring the contents with wooden hoes.

"You want another turn at it?"

"All this work. I think we're underpaid, charging for this like a simple kidnapping. Between the hauling, the mixing and the rest I swear stone cutting's an easier living."

"Where is he anyways?" the third one put in. "I want to count me money and see the back of this job."

"We're supposed to meet him at Bottomless Gorge, and we're still a good half mile from Bottomless Gorge."

"And who was it who decided we'd stop and do it here, eh?"

"I didn't decide. Here's where the cart broke down."

"I knew it would," the third one said gloomily. "Overloaded it was, and as soon as we got off the main road . . ."

"It will ride lighter with nothing but him in it," the tall one told them. "Just get that stuff mixed up good and we'll have plenty of time to fix the cart while it sets hard. Meanwhile our client will just have to wait."

"I dunno. Not good business practices to keep a client waiting. How's that cement coming?"

"Still more like soup than cement."

"You put too much water in," the tall one said from where he held the sword on Wiz.

"I did not!" the shorter man retorted.

The third one stuck his hoe blade in the trough and watched the milky concoction run off the end. "This lot's got chalk mixed in with it. Adulterated, that's what it is."

"Came right out the city warehouse, it did," the short man said morosely. "Councilman Hanwassel's best. You can't trust no one nowadays. The decline in honesty in our society is shocking. Positively shocking. Me, I lay it all to the parents."

"Me, I lay it all to you," the tall one said acidly. "Last time I let you get the supplies for a job!"

"And who was it who was too busy nattering over his ale in the Blind Goat to go out and get the necessaries?"

"That was planning," he answered loftily. "Something like this takes planning—and delegation. It's up to the subordinates to fulfill the tasks delegated to them."

"You can delegate all you want," the short man answered sullenly. "But next time *you* steal the flipping cement."

The other one started to reply, but the third man gestured them to silence.

"Hsst. Here he comes."

Pieter strode into the firelight.

"Where have you been?" he demanded. "And what are you doing here?"

"Cart broke down," the tall one told him. "We figured we'd set him up here and then take him the rest of the way." But Pieter had quit listening as soon as he caught sight of Wiz.

He stood in front of Wiz, arms akimbo. "So Wizard, not so high and mighty now, are you?" He followed it up with a stinging slap to the face.

At least Pieter's hand stung. It was like slapping a rock and the young man winced in pain.

"He can't hear you," one of the footpads said.

"Can't feel what you do to him either," another one added.

"Well, wake him up then. I want him to know the author of his fate."

"Wake him up?" the shortest one quavered. "He's a wizard."

"And he's tied so tight he can't wiggle a finger and gagged so tight he can't utter a word. Release him, I say!"

Hesitantly the one with the sword removed it from Wiz's ribs.

Suddenly Wiz was there again, tied up, gagged, surrounded by three armed thugs and a grinning Pieter, and up to his knees in cement. Not for the first time it occurred to him that the protection spell's definition of "mortal danger" left a lot to be desired.

The short, balding one, whom Wiz mentally tagged "Curly," was edging away from the reanimated wizard. The one beside him was holding his sword warily, ready to thrust it between Wiz's ribs at the first sign of movement. The tall one was looking back and forth between Wiz and Pieter.

"Throw me out of the house, will you?" Pieter snarled and drew back his hand to slap Wiz again.

The blow never landed. Wiz was gagged, but that didn't matter. He could form the words in his throat and that was all it took.

The spell for "loose knots" worked in part by making things self-repulsive and in part by reducing the coefficient of friction of everything in the neighborhood to something less than teflon on plate glass lubricated by greased owl shit. Which is to say that any friction fastening in the vicinity stopped working instantly.

Which is to say that everyone's pants fell down as their belts came untied. Actually it is to say more than that. Sewing can be loosely defined as a form of knotting, so the clothes not only fell off, they fell to pieces.

That left Wiz, Pieter and his three henchmen standing there stark naked. In this crisis the thugs reverted to their natural behavior: They turned to run like frightened rats. Pieter just stood with his hand stopped in mid-air and his mouth open. Wiz spoke another word and all four of them were frozen in place.

Wiz took a step forward and nearly tripped over the edge of the tub he was standing in.

light exe he commanded and a witchfire globe cast an even blue light over everything.

It made an interesting tableau. The tall man had lost his footing and fallen to his hands and knees. The balding one was trying to scramble over the tall one's back, which left them poised as if playing a slightly obscene game of nude leapfrog. The middle-sized one was straightening up with arms pumping, like a sprinter coming out of the blocks.

Wiz shook the wet cement from his legs and considered his next move. A chill evening breeze reminded him that his first priority was finding something to wear if he didn't want to catch cold. He looked at the piles of fabric littering the ground around them but none of them were large enough to cover much.

The cart had been outside the range of the spell, so the horse was still placidly cropping grass. Wiz pulled off the horse's blanket and, ignoring its condition and its odor, draped it over his shoulders toga style.

Leaving Pieter frozen, he gestured to unfreeze his stooges. The three returned to awareness facing a wizard surrounded by glowing blue light and wearing a tattered horse blanket. Just then Wiz's sartorial shortcomings meant less to them than his obvious power.

Their first act was to collapse in a heap as their momentum caught up with them. Curly covered his head with his hands and moaned.

"Stand where you are!" Wiz commanded in a stern and majestic manner—or as stern and majestic as you can be when the cold night air is nipping at your bare backside. "Go on, stand up, all of you."

The three thugs pulled themselves erect and sorted themselves out facing Wiz. They were all about the color of the cement in the tub and Wiz didn't think they were shivering because they were cold.

"I ought to turn you all into frogs," he said sternly. The tall one blanched and the short one whimpered more loudly.

One of these days I've got to write a spell to do that, he thought. However, just now the threat was enough.

He pointed at the trough. "What's this stuff?"

"Cement, My Lord. It's a little thin because . . ."

Wiz cut him off with a wave of his hand. "Okay, you're going to take this cement and you're going to paint a coat of it onto Pieter here. All over, so he's thoroughly covered. Then, when it's dry, you're going to load him into the wagon, take him back to town and set him up in the square in front of the town hall. Got that?"

"The wagon's broke," Larry said sullenly.

"Then carry him," Wiz said and turned away into the night. He took two steps and then turned back to them. "But if he's not standing in the square by noon, you're all going to be pigeon roosts by evening."

He took two more steps and turned back again.

"Oh, and one more thing."

The three quailed before him.

"Which way is it to town?"

God what an evening, Wiz thought as he trudged down the dusty road toward town. The moon gave

enough light to keep him on the road and out of pot-
holes, but not enough to see every rock and tree root.
As a result he had stubbed his toes and bruised his heels
a half dozen times before he had gone as much as a
mile.

*The only good thing is, it's too late for anything else
to happen to me tonight.*

Just then a shadow passed over the moon. Wiz looked
up to see a dragon settling down on a hillock beside
the road. The moon was behind the creature so it loomed
nightmarishly large and black before him.

"Starting a new fashion, Wizard?" Wurm's "voice" rang
in his head.

"Right now I'm trying to get back to town."

"Still, this is opportune. I have been meaning to speak
to you at a time and place which would not upset your,
ah, clients."

Wiz had a sudden premonition the night's events so
far had just been a warm-up. "What do you want?" he
asked wearily.

"An opportunity to discuss your progress, and perhaps your future actions. I understand for example that
you personally convinced one dragon to give up his prey.
That in itself is a notable accomplishment."

"Ah, to tell you the truth it wasn't that difficult. Not
with that particular dragon."

Wurm nodded his enormous head. "Griswold is a
moron. Even for a hatchling."

"Well, at least my run-in with him helped get me in
solid with the council."

"Oh, you have accomplished more than that," Wurm
said, amused. "In two days there will be a dragonmote
to decide what to do about you."

"Dragonmote?"

"A meeting of dragons, or of all who choose to attend."
He cocked his enormous scaly head. "Quite an honor

actually. The first dragonmote in several hundred years. Dragons dislike gatherings and prefer single combat to the constant clumping and bickering of humans. Besides, dragons seldom feel the need to take concerted action."

Suddenly it got even colder under the horse blanket. "Concerted action?"

Wurm nodded again. "I believe the currently favored solution is incinerating the town and you with it."

"Is this where I came in?" Then he thought furiously. "Look, can you get me in to that meeting? To speak to them I mean."

Wurm cocked his enormous head. "I think it can be arranged." The way he said it left Wiz no doubt that had been his plan all along.

TWENTY-THREE

DRAGONMOTE

*The number of screw-ups in a presentation is
directly proportional to the importance of the
audience and inversely proportional to their belief
in what you're selling.*

—*The Consultants' Handbook*

*Never meddle in the affairs of dragons, for they are
subtle and see right through bullshit.*

—Marginalia in a copy of *The Consultants' Handbook*

The place was a narrow chasm between two tower-
ing sandstone cliffs. When it rained the sandy bottom
was probably under several feet of water. About twenty
feet of water, Wiz judged from the bits of driftwood and
debris caught in cracks and ledges up the wall. He
devoutly hoped it didn't rain while the dragonmote was
in progress.

Not that it would matter to the dragons. They dropped
in through the narrow crack of sky above and settled
themselves along the cliff faces, hanging head-down like
bats.

The smell of snake and sulfur was well-nigh

overpowering and garbled bits of dragon speech rang in his head.

With a minimum of hissing and squabbling the dragons settled into their places. There didn't seem to be any strict hierarchy, but the larger, older dragons clearly got the best seats in the house.

A smallish dragon slipped in through the crack of sky, but instead of choosing a spot on the sandstone walls, it dropped down onto the sand next to Wiz. All dragons looked pretty much alike to Wiz but as soon as the creature "spoke" Wiz recognized Griswold.

"You cheated me!" the young dragon said. "Cheated me out of my rightful prey. That spell you showed me was a phony."

"No it wasn't."

"But it doesn't do anything!" Griswold protested.

"I never said that it did," Wiz said blandly.

"But, but, but . . ." Griswold did a fair imitation of a turkey gobbling. Wiz just smiled sweetly.

The young dragon drew back his head as if to say something else, but Wiz shushed him as the meeting came to order.

"This mortal is here under my protection," Wurm declared as the dragons settled in. "Are there any objections?" There was a certain amount of shifting and hissing, but apparently no one objected strongly enough to try to tackle Wurm.

There was no introduction. The dragons fell silent and stared at Wiz, waiting for him to begin.

Wiz gestured and his equipment appeared. It included an overhead projector, complete with a green demon to operate it, a screen, and a large easel holding flip charts. *Beats heck out of lugging this stuff down the hall,* he thought. He picked up the pointer lying on the easel and launched into his prepared spiel.

"Uh, good afternoon ladies and, uh, well dragons. My name is . . ."

"We know who you are," a steely voice rang in his head. "Get on with it."

"Certainly, Mr. ah . . ."

"Ralfnir," came the cold voice. Looking up and to his right Wiz identified the "speaker" as a dragon nearly as large as Wurm and just as ferocious looking.

"First slide, please. Now, as you can see here . . ."

The demon flipped on the projector and a gorgeous rainbow-tinted slide appeared on the screen. It was not, however, the title slide. Wiz didn't recognize it at all. Then he looked harder and realized it was in upside down. At least it seemed to be upside down. Since it was titled in Japanese it was hard for Wiz to tell.

"Uh, next slide please. Now, as you can see here . . ." He stopped. This one was the Miss July picture from the presentation to the council. Trying to look at the slide from the dragons' perspective, Wiz realized her pose and lack of clothing made her resemble something on a buffet. The dragons seemed mightily unimpressed.

"Uh, next chart please."

Finally, mercifully, the demon got the right slide.

"Now as you can see . . ." But that was as far as he got. Ralfnir drew back his head and aimed an incandescent blast of dragon fire down at him.

The world blinked as Wiz's protection spell cut in. When it cut out Wiz found himself standing beside a heap of smoking ashes holding the charred stub of a pointer. Behind him the reflected heat from the canyon wall warmed his back unpleasantly.

Damn. There have been times I've wanted to do that to a presenter.

"Ah, perhaps it would be better if I dispensed with the visual aids," he said weakly.

"Now," said another frigid, metallic "voice," "tell us something we wish to hear or begone."

Always stress the advantages to the client. But he couldn't think of any.

"All right," he said desperately. "I'm here today to talk to you about a matter of mutual concern between humans and dragons."

"Not all dragons think there is a problem with humans," Ralfnir put in, looking at Wurm. "Humans multiply and dragons eat them."

Wiz got the strong impression that Ralfnir and Wurm were rivals in some way. The very fact that Wurm was sponsoring him seemed to make Ralfnir oppose him.

"You have until now," Wiz said. "But things are changing among the humans."

"Oh yes," Ralfnir said, "the 'new magic' we have heard of. Why should we fear anything you humans do?"

"It's already defeated two of you," Wiz said levelly.

"That's a lie!" Griswold "shouted" so loud Wiz flinched. "I was hornswoggled, not defeated."

There was a ripple of laughter from the other dragons. Griswold bridled with rage, but Wurm checked him with an easy gesture of his wingtip. The young dragon subsided, glaring murderously at Wiz.

"The point is," Wiz went on, "that humans are much more potent magically than they have been. It would be in all our interests for dragons to recognize that and to renegotiate your contract with humans."

That produced a babble of dragon speech that made Wiz's head ring. Finally Ralfnir cut through the din.

"Nonsense!" he roared. "I have no 'contract' with humans." There was another head-splitting chorus of assent from the dragons up and down the canyon walls.

Gradually the noise, both acoustic and mental, died away. "Not all of us are afraid of humans," Ralfnir continued, turning his head to look at Wurm. "Dragons dealt with your kind for ages and dragons will deal with them for ages more. Magic or no, dragons will continue to handle humans as it pleases us to do so."

"That won't be as easy with the new magic," Wiz said.

"So far, your 'new magic' has only disturbed Shulfnim at his nap." He paused and nodded toward Griswold. "Oh yes, and bested that one."

Griswold's renewed protest was cut off by a roar of dragonish mirth. The other dragons flapped their wings and slapped their tails against the rock to show approval.

Ralfnir waited for the noise to die again before he went on. "I do not think we have to fear such powers as these."

"This was just a taste," Wiz warned. "The new human magic is very powerful. You will have to reckon with it or I cannot be responsible for the consequences."

"If humans interfere with us," came another steely voice, "it will be we who are responsible for the consequences—to the humans."

Another cacophony of approval with more wing-flapping and tail slapping burst out from the assembled dragons.

"But if you look at the long-term trend . . ." Wiz began, but Ralfnir cut him short.

"A human talks to dragons about the long term? We who live for age upon age?"

Wiz gathered his remaining courage and tried again. "Even dragons can die," he pointed out. "They can be killed by magic and humans now have magic that can, ah, severely limit your scope of action."

"Then prove it," Ralfnir said. "Show me the power of this new magic you think of so highly."

"I'll be glad to demonstrate," Wiz said. As soon as the words were out of his mouth he realized he had made a mistake. "Uh, what did you have in mind?"

"Why," Ralfnir purred, "if this new magic is so dangerous to us, surely you cannot object to a simple duel."

Having no lips, dragons cannot smile. But Ralfnir did an excellent imitation, drooping his lids over his golden eyes and opening his mouth slightly to run a blood-red forked tongue over his gleaming ivory fangs.

Wiz looked at Wurm but the great dragon remained impassive. The chasm had gone very, very quiet.

"Okay," Wiz lied. "How about tomorrow?"

Their business concluded, the dragons left the canyon like a cloud of startled bats. At last only Wurm and Wiz remained.

"It was perhaps unwise to challenge Ralfnir to a duel," the dragon said in a tone of mild reproof.

"Did anyone ever mention your genius for understatement?" Wiz said sourly.

"This was not your object, then?"

"No. I was suckered. What now?"

Wurm seemed surprised by the question. "Why, that is up to you. You can fight him or not."

"Any advice?"

"Advice? That would be presumptuous indeed of me. You must do as you think best."

Wiz thought Wurm had been presumptuous as hell already by getting him into this mess. However he didn't see any point in saying so.

"But if I fight him and he kills me, I haven't solved the problem."

Wurm considered. "Your death would be a solution of sorts."

For an instant Wiz wondered if this entire episode might have been Wurm's elaborate plot to get him to commit suicide. He dismissed that as unnecessarily baroque, even for a dragon.

"I don't suppose I could talk him out of this?"

Wurm cocked his enormous head. "Unlikely. The challenge was formally issued and accepted. Now it is a matter of honor." He paused, as if considering. "True, there is not much honor to be gained by killing a single human, but Ralfnir enjoys sport for its own sake."

"But if I win do I have a deal?"

"Why should you? If you win you will only eliminate Ralfnir."

"Then what's the point?"

"No point, really," Wurm said, "unless you like slaying dragons as much as Ralfnir likes slaying humans. I told you before, Wizard, dragons do not form groups as humans do. There is none who can speak for all of us."

"So why should I even show up for this duel?"

Wurm gave a mental "shrug." "Perhaps no reason at all. Save that if you do not Ralfnir will undoubtedly hunt you down and quite likely burn down that town you humans are so fond of in the process."

"And if I do face him?"

"If you win you have nothing to fear from him. If you lose—" again the "shrug" "—he will probably not bother with the town."

"Great. And if I do beat him, I'll still have to best every single other dragon in order to get them to leave the people alone?"

Wurm paused, as if considering. "Probably not. I imagine that after you have slain forty or fifty dragons most of the rest will decide humans are not worth bothering with." He cocked his head. "It would be an effective strategy, were you able to carry it out."

"There's gotta be a better way," Wiz muttered.

"If there is I would suggest you endeavor to find it," Wurm said. "It would be best if you found it ere dawn tomorrow."

"I'm working on it," Wiz told the dragon and turned to start down the canyon.

"Oh, and Wizard . . ." Wurm's "voice" rang in his head. Wiz turned back to the dragon.

"Do not count on your ring of protection. Even a hatchling could defeat that spell."

"Thanks," Wiz mumbled, and turned his face again toward town.

TWENTY-FOUR
NET GAINS

The essence of successful consulting is knowing when to bail out.

—The Consultants' Handbook

Wiz spent most of the night staring at the screen and doodling meaningless bits of code. He knew he should be coming up with some dynamite dragon-killing spell, but instead he kept reviewing the spells he did have.

Let's see. I've got lightning bolts . . . probably not much good against a dragon . . . suck energy . . . maybe that would do something . . . frictionless surface . . . nope, not against a flying creature . . . attract fleas . . . I wonder if dragons get fleas? Occasionally he would compound something out of the spells at his command, combining the old spells to be called in sequence or simultaneously by a single code word. He spent rather more time working on a fire protection spell that looked pretty good. But mostly he just sat at the terminal and stared into space.

Time and again his fingers would stretch to the keyboard and he would start the sequence to reach the Wizard's Keep over the Internet. Time and again he hesitated and his hands dropped away. He knew he wasn't thinking clearly but trying to think more clearly only made things less clear. *Like trying to squeeze a handful of jelly,* he thought morosely.

Anna spent the night sleeping the sleep of the completely unworried—or the really stupid, which may have been the same thing in her case. Bobo spent the night doing tomcat things. No one knew how Widder Hackett spent the night except that she wasn't talking to Wiz.

The only really active one in the house was Malkin. She spent most of the hours before first light gathering up the booty she had secreted about the place. Even though she'd turned most of it to gold coins through One-Eyed Nicolai it still made a substantial load.

Live for some time on that, she thought as she swept the last of the gold into a leather sack. *Time to move on anyway. I was tired of this town.* The prospect wasn't very satisfying somehow and Malkin realized it wasn't just because this was where she had been born. With a sigh of frustration she dropped the bag on the table. It toppled and spilled a cascade of coins onto the tabletop. Malkin didn't bother to sweep them back into the bag.

Restless, she wandered down to the kitchen to get something to eat. Once she descended the narrow steps she found she wasn't hungry. Maybe a cup of hot mulled wine would help her sleep.

She busied herself blowing up the fire and drawing wine from the small cask on the sideboard. She took down a lovingly polished saucepan and put in the wine with cinnamon, cloves and other spices to steep over the still barely glowing coals.

"Smells good," came a voice behind her. "Can I have some?"

Malkin whirled and there was Wiz, dressed for traveling with cloak and staff.

"Startled me," the tall girl said. "But yeah, there's plenty."

"On second thought I'd better not. I'll need a clear head this morning." He didn't sound at all confident.

Malkin ladled out a cup of the hot, spiced wine. "Getting an early start eh?"

"No sense in postponing things." Malkin just nodded and sat down at the table.

For several minutes neither of them said anything or moved, Malkin drinking her wine at the table and Wiz standing on the stairs.

"Look," he said at last. "I'm not much good at these things, but I just wanted you to know that you've really helped me here. And I wanted to thank you for that."

Malkin only nodded, not trusting her voice.

Wiz sighed heavily. "Well, I'd better get going if I'm going to make the spot by sunup. Thanks again."

"Good luck Wizard. And thank you." Then she stared down into her wine cup so Wiz couldn't see her tears.

Wiz went back up the stairs. A moment later she heard the front door open and close.

Well, she thought to herself, *that's that.* It was possible Wiz would beat the dragon, of course. But in Malkin's world winning a fight with a dragon was a near-impossibility. Besides, the wizard hadn't sounded nearly as confident as he had when he'd been tackling human foes.

She sighed and drained the last of the wine. She still wasn't sleepy so she poured the rest of it into her cup and headed back upstairs with it. She still had packing to do.

Wiz had left the workroom door ajar and his work-station on. The colored light from the screen saver pattern streamed onto the floor in rainbow patterns of cold fire. Malkin paused at the door, intrigued. A combination of thief's caution and a certain sense of honor had kept her away from Wiz's work table so far, but now Wiz was gone and she was going as well. She no longer felt bound and the thing had always intrigued her.

A glance out the window showed the sky just turning pink, so she had a while. She spoke the word that turned off the guardian demon. Then she slipped into the chair, set the wine cup on the desk and started to experiment.

Unlike most of the non-magicians in her world, Malkin could read. Literacy is a handy skill for a thief who wants to know what she is stealing. Thus the keyboard on Wiz's workstation wasn't completely alien to her. Further, burglary is as much a matter of attitude as technical skills. Malkin knew nothing about computers and security, but she had seen Wiz type his log-on sequence repeatedly and she had memorized it.

Unfortunately her memory wasn't that good. The keys were small and fairly close together. What's more, Wiz's program didn't echo the password on the screen and to top it off, Malkin's typing technique was primitive. Twice she blew the password and she was hesitating with her index finger hovering over the keyboard when Widder Hackett took a hand.

"Not that one dummy!" the Widow Hackett screamed in her ear. Malkin didn't hear of course, but Bobo jumped up on the desk and walked across the keyboard, placing his paws very deliberately.

Malkin sneezed as the cat's tail brushed under her nose and when she opened her eyes she was in.

The fiery letters above the desk formed a list of items, each with a number after them. At the top of the list, blinking in and out of existence, was a tiny black demon with a spindly tail and long nose wearing red shorts with two big white buttons in front. When she moved the steel mouse on the table the demon moved. Obviously it was what Wiz called a "mouse," although it looked like no mouse she had ever encountered.

She moved the mouse and the on-screen mouse skittered over the first item on the list. As she had seen Wiz do so often, she pressed the steel mouse twice. The screen changed and she saw a series of messages. Another push on the mouse and the mouse demon on the screen flipped the first message down to reveal the next one. Malkin started going through them and puzzled out the messages as they came up.

What she got was extremely confusing. The first group of messages seemed to be jokes, except they were about pieces of knotted string—frayed knotted string—and mouse testicles. Malkin couldn't understand why that was supposed to be funny and most of the stories didn't make any sense anyway. There was another series which consisted mostly of a four-way argument with the participants hurling vituperative abuse at each other. The subject was obscure and she didn't recognize all the words but she guessed that a complete translation would have made a fishwife blush.

The next batch of messages consisted of a host of extremely creative ways to kill off a being who was apparently some kind of demon—at least it was described as large and purple and the only things Malkin could think of that matched that description were demons. Judging from the hatred in the messages it must be an exceptionally evil demon. It also seemed to have a fondness for children. Perhaps it ate them, she couldn't be sure.

Several of the messages mentioned a being called "Kibo" who seemed to be an extremely powerful demon. At least these people seemed to believe that mentioning the name brought them luck.

There were even some messages that seemed to bear

upon magic. But they were obscure and often couched in strange combinations of runes which made her eyes water just to look at them.

Finally, unknowingly, she clicked out of the stored messages and into the next item on the menu, which happened to be chat mode.

Jerry was working late. Which meant it was dawn and he was still at his desk. He was deep in a piece of code when a slate-blue demon wearing a dress and sporting a telephone headset in her 1940s hairdo popped up at his elbow. "Wun-ringy-dingy," the creature pronounced in a nasal voice, "teew-ringy-dingy."

"Gotta get a new chat demon," he muttered. Then he saw who was asking to chat and hit the call button for Danny and Moira.

Danny had been in the kitchen getting a snack before he went to bed. He showed up with a slab of gingerbread liberally smeared with butter in his hand, a mouth so full he could barely breathe and a generous trail of crumbs leading down the hall.

Moira was right on his heels. Her face was puffy, her red hair a tangled mess and a green silk robe had been wrapped hurriedly around her.

"He's on IRC," Jerry said over his shoulder. "But so far he hasn't said anything."

"Here," Danny said around the gingerbread, "let me take it."

"But . . ."

"Get the search demon started," Danny hissed. "Use my workstation." Somewhat reluctantly Jerry gave up his seat and Danny set down his snack and began to type.

A message formed itself in fire at the level of Malkin's eyes.

"How you doing?" it said.

Malkin had seen this happen with Wiz before but it was still a little surprising.

"All right," she picked out on the keyboard.

In chat mode a person's method of typing is almost as distinct as a telegrapher's "fist," especially when you're expecting a very fast typist and you get someone whose method is obviously more hunt than peck.

"You're not Wiz," Danny typed.

"Shut up," Jerry hissed. "Keep him on the line until we've got the location." Beside him the tracing demon was scribbling furiously as it unraveled link after link.

"Right about that," came the laborious reply. "I'm Malkin."

"Where's Wiz?"

"In over his head is where," Malkin typed. "He's out fighting a dragon."

Moira gasped, Danny paled and Jerry craned his neck to read the message from Danny's workstation.

"Is he all right?" Danny typed.

Moira snorted when she read the question. "I told you he's fighting a dragon," she picked out. "In these parts that ain't healthy. Who are you?"

"I'm Jerry," Danny lied, "Wiz's best friend. It sounds like he can use all the help he can get."

"You got that right," came the reply.

"Look, he's under a spell cast by a dragon to keep him from telling us where he is. Can you tell us where he is?"

Malkin hesitated, then her thief's caution won out.

"Look, I don't know why but for some reason Wiz didn't want you to know where he is. I don't think I should tell you either."

"Shit," Danny muttered as he read the message.

Behind him Moira said something considerably stronger.

"But he's under a spell," he typed.

"So you say," was the answer. "Maybe you're telling the truth and maybe you're not. But it's not for me to give away his secrets."

Danny looked over his shoulder and tried to gauge the progress of the tracking demon. "All right," he typed. "I guess we have to respect that."

Back in Wiz's workroom Malkin had a sudden flash of insight. "You can find me through this, can't you?"

"How could we do that?" came the hasty response. "We just want to talk is all."

"No," Malkin typed, "I've talked too long as it is. Goodbye." With that she moved to sign off.

"NO YOU IDIOT!!!" shrieked Widder Hackett but no one could hear her.

It was Bobo who rose to the occasion—literally. Before Malkin could complete the logoff sequence, he uncoiled from his spot on the windowsill, levitated across the room in a single bound and skidded to a four-point landing on the table next to the "computer." A quick lash of his powerful tail sent the cup of hot mulled wine splashing into Malkin's lap.

With a curse Malkin jumped to her feet. Bobo hopped off the table, clawed her solidly on the ankle and ran out yowling. Malkin grabbed the fireplace poker and chased the cat down the hall. She didn't realize she had forgotten to log off.

Back at the castle the programmers realized it immediately.

"Line's still live!" Danny shouted. "Quick, get the trace going."

"That will take hours!" Jerry didn't exactly shove Danny out of the chair but he squeezed in so quickly the smaller programmer almost landed butt-first on the floor.

His fingers blurred as he rattled through a sequence and the fiery letters flew from the demon's pen.

"What do you think you're doing?" Danny demanded as the message began to take shape.

Jerry stopped typing and backspaced over a mistake. "I've turned off the routine that splits spells into pieces on the screen so you don't activate them just by entering them."

"I can see that."

"As soon as this spell appears on Wiz's terminal it will activate. Just printing it out is the equivalent to reciting it." Another pause and more frantic backspacing. "It'll produce a big flare of magic to show us where Wiz is."

"It is also gonna produce a big flare of magic here," the younger programmer pointed out. "That's likely to raise all kinds of hell with the spells around here."

Jerry didn't take his eyes off the screen. "I know."

"Bal-Simba is not gonna like this."

Jerry hit the last key and completed the spell at the Wizard's Keep, and sent it on its way.

The magical lights in the workroom dimmed and then came back with an unhealthy greenish pallor. There were various poppings and cracklings, unearthly wails and one or two outright explosions from other parts of the Wizard's Keep, accompanied here and there by yells from wizards who had been working late or were at work early.

At the abandoned terminal in Wiz's office Jerry's typing poured out of the screen. There was no one there to read it, but since it was a spell and not a message that didn't matter. Unknown to the inhabitants of the house, magical forces gathered and twisted around them as an invisible tornado of magical energy rose toward the heavens. The emac reached the last line of the spell and sent the requested acknowledgment.

"It worked!" Jerry yelled triumphantly. He spun to face Moira. "Quick, tell the searchers to scan the World for a flare of magic. Big magic." Moira nodded and dashed from the room.

"And tell Bal-Simba too," Jerry called after her. He raised his voice to follow her down the hall. "And apologize to him for the mess, will you?" Then he turned to Danny. "Get your staff. I think we're going to fight a dragon."

When a dragon says dawn, does he mean daybreak or sunrise? Wiz wondered.

It was past first light and already the sun was peeking over the eastern hills. There was still no sign of the dragon. Wiz didn't know if that was because the duel wasn't supposed to start until sunrise or if it was a psychological move on Ralfnir's part. If it was psychology, Wiz thought, it was sure effective.

The dawn air was heavy with dew and still as death. Not so much as a zephyr ruffled the tall green grass or the yellow meadow flowers. A few puffy clouds hung high in the summer sky and here and there a butterfly or bumblebee went about its business among the patches of buttercups and field mallow.

Wiz licked his lips, took a tighter grip on his staff and nearly died in an eyeblink.

With a pop of displaced air Jerry, Danny, Moira and Bal-Simba flashed into existence in Wiz's workroom. A quick glance showed them the room was empty but the sound of cursing downstairs told them there were people about. As one they dashed for the door.

Malkin was standing at the sink, sponging the wine out of her dress and describing in lurid detail all the things she was going to do to Bobo, when Bal-Simba and the others came pounding down the stairs with Jerry in the lead.

"You're Malkin, aren't you? Where's Wiz?" he got out in a single breath.

Malkin's mouth fell open.

"My Lady, please," Moira said as she pushed around Jerry. "Where is Wiz?"

"Where, Lady?" Bal-Simba demanded over Jerry's shoulder.

No one argued with Bal-Simba. Not only did he have the presence and voice of a mighty wizard, he was nearly seven feet tall with bulk to match his height. For the first time in her adult life Malkin found herself dwarfed and intimidated by another person.

"Tell them, girl!" shrieked Widder Hackett.

Over in the corner Anna gaped at what had invaded the kitchen.

"At the dueling field," Malkin stammered. "You take the west road . . ."

"No," Bal-Simba commanded. "No time for words, just think of the place. Think clearly."

"Got it!" Danny shouted. "Let's go." The four gestured as one and vanished.

There was a *pop* of inrushing air and the kitchen was empty again save for its normal inhabitants.

"Fortuna!" muttered Malkin. The stains on her dress forgotten, she reached for an empty wine cup, eyed it, tossed it back on the drainboard and took a beer tankard down from its peg. She filled it to the brim from the wine keg and downed nearly half of it without taking the tankard from her lips.

"Excuse me, My Lady," Anna quavered when Malkin came up for air, "but who were they?"

"Friends of the master's."

"How did they get here?"

Malkin shrugged.

Bobo sauntered into the kitchen looking pleased with himself. But since Bobo always looked pleased with himself neither woman noticed.

Malkin took another long pull on the wine. "Best prepare the spare bedrooms, girl. We're going to have company this night." *Either that or dragon fire ere sundown* she thought as she turned away. But no sense in saying that. Nothing they could do about it and the poor child was already frightened near out of what little wit she had.

TWENTY-FIVE
WE WHO ARE ABOUT TO . . .

The essential difference between a consultant and an owner is that it's not the consultant's butt on the line.

—The Consultants' Handbook

And if it is your butt on the line you've screwed up big time.

—Marginalia in a copy of The Consultants' Handbook

Wiz sensed rather than heard the movement behind him and flung his staff out in an instinctive warding gesture. A wall of flame washed over him, charring the grass and scorching the earth beneath. The sky darkened for an instant and then the shock wave nearly knocked Wiz off his feet.

Shaking his head to clear it, Wiz realized Ralfnir had come in behind him right at ground level and very fast. His instinctive guard was the only thing that had saved him. Looking the way the shadow had gone he sought Ralfnir. At last he saw the dragon, so far away it was only a speck in the blue. The dragon hauled around in a tight turn, mighty wings beating the air. Then he seemed to drop down on Wiz like a stooping hawk. Again Wiz raised his staff and this time he didn't let the dragon close.

Bolt after bolt of lightning struck Ralfnir square on and splattered harmlessly off his armored chest. The dragon replied in kind and Wiz's anti-fire spell glowed dull red around the edges. Wiz turned his head away from the blast of heat radiating off the shield and countered with a rainmaking spell. The dragon steamed and sizzled in the sudden downpour, but shook off the water like a dog and kept coming.

Wiz raised his staff and gestured again. Four things like old-fashioned beehives made out of steel appeared at the cardinal points around Ralfnir. As soon as they winked in they exploded, releasing a horde of steel bees aimed straight for the dragon. Ralfnir shot a great gout of flame, slewing it back and forth to play over the oncoming metal insects. Most of them glowed red, then yellow, then fell from the sky like a rain of molten steel. The few that penetrated Ralfnir's defenses bounced harmlessly off the beast's armored hide.

Now he swooped close and reached out with gaping jaws. Wiz dropped flat on the ground and heard the dragon's jaws close above him like a rifle shot. The pressure from the wingbeats made Wiz's eardrums ring and then the dragon was gone again with a lashing of lightning bolts to speed him on his way.

Ralfnir winged over and dived behind the hill. For an instant Wiz thought he had gotten him, but the dragon popped up seconds later, spraying Wiz with fire from close range and jinking down again before the human could get a spell off.

backslash spindizzy exe! Wiz muttered. A blue haze enveloped him and he rose, a hundred, two hundred, three hundred feet straight into the air. The ground fell away from him and the hilltop where he had stood became a black smear on the rolling green meadow.

It was a calculated insult. Dragons hate other flying things near them, especially flying humans. Ralfnir swelled his neck and hissed like a runaway steam whistle. Then he dove for Wiz with all his strength.

Jaws agape and talons spread, Ralfnir dived for Wiz Zumwalt. With a mighty roar he struck the flying wizard square on with the full force of his two-hundred-foot-long armored body.

Wiz bounced. Bounced and skittered away from the dragon, light as a windblown leaf. Ralfnir clutched at him with his talons but Wiz popped out of his grasp like a watermelon seed.

The dragon roared in frustration and fury and unleashed a column of fire straight at his would-be prey. The incandescent blast curled around the blue haze and Wiz was simply borne away like a feather on a puff of breath. Again and again Ralfnir spewed mighty gouts of flame at his victim. Each time Wiz was borne lightly away by the force and unharmed by the flame.

Hot damn! It's working. When he had developed the spell it had seemed just too tricky, but it was not only protecting him, it was obviously puzzling the hell out of the dragon. The bubble-of-force component kept the searing heat of the dragon's fire away from him and the repulsion spell kept the dragon from grabbing him, but the real secret was the inertia-canceling spell. Without inertia the dragon couldn't hurt him no matter how hard he hit. Even the force of Ralfnir's fiery breath simply blew him gently away.

Now maybe he'll get tired and give up.

Ralfnir hung motionless, wings beating and armored chest heaving. He cocked his head and considered the human in the blue bubble floating a few hundred feet away. Then he straightened his neck as if he had reached a decision.

On the other hand, Wiz thought, *maybe he won't.*

Slowly, methodically, the dragon began to stalk the human across the sky.

If Ralfnir couldn't harm Wiz, he quickly discovered he could knock him around a lot. The dragon batted Wiz in his blue bubble from paw to paw and then lashed him with his tail. The force of the blow drove Wiz down to the earth. The spell bounced him back up again like a rubber ball and rattled Wiz's teeth, spell or no.

Again and again blows from Ralfnir's tail hammered Wiz to the ground, and again and again he bounced back up. In effect Ralfnir dribbled Wiz the length of the meadow and back.

His spell might have rendered Wiz immune from physical force, but it did nothing at all for his inner ear. Somewhere between the second and third dribble Wiz discovered a hitherto unknown predilection to airsickness.

While he fought to keep his stomach in place Wiz realized he hadn't been as smart as he had thought. He couldn't even think straight in the middle of all the bouncing, much less cast spells. Perhaps worse, the protection field severely limited the kinds of spells he could cast at all. The best he had was a standoff and he had a suspicion that wouldn't last forever.

It didn't. After bouncing Wiz off the terrain one last time the dragon lay back and regarded him briefly. A garbled bit of dragon speech formed in Wiz's mind and suddenly his bubble burst, leaving Wiz hanging unsupported and unprotected several hundred feet in the air.

There was a brief, sickening drop as the world rushed toward him.

backslash paracommander exe! Wiz cried and his fall slowed to an easy descent. Ralfnir, however, didn't. The dragon dived again on the now-helpless wizard, intent on finishing him before he reached the ground.

Wiz sucked in his breath when he saw the dragon coming. *Doesn't shooting a man in a parachute violate the Geneva Convention or something?* He realized Ralfnir had probably never heard of the Geneva Convention and wouldn't abide by it if he had.

Wiz watched the dragon bore in on him, looming ever larger in his vision. **backslash uncommander.exe!** he whispered and the spell released him, letting him fall free again. The sudden burst of speed confused Ralfnir and instead of nailing Wiz squarely, he passed several feet over Wiz's head. As the dragon spread his wings to brake and come around again he twisted his head over his shoulder and shot a quick burst of fire at Wiz. The shot was badly aimed and missed, but it came close enough to fill Wiz's nostrils with the reek of singed hair.

Wiz was so intent on watching Ralfnir he almost forgot to reactivate the spell. He was only a few feet off the ground when he switched it back on and hit hard enough to drive him to his knees. He barely had time to grab his staff before the dragon was on him again.

This time Ralfnir settled to the ground with two mighty wing beats that threw up so much dirt Wiz flinched away. Then slowly, ponderously, he waddled across the meadow to confront his adversary.

A quick spell reduced the friction beneath the dragon to almost nothing, but the dragon simply glided on like a skater on ice. He nearly fell into the gaping pit that opened before him, but he hopped over with a quick half-flap of his wings. Tendrils of meadow grass tugged at his feet, but the dragon broke their grip without seeming to notice. Wiz used an illusion spell to fill the meadow with duplicates of himself. Ralfnir ignored them and came straight for the real Wiz.

A basketball-sized meteor blazed out of the sky and struck the dragon squarely between the eyes. Ralfnir shook his head as if to dislodge a fly. An iceberg congealed around him and shattered instantly. Ralfnir plowed through the pile of ice shards and kept coming. Barely a dozen feet from Wiz he stopped, raised his head high over Wiz and looked down at him.

Wiz felt as if he was suffocating. The dragon's glare seemed to press down on him like a rock on his chest. He felt his will, his magic and even his life draining away from him under the impact of those great yellow eyes.

Gasping, Wiz managed to form one more word and the world went black and freezing cold.

Ralfnir roared in rage and frustration as his prey disappeared in the rapidly expanding black cloud. He drew his head even higher and breathed a gout of flame at the spot where Wiz had been.

The resulting fireball blew Ralfnir clear across the meadow. Technically it was a misfire since the carbon black and liquid oxygen Wiz's spell had dumped around him hadn't had time to mix fully. However, the result was impressive enough. The carbon was very finely divided, almost monomolecular, and the liquid oxygen not only propelled the carbon black outward in all directions, shutting out light, it also made a dandy oxidizer for the carbon fuel.

Another part of the spell protected Wiz from the explosion. Ralfnir wasn't so lucky. He lay stunned for an instant where the blast had flung him. As he rolled to his feet Wiz saw he was moving slowly, as if in pain. But he sprang into the air as agilely as ever.

This time the attack was purely magical. Again the dragon closed in on Wiz, beating and battering at him with magical blow after magical blow. Wiz was able to deflect some of them with his staff, but there were so many and they came so quickly he could not ward them all off. Under the inexorable pressure Wiz was beaten to his knees, waving his staff in one hand in an increasingly futile effort to protect himself. His chest constricted, his vision blurred and he gasped for breath, leaning on his staff to keep from falling. Ralfnir came ever closer, moving in for the final kill.

There was a sound like machine-gun fire from the edge of the meadow, four quick sharp explosions.

And Jerry was there.

And Danny.

And Moira was there.

And Bal-Simba was there.

As one the quartet raised their staffs and hurled death and destruction at the dragon bearing down on Wiz.

If he'd had time to prepare Ralfnir might have had a chance. He was an old dragon and greatly skilled in magic. But he was in the midst of battle and he was focused on Wiz with a predator's intentness. He barely noticed the other humans before their spells hit him.

Bal-Simba was quickest off the mark. A bolt of black lightning flew from his fingertips and wrapped itself around Ralfnir. The dragon was brought up short in mid-swoop as if he had been lassoed, and he jerked violently against the sooty black bonds drawing tighter and tighter around him. The more he struggled the more closely he was held. Before the others' spells could reach him he was already weakening and sinking toward the earth.

Jerry's spell was an outgrowth of his speculations about the physical nature of dragons. It enclosed Ralfnir in a perfectly reflecting sphere that rapidly brought its contents to the black body temperature of a dragon. Of course, since there was no energy sink available in the sphere, the dragon died a heat death, which is sort of the thermodynamic equivalent of heat stroke.

Moira wasn't fancy. She just threw the three worst death spells Wiz and his friends had taught her. She topped it off with the worst spell in the old magic she remembered from her days as a hedge witch—a spell guaranteed to give the victim a case of hives.

Danny's spell was probably the most ingenious. It took all the random molecular motion in the dragon's body and pointed it in one way—toward the highest gravity potential. What was left of Ralfnir didn't just drop out of the sky, he hurtled with ever-increasing speed. In the space of a few hundred feet the dragon went from zero to Mach eight. Straight down.

Where he hit, Ralfnir literally left a smoking hole in the ground.

Wiz sagged against his staff and stared dumbly at the hole where the dragon had been. Then he stared at his friends coming across the meadow to him. Neither event registered very strongly.

"You shouldn't have come," Wiz mumbled as Bal-Simba reached him slightly ahead of the others. "You weren't supposed to come. I didn't want you here. You've ruined everything."

He was still mumbling when Bal-Simba laid a huge hand on his shoulder. "Sparrow look at me," he commanded. Wiz met his eyes and his mouth dropped open. He shuddered, staggered and would have fallen if Bal-Simba had not taken his arm.

"Wha. . what . . .?"

"A geas," Bal-Simba said. "A magical compulsion. Laid on you, I have no doubt, by a certain dragon."

Wiz's jaw dropped again. "Oh," he said. "So that's . . ." He didn't get a chance to finish. Moira was in his arms, kissing him and crying and all he wanted to do was hold her close forever and ever.

"Hey, Wiz," Danny said after an appropriate interval.

Wiz raised his face from Moira's mane of copper hair. "Thanks guys. I think you just saved my life."

The giant wizard made a throw-away gesture. "It was a piece of pastry."

"That's 'piece of cake,'" Danny corrected.

"Whatever."

"Come on love," Moira murmured in his ear, "let us leave this place.

Wiz shook his head without taking his nose out of his wife's hair. "I can't just yet. There are a couple of loose ends I need to tie up here."

Moira looked over Wiz's shoulder at Bal-Simba.

"No geas," he told her. "Only a sense of responsibility."

"Responsibility to whom?" Moira asked.

"The town council," Wiz told her.

"The town council?"

"Yeah, I'm a consultant to them on dragon problems."

"Sparrow," the giant black wizard rumbled, "I am almost afraid to ask what you have been doing."

"Well," Wiz admitted, "it's kind of complicated."

Bal-Simba eyed his friend. "Now I *am* afraid to ask."

"I'll explain it to you when we get back to town," he said. "It's really not that bad." Then he stopped. "At least it seemed like a good idea at the time. But it's not dangerous." He stopped again. "Well, okay, there are these three thugs who were trying to kill me and a couple of people on the council who want my hide. And I guess Pieter, the guy in the cement overcoat who's standing in the town square, is going to come looking for me once he gets unfrozen. But it's really not that bad." He realized all four of his companions were staring at him, hard. "Honest," he finished lamely.

"You had best tell us about it when we get back to town," Bal-Simba said.

"Uh, I've got to make a kind of a detour first." Wiz looked over his shoulder at the trickle of smoke coming from the fresh crater in the sod. He took a deep breath.

"Okay, now for the hard part."

TWENTY-SIX
DRAGON DECISIONS

History does not always repeat itself. Sometimes it just yells "Can't you remember anything I told you?" and lets fly with a club.

—John W. Campbell

Again Wiz Zumwalt faced the assembled dragons. This time he had arrived under his own power along the Wizard's Way. He had come alone, but Bal-Simba and the others were watching him closely.

This meeting being called on short notice, there weren't as many dragons along the walls of the canyon as there had been the day before. But there were still a satisfying number.

"Well," he said to the mass of monsters, "you've had your taste of the new magic. Satisfied?"

"It was not a fair duel," one of the dragons complained. "You had help from others of your kind."

"Not fair at all," Wiz agreed cheerfully. "But then you're not going to get a fair fight with a human. Don't you see? Humans cooperate. They work together naturally." He thought of the town council. "Maybe not always easily and not always well, but they manage to do it."

He threw his head back to look up at the assembled dragons and raised his voice so his words echoed off the cliffs. "It won't be one dragon against one human. It will be one or a few dragons against every human in sight. And most of the time the humans will win with the new magic."

There was a great shifting and slithering as the dragons absorbed the idea.

"Then we should kill you all now," a voice rang harshly in his head.

"You could try," he said levelly. "But there are many more humans than there are in this valley and a lot of them already have the new magic. Even if you got every human in the valley, others would replace them."

More shifting and slithering.

"What do you propose then?" a new voice asked.

"Simple. You're going to make a treaty with the people in the valley. And this time you're going to abide by it." He turned round to face the mass of assembled dragons. "All of you."

"And how shall we bind all dragonkind by our agreement?" a "voice" like an iron kettledrum asked.

"That's your problem. Maybe the seniors could take turns patrolling the border. But you're going to solve it or in a few generations there won't be any dragons left in the Dragon Lands."

He looked up at the assembled monsters. "Think it over," he said. Then he turned on his heel and left.

It wasn't yet noon but the group was worn out by the time they returned to the house. They were too tired to walk so they took the Wizard's Way back and popped into the front hall just as Anna came up the stairs from the kitchen.

She wasn't the least fazed by the apparition in her front hall. These were wizards, wizards did strange things, therefore anything wizards did was normal. She merely curtseyed.

"Will there be anything you need, My Lord?" she said to Wiz. As usual Anna looked utterly charming in a brown work dress and dirty apron. There was a smear of soot on her cheek just below one china blue eye and blond curls peeked out from the kerchief that protected her hair.

"No, nothing now, thank you," Wiz said. "There's ale in the keg in the kitchen isn't there? We'll probably be down there for a while."

Anna curtseyed again. "I'll finish preparing the guest rooms, then, My Lord." With that she turned and hurried up the stairs, oblivious to Moira's eyes boring into her back.

"Who," Moira demanded, "is she?"

"That's Anna. She's my housekeeper."

The red-haired witch fixed him with a fishy eye. "Your house had better be all she has been keeping. My Lord."

In the event the explanation in the kitchen took somewhat longer than Wiz had anticipated. About three hours, in fact, by the time he answered all the questions, straightened out everyone's chronology, found out about Judith's troubles with the FBI, and gave Jerry and Danny a very detailed and highly technical explanation about exactly how to gimmick an Internet router.

"What do you intend to do about this Pieter, the one you left in town square?" Bal-Simba asked when he finally ran down.

"Well," Wiz said, "I don't suppose it would be really right to leave the little oinker frozen for all eternity." He sighed with genuine regret. "So I guess I'll have to take the spell off him."

"I would suggest doing it the last thing ere we leave the town," Bal-Simba said. "Otherwise he will like as not try to attack you again."

"Oh, I wasn't thinking of being around at all," Wiz said. "I figured I'd create a timer demon to unfreeze him after we've left."

"Wise," Bal-Simba nodded.

"I was thinking of having the demon unfreeze him— oh, I dunno, say at high noon on the next market day. The square should be nice and crowded about then."

"That's nasty," Danny said. "I really like it."

"You get that way when you play consultant," Wiz grinned back. "That and hanging around politicians." He snapped his fingers. "Speaking of which, I'd better get down there and set up the spell. Don't want to leave it to the last minute. Also I've got an errand to run at the town hall."

Bal-Simba cocked an eyebrow. "More consulting?"

"No," Wiz told him as he stood up from the table, "I've got to see a man about a house."

Wiz's errand at the town hall took somewhat longer than he had expected. *But not nearly as long as it would take in Cupertino*, he thought as he pushed his front door open. The council may have had politics down to a blood sport but at least they hadn't invented lawyers yet. As part of his efforts to gum up the works Wiz had considered introducing them to the concept, but he had saved it as an emergency tactic if things really got dire. *Common decency if nothing else*, he thought. Llewllyn hadn't been in his office at the town hall and Wiz was just as glad.

As he tugged the front door closed Malkin came up from the kitchen.

"Where is everyone?" he asked as she reached his floor.

"Oh they're around," she said breezily. "Your wife's down in the kitchen, 'helping' Anna."

"'Helping'?"

"Allaying her suspicions about what you've been up to with her. The big black wizard is in the front parlor, along with one of your friends." She grinned. "They're supposed to be meditating, but every so often they get so deep in thought they start to snore. Your other friend is upstairs working at your desk. Says he's surfing, but there's not a wave to be seen."

"That's just a figure of speech," Wiz told her. "What about you?"

"Oh, I've got some errands to run." She paused. "Leaving, eh?"

"Probably tomorrow. I'm done here."

She nodded. "That's the way of it."

There was a longer pause.

"What about you? What are you going to do once I've left?"

Malkin laughed. "Oh, I'll go back to the Bog Side, away from all these high-toned folk like the town council and their fancy ways. I'll be taking the air, as you might say. You've stirred up a right hornet's nest here and I'm minded to see how it goes on for a bit."

"I mean, you'll be all right and everything?"

Malkin laughed again and Wiz thought it sounded a bit brittle.

"Me? Fortuna, I've looked out for meself all these years. I'll do just fine on my own. Now if you'll excuse me, I've got an errand to run." She loped up the stairs toward her room.

"Malkin."

The tall thief paused at the top of the stairs and looked back. "Yes?"

"I meant what I said about appreciating your help. Thanks again."

"Any time, Wizard. Any time." With that she disappeared down the hall.

As Wiz turned back toward the kitchen there was a hammering on the front door.

"What in the . . . ?" Anna was halfway up from the

kitchen, but he waved her back and tugged the door open himself.

As soon as the door cleared the latch it flew open, sending Wiz reeling backward. Llewllyn burst through, waving his arms. He was flushed, sweaty and almost completely out of breath.

"Flee!" he gasped. "There's a dragon . . . Anna. Run. We must . . . run or be . . . burned where we stand."

He tried to push past to the kitchen but Wiz put his arm around him.

"Relax. The dragon's dead. It's all over."

Llewllyn turned back to Wiz and blinked. "Dead?"

"Very dead. There's no danger."

"But . . . but, but . . ."

"Look, we've got houseful of company, so if you can just put off seeing Anna until tonight I'm sure she can explain the whole thing." He gently turned the some-time bard and would-be magician around and guided him back toward the front door.

Wiz almost had him out the door when Bal-Simba came out of the parlor, rubbing the "meditation" from his eyes.

"Sparrow, I . . ."

Llewllyn gaped. He might never have been near the Wizard's Keep, but even people who had barely heard of the Council of the North recognized its leader on sight. Even in our world how many six-foot-eight, 380-pound guys do you see—outside of the NFL? And even NFL linemen don't file their teeth to points.

"I am sorry, Sparrow," the huge wizard said, "I did not know you had a visitor."

Llewllyn's head was swivelling back and forth between them convulsively. His mouth hung open and he had suddenly gone pasty white.

"Uh, leave us for a minute will you, My Lord?"

"Of course," Bal-Simba rumbled. "I will be in the parlor."

"You knew," Llewllyn said dully as soon as Bal-Simba closed the parlor door. "You knew what I was all along."

"It was a little hard for me not to," Wiz said dryly.

Llewllyn struck a noble pose, chin-high. "Well, go ahead. Denounce me to the council. Have them stake me out for the dragons to rend and tear. Or will you simply turn me into a toad?"

It was awfully tempting, but Wiz shook his head.

"I've got a better idea. I'm leaving tomorrow and I'm going to make you my successor."

Llewllyn stopped posing and gawked. "But, My Lord, I am a liar! A charlatan! A back-stabbing schemer!"

Wiz smiled and clapped him on the shoulder. "I can't think of a better set of qualifications for this job."

It is also, he thought, *called making the punishment fit the crime.*

"Besides," Wiz continued, "Anna needs you."

Llewllyn looked blank. "Anna, My Lord?"

"My housekeeper. You know, the woman at whose merest whim you'd lay down your life. The very light of your existence. You are in love with her, aren't you?"

"You know I am, My Lord," Llewllyn said quietly. "But why is she your concern now that you are leaving?" His eyes narrowed. "Or was there something between you?"

"Would it make a difference to you if there was?"

Llewllyn looked at him levelly. "Only that I'd have your heart for trifling with her, be you wizard or no."

Wiz suddenly discovered Llewllyn could be amazingly convincing under the right circumstances.

"No, there was nothing between us. But she's a good kid and she deserves to be happy. You are apparently what makes her happy, so . . ." He shrugged.

The blond man bowed. "I will endeavor to see that she is happy, My Lord."

"Do that. Meanwhile, come back later." With that he pushed him out the door.

TWENTY-SEVEN
DRAGON TALE HOME

Always end projects on a positive note, no matter what they were like.

—The Consultants' Handbook

"Excuse me, My Lord," Anna said from the top of the kitchen stairs. "But Llewllyn, what did he want?"

"Mostly to tell you about the dragon. I asked him to come back this evening."

Anna frowned, prettily. "The one you killed? But I already knew that."

"Yes, but he didn't."

"My Lord?" It was a good thing Anna looked so pretty when she was confused, Wiz thought, because she spent so much time being confused.

"He'll explain it to you this evening. But I wanted to talk to you anyway."

A shadow darkened the maid's beautiful, empty brow. "Have I done something wrong, My Lord?"

"No, no. Not at all. It's just that . . . Look, you know I'm leaving here tomorrow with my friends?"

The maid nodded. "I know and I'm so happy." Then

she went crimson. "Oh, that's not what I mean at all. I mean . . ."

"I know what you mean," Wiz said reassuringly.

"I mean it has been a pleasure serving you, My Lord, but I, I mean," then the words came in a rush. "I mean Llewllyn has asked me to marry him and I said yes and oh, I'm the happiest girl in the world!"

Wiz ignored the disembodied snort from over his shoulder. "Congratulations. When is the happy event?"

"As soon as can be." Her eyes sparkled. "He is wonderful and I love him so. Besides," her voice dropped. "I have been so alone since Grandma died. Oh you have been kind, My Lord, but there's been no one for me to turn to for advice and Llewllyn," she sighed, "why he knows *everything*!"

Wiz held up his hand, checking the explosion of spectral wrath behind him.

"Well, since I'm not going to be here for the wedding, I'd better give you your present early."

The girl flushed again. "Oh My Lord, that is not necessary."

"Still, I am going to give you this house. As a wedding present, you might say." Anna's jaw dropped and her face lit up like a child's at Christmas. He waved a finger. "Now mind, I am giving this to you personally. Not to the two of you. I've arranged it with the council that it shall be yours alone."

Anna hugged him and started to cry into his shirt pocket. "Hey, it's okay," Wiz protested and tried to move her away. "It's all right."

"Well, My Lord," Anna said with a smile and a sniffle. "I'd best go and finish in the kitchen."

"Yes, do that." *Before Moira catches you hanging all over me and turns us both into toads.*

"Smart," Widder Hackett said at last. "If she owns

the house I'll be able to advise the poor child. And she'll need it, married to that empty-headed popinjay."

"That's kind of what I was thinking," Wiz said. *That and I don't want to find out if the ghost stays with the owner if he leaves the house.*

Malkin was gone for a long time doing Malkin-ish things. The principal one of those things was a visit to her fence to turn the last of her swag into gold. Since One-Eyed Nicolai didn't open for business until after dark, she took her dinner at a dingy little food stall in the Bog Side. On the way home she was diverted by a couple of opportunities to ply her trade and ended up returning with more loot than she left with, plus the gold from the fence, and coming in quite late to boot.

Thus it was that Malkin was sneaking up the back stairs with her latest acquisitions when a looming shadow blocked her way.

Jerry, who was wide-awake after the day's nap, had been net surfing on Wiz's workstation. He had taken a break to stretch his legs—and see if there was anything to eat in the kitchen. He wasn't expecting to meet anyone on the stairs and he nearly stepped on Malkin before he could stop. As it was he half-stumbled, half-fell into her and they ended up clinging to each other to keep from falling completely downstairs.

"Oh hello," Jerry said mildly, releasing his hold on the girl.

"Hello yourself," said Malkin, looking up at him. Not only was she one stair lower on the stairway, but even on the level Jerry overtopped her by perhaps half a head. "Let's see, you're the one called Jerry, right?"

"That's me."

"And you're a wizard too?"

"Well, a programmer but around here it pretty much comes to the same thing." Between the darkness in the stairwell and Malkin's dark clothing Jerry couldn't see much of his new acquaintance, but the combination of dark hair working its way out from under the knit cap, the pale, fair skin and lithe figure he had wrapped his arms around to keep from falling all made a very favorable impression.

"I was just taking a break," he explained. "From work on the computer, ah, workstation, I mean." It occurred to Jerry he was babbling, but if he shut up she might just pass him by on the stairs. "I do that a lot. Work, you know. Besides I'm kind of a night person," he explained. "I do most of my best work then."

Malkin smiled up at him. "I know just what you mean. I'm that way myself."

Somehow the big programmer and the tall thief ended up sitting side by side on the stairs, talking. Somehow it was getting light outside before they reached a stopping place in their conversation and went their separate ways.

It is possible they were overheard. But Danny was sleeping in the front parlor and Wiz and Moira were far too occupied to hear anything. If Bal-Simba heard he gave no sign. Widder Hackett didn't talk about it and Bobo just looked smug.

It was barely dawn, but Wiz was already up and packing to go. He was taking clothes out of the wardrobe, folding them more or less neatly and putting them in a thing he persisted in thinking of as a duffel bag, even if it was made out of sueded leather rather than canvas. There wasn't much besides a few clothes. He hadn't accumulated many possessions in his time here, just as he hadn't grown particularly attached to the place.

There was a shadow at the window, as if a cloud had passed before the rising sun. But a cloud doesn't usually send the early risers in the street running and screaming. Nor does a cloud rattle the windowpanes.

Shirt still in hand, Wiz went to the window. There was a dragon settling daintily into the square, oblivious to the townsfolk scattering like a herd of terrified sheep. He didn't have to be told it was Wurm.

"Leaving, wizard?" the dragon's voice came in his head.

"Yes, now that I'm free of your damned geas."

Wurm waddled across the square until his head was just outside Wiz's room. It was a small square and Wurm was a large dragon, so it was only a few steps.

Wiz watched him come. He discovered he wasn't intimidated by dragons any more, but he was awfully tired of them.

"You had solved the problem so I would have removed that anyway."

"Big of you," Wiz said and turned back to his packing.

The dragon cocked an enormous golden eye at Wiz through the window.

"You have not claimed your fee."

Wiz put a stack of shirts into his pack and hissed in irritation as one of them slid onto the floor. "I'm not interested in a fee," he said stooping down to pick up the shirt.

Wurm raised an enormous eyebrow. "If you are not paid how do you expect to remain in business?"

"I'm out of business as of right now," Wiz told him. "The next time I feel the urge to do this I'll take up a more honest branch of the profession, like television evangelism."

"Nevertheless, you are entitled to payment."

"The only payment I want is a little peace and quiet, like about fifty years worth. I don't want ghosts screeching in my ear, I don't want to have to worry about the cops busting down my door because of my housemate's

hobbies, I don't want to have to put up with a bunch
of quarrelsome children masquerading as politicians."
He threw the shirt into the bag and it promptly slid out
again. "And most of all, I don't want to have to deal
with dragons."

"That is a rather large reward indeed," Wurm said.
"Even for a task such as you have performed."

Wiz stuffed the shirt into the bag again, more carefully this time, and turned to face the dragon. "You knew
this, didn't you? You knew the new magic was spreading to the north and you knew that with it humans could
beat the dragons."

"Let us just say I found the probabilities inoppor-
tune," Wurm said lazily.

"So you went right to the source of the new magic
and kidnapped me to fix things before they got out of
hand."

"And you fixed them. That is vindication enough, I
think."

Wiz opened his mouth to protest and then closed it
again. Dragons being cold-blooded in more ways than
one, nothing else was likely to matter to Wurm, least
of all the danger Wiz had been in.

"So you dragged me in here against my will to help
the humans with their dragon problem."

"I prefer to think of it as dragons having a human
problem," Wurm said.

"Well, why didn't you just tell me that?"

Wurm's "voice" was coldly amused. "Would you have
bent all your skill to protecting dragons from humans?
Even under geas?"

There was enough truth in that that Wiz didn't have
a reply, so he changed the subject."By the way, what
are you going to do?"

"I? Oh, you mean dragonkind. We will solve our own
problem—now that we agree it is a problem." The

dragon sounded amused. "That is the essence of consulting, is it not? To, ah, 'borrow someone's watch and tell him what time it is'?"

Wiz wondered where the dragon had heard that. He had an uneasy feeling Wurm had heard, and knew, a lot more than he was telling.

"Goodbye Wizard. I do not think we will meet again, but I predict you will have an extremely interesting future." With that Wurm turned sinuously, took three running steps and launched himself into the air with a beat of wings that rattled the windows and made the shutters bang against the walls.

"If I have anything to say about it," Wiz said to the dragon's rapidly dwindling back, "my future will be about as exciting as watching grass grow."

"I see you had a visitor," Bal-Simba said as Wiz came down to breakfast in the kitchen.

Wiz leaned over and kissed Moira soundly before replying. "Yeah, Wurm. He wanted to say goodbye."

Moira arched a coppery eyebrow and the big wizard accepted this without comment. Wiz helped himself to the porridge on the tile stove. He added some sliced apples and peaches from a bowl on the table and drizzled honey over the mixture.

It was a remarkably full kitchen, considering the programmers' normal working hours. Anna was still bustling about finishing up the last of breakfast. Moira was sitting next to Bal-Simba and Jerry and Malkin were off to one side, talking intently. Only Danny hadn't come down yet and that wasn't surprising. Yesterday was probably the earliest he had gotten up in months.

Wiz took a mouthful of porridge and fruit and sighed. "A few more hours and we'll be back at the Wizard's Keep and peace and quiet."

Moira raised her eyebrows and gave Wiz one of her

patented smoldering looks with her enormous green eyes. "So it's peace and quiet you want, My Lord?" Bal-Simba guffawed.

Wiz reddened. "Relatively speaking, I mean. And speaking of relations . . ."

Anna set another bowl on the table and Moira looked at the girl significantly. "We shall have plenty of time to discuss that when we get home."

"Home," Wiz repeated. "I can't wait to get back. I've missed you so much. I've missed all of you." He quirked a smile. "Heck, I even got to missing Little Red Dragon, I mean Fluffy."

Moira raised an eyebrow and smiled. "I take it you have not enjoyed your adventure? Seeing strange lands? Battling dragons? Doing great deeds of heroism?"

Wiz smiled back. "I only battled dragons when it was absolutely necessary, I rigorously avoided deeds of heroism, great or otherwise, and this place may be strange enough, but I wish I'd never seen it and I bet you all do too."

Moira turned to where Jerry and Malkin were deep in conversation.

"Well, not all of us perhaps."

Watching the pair Wiz felt a sudden chill.

"Well, we'll be out of here soon enough. Let me finish eating, grab my staff and we'll be leaving inside a half-hour." He smiled at the prospect and leaned back to take another pull from his mug of tea.

"Oh, that reminds me," Jerry said. "I've got some news too. "Malkin's agreed to come back to the Capitol with us."

Wiz spewed tea all over the table.

"*WHAT?*" he demanded indignantly and lapsed into a coughing fit that somewhat diminished the effect.

"I have decided to come with you," Malkin said gaily.

"This Capitol of yours sounds like an interesting place. Full of opportunities."

Wiz thought of Malkin's definition of "opportunity" and blanched. "I don't think you'll find any opportunities in the Capitol. Nope, no opportunities at all. It's a dull place really. Full of all kinds of boring guards and burglar alarms and . . ." He trailed off when he saw he obviously wasn't making an impression. Then he looked at her more closely, over at Jerry and back at Malkin. "There's more to it than just opportunity, isn't there?"

Malkin looked shy. "He's the first man I've ever met I didn't have to look down on."

Wiz was tall by this world's standards and Malkin could look him square in the eye. Jerry was a head taller than Wiz, which made him about the biggest man around, save Bal-Simba. He was still heavy, but after several years of more exercise and the diet full of vegetables, grains and fiber eaten in this world he was no longer exactly fat.

Wiz looked at his friend.

"I've never met anybody like her before," Jerry said simply.

Considering that Jerry had never been in jail that was probably true, Wiz reflected.

Wiz turned to Moira. "I don't suppose this is some kind of infatuation spell?" he asked with a tinge of desperation in his voice.

Moira looked amused. "Infatuation, yes. A spell, no. Only the age-old magic between man and woman."

Wiz put his head in his hands and moaned.

"Is there aught I can do?"

"Yes, warn the people at the Wizard's Keep to nail down anything they want to keep." He considered. "And tell them to use *big* nails."

Jerry and Malkin had moved to the corner, intent on some private matter and oblivious to the other people in the room. She had her hands on the rough stone walls and was apparently explaining to him how to scale a wall at a corner. Jerry was just looking at her, ignoring what she was saying.

"I think Jerry has finally met his match," Moira said approvingly. "She seems quite taken with him as well."

"She probably just wants a place out of jail," Wiz said sourly.

Moira looked speculatively at the couple in the corner. "No, she is really in love, I think."

"Worse," Wiz groaned.

"Well," rumbled Bal-Simba. "At least it shall not be boring."

"That," said Wiz Zumwalt, "is exactly what I am afraid of."